A Dimensional Tune

Rita Redswood

Acknowledgements

Thank you to all my family and friends, who have supported all of my writing endeavors over the years and have given me countless bucketfuls of motivation. I'm eternally grateful. Thank you as well to everyone who has given me feedback on my work. Such words have been invaluable to me, and I appreciate them greatly.

Chapter One: A Child's Music box

Ever since Nix Winfire was a child, she danced alone in her room to the sound of her music box, which played a delicate tune. This tune was reminscent of dancing in the middle of a fairie circle while the small creatures played flutes and harps. Some days, she would pretend that she was a nymph dancing in the forests and allowing the summer breeze to glide through her wavy, shoulder length and dark brown hair as the warm air guided her movements. Rich green grass tickled her toes, and the peaceful sound of a nearby waterfall filled the air. The rhythm of the falling water aided her in her secretive dance.

She loved her music box dearly, and she adored examining every intricate detail inside. From the small purple-roofed house to the cat that stood on the cobblestone path. The music box had always seemed to be in her life. Nix didn't remember a day when she didn't have it. It was her most treasured possession. It transported her to another world: a world without worries or the constant yelling between her aunt and uncle, who adopted her at the age of five after her parents had died in a plane crash.

Nix remembered them promising to bring her back souvenirs from England. One of those souvenirs being a porcelain tea set, but she never received that tea set. Instead, she was brought into a house that never became quiet; there was always yelling. It was still somewhat of a home, though. With her music box, she could daydream in her small room.

As she grew older, her imagination could no longer drown out the fighting. Winding up the music box time after time would help dull the fighting but never block it entirely, especially, since her aunt and uncle brought her into their fights, which had nothing to do with her. Bruises piled on her body while she piled on the layers of makeup, wanting to hide the purplish- black marks on her skin. The music, however, drowned out her tears, permitting no one but herself to hear them. How she craved to live in that peaceful world within the music box.

At the age of sixteen, something peculiar appeared in her music box, though. A small girl stood in the box's garden. Her sunhat and simple orange dress complimented her rich brown eyes and golden locks. Nix had no idea how the girl came to be there, but she found that the small child fit the scenery well. She wished to question her aunt and uncle on it, but she figured that the pair would accuse her of stealing. So, she kept quiet about the girl and let it be.

Another two years had passed since then, bringing with it more yells and attacks, but her music box could no longer save her. For that day, her aunt came bursting into her room when she wound up the cherished possession. The older woman's eyes were the definition of madness as she stared at the intricate music box. Noticing the woman's gaze, Nix darted for the box on her dresser, but her aunt reached it first.

Grabbing it in her hands, the woman stared at Nix's form and smiled as she gazed upon worried dark brown eyes. Those eyes begged the older woman to set down the box. A grin spread across her aunt's face. "Do you know how long I've had to listen to this stupid thing play. Day after day this tune invaded my mind, but I allowed you to play it, hoping that one day you would grow out of it, grow out of your childish ways. That never happened, though. How I wanted it to end; how I wanted the tune to stop playing as my husband yelled at me. Its sickening tune never stopped. Today, however, that will end!" Raising the box above her head, she slammed it against the floor.

Cogs flew out of box's bottom as the cat's head broke off from its body and rolled across the carpet floor. The purple-roofed house tilted over as its roof was now detached. As the box broke, the tune slowed down, morphing into a dreadful combination of notes until even that sound became nonexistent.

Her aunt began to dance crazily around the room, shouting "I'm free! I'm free from that awful sound! No more music will ever come from this room!" She began laughing quietly until her laugh transformed into an onslaught of crazed chuckling. Nix's escape had vanished completely, and she was left with the sounds of a mad woman who abused her on a daily basis.

Finally, her laughing died down as she gave Nix one last crazed grin. By now, Nix was collapsed on the floor, trying to piece the music box back together. Walking up to her niece, Nix's aunt kicked the broken box from her hands and rested her hands on Nix's shoulders. Smiling, the older woman took one of her hands and ruffled the younger's hair. "Aww, don't worry Nix. You'll get over it soon enough." Leaving the room, her aunt slammed the door behind her and made it seem as though the wall would break from the harsh closing of the door.

There was no chance that she would ever get over her music box; it was one of the presents that her parents had given her. That didn't stop her, however, from trying to fix it. Grabbing a glue bottle, she collected all the pieces, which were scattered about her room, and began her repairs. She managed to glue everything back to the way it was except for the cogs. No matter how hard she tried, she couldn't get the cogs to go back into their proper places, rendering the tune of the music box forever lost. It was evening when she stopped working on it. She refused to leave her room, not wanting to see her aunt or uncle or catching sight of her aunt's crazed face again.

Crawling over to her bed, she lay the box on her stomach and peered into its small world. Sighing, she placed it on her nightstand and turned off the light. Her room was cast in the calming light of the moon. She rested her left arm over her eyes, closed her eyes and wished outloud to be rid of this world and to go into the world of the music box.

Once her wish left her lips, she heard the sound of a key winding up. In moments, she heard a familiar tune resonate throughout her room. Turning her head slowly, she looked over to the music box. There was no mistaking it; it really was playing, but how? She knew that she hadn't turned the key. Besides, some of the cogs were missing.

Sitting upright, she grabbed the box and inspected it . Upon making contact with it, she felt a force tugging on her and pulling her into the music box. A final tug was made, and she felt the world around herself change. Closing her eyes, she waited until the tug on her stopped.

Opening her eyes, she gazed around at her surroundings. They were identical to the ones in her music box. She was standing in the flower garden. Gazing beyond the music box, she looked upon her room, which seemed massive and like a giant lived there instead of her. Pinching herself, she found that she wasn't dreaming. The sound of water penetrated her ears, and she looked behind her. Nix saw the cat watering the flower garden as he stood on the cobblestone walkway.

He noted her staring at him and waved one of his arms, but there was no glue present; the cat had returned to its original state. In fact, the entire music box looked as it did before her aunt had smashed it. "How can this be?" she muttered to herself.

"Because, you wished for it," a sweet voice said from the other side of the garden.

Following the sound, her eyes met with the girl in the sunhat and orange dress. "I'm afraid I don't understand," Nix stated, still staring at her.

Her short, golden blonde hair bounced as she giggled lightly to herself. "You don't need to understand, Nix. Like I said, you made this wish, so it came true. It's an honor to finally be able to speak with you."

Realizing that she was not going to clarify anymore on the situation, Nix sighed and decided to be content since this world was better than her old one. Soon, though, her brief peace was interrupted by thunderous footsteps. Covering her ears, she watched as her aunt opened the room door so roughly that it almost tore off of the hinges.

The older woman stared angrily at the music box, not even noticing that her niece wasn't present in the room. Grabbing Nix's hand, the sunhat girl began to shove her towards the purple-roofed house. "Hurry! You must get inside, Nix, before your aunt reaches us."

"Wait, how is that going to help? The house is still apart of this music box," Nix yelled as the sunhat girl continued to shove her forwards. The footsteps increased in volume, making her head ache in pain.

"Stop asking questions. Just get inside before it's too late."

Before Nix could protest anymore, the sunhat girl opened the door and pushed her inside the house. For just a second, however, before the girl shut the door, Nix saw her smile twist into a more sinister one. The door's latch clicked, locking her inside, yet she still heard the booming footsteps of her aunt.

Running over to the window, she gazed outside and saw that her aunt finally reached the music box. It felt as if she were suddenly thrown into a moving elevator when her aunt picked up the item. Nix rolled across the purple and black tiled floor, knocking over a round table and chairs. Dragging herself back to the window, she peered out and saw her aunt raising the box above her head. The older woman threw the box, causing Nix to crash into the wall opposite of her. She heard the box smash against the floor as a chair slid into her, knocking her unconcsious. The last thing Nix saw was the sunhat girl smiling at her in a wicked way.

When she awoke, Nix found herself on black and white tiles. Glancing around, she saw that it looked like the inside of the purple-roofed house but slightly changed. Besides the one color of the tiles changing, there was no furniture present within the room. Only crimson walls surrounded her as paintings decorated the walls. Each painting, however, only portrayed an endless void, seeming to suck the viewer inside if they stared for too long.

Two doors were in front of her, though; one blue and the other red. Walking up to them, she examined each and wondered which door to go through. It was better than staying in this strange room. While she was inspecting the doors, she didn't notice the four eyes watching her from above.

"Diamond, it looks like our new plaything has finally arrived after nearly two years of waiting."

"Yes, it does look that way, Heart. I'm looking quite forward to the entertainment ahead."

Both brothers stared at her, waiting for her next move and what door she would choose.

Chapter Two: The Blue Heart

Looking between the two doors, Nix first examined the blue door. It was painted in a blue-grey hue, and the paint was starting to peel away, giving the door an antique feel. The doorknob was composed of a blue, circular crystal with a blue butterfly frozen within the doorknob. On the other hand, the red door was painted in a rich crimson, looking brand new as though it had been painted yesterday: the new paint almost resembling fresh blood. Its doorknob was made entirely out of brass, shining brightly in the strange room.

Backing away from the two doors, she finally decided to enter through the blue door. Resting her hand on the doorknob, she slowly turned it as the door creaked in response. The room behind her began to fade as she entered into a new realm.

~ ~ ~ ~ ~ ~ ~ ~ ~ ~

"Seems that she chose your door, brother. I'm quite jealous," came the voice of the older of the two.

"Yes, I must greet our new plaything. I wonder how she'll react to my opening act?" questioned the younger.

"Don't get too carried away. We don't want to terrify her too much."

"Don't worry, I won't. Until we meet again, my dear brother."

Heart vanished from his brother's sight, leaving him alone in the strange room. Diamond couldn't wait until she reached the next checkpoint where she would meet him. It had been a long time since they had a visitor, so he grinned in anticipation at meeting her and vanished from the room.

~ ~ ~ ~ ~ ~ ~ ~ ~ ~

Once through the door, it slammed behind her and disappeared, forever preventing her from going backwards. She was forced to wander deeper into the mysterious world before her. Focusing her gaze on what was in front of her, she saw an enchanting but eerie forest.

Trees twisted their dark branches, blocking out any light from above. Delicate blue lanterns hung from some branches and illuminated a quiet stream. Fireflies hovered in the air, glowing like specks of light. Spider webs were nestled in the trees while, in one of the nearby ones, a spider slowly consumed its prey: the moth struggling to get away but failing horribly. Birds that made strange noises watched from the trees, some hidden while others apparent. They seemed to follow her every move, and she dared not go any closer to them.

What terrified her the most, though, was the blue mist, which crept around the forest floor, bringing shadowy figures along with it. The shadows didn't seem to notice her and wandered aimlessly in the forest as if they were lost souls, who had no purpose in the world.

Not seeing a path of any form, she decided to follow the stream and permittied it to guide her through the forest. Many times it broke off in several ways, but she kept choosing the way that had no shadows. Despite them not noticing her, she didn't want to risk getting too close to them. She had no concept of time as she walked through the forest; she only wished to find a way out of it. Nix wondered how this world could even fit within the music box. Then again, she did manage to wish herself into the item, so she figured that anything could happen at this point.

The image of the sunhat girl's smiling face kept filling her mind. Why was the girl grinning like that? Nix wanted to know, but, at the same time, she thought it best to keep her distance from the girl because who knew what lay behind that smile of hers. From her experiecne with her aunt, she knew that a smile didn't necessarily mean a good thing.

Focusing her attention back in front of her, she heard something rustling in the trees above. A light chuckle soon followed. At first, she thought that it had been one of the weird birds, but none of the birds had chuckled before. Hesitantly, she peered upwards into the trees and noticed a person sitting among the tree branches.

From where he was sitting, she couldn't see too many of his features, but she could tell that his clothes were that of a jester. She narrowed her eyes, trying to get a better view of the male. He only chuckled at her curiousity before jumping down from the tree. Startled, she moved back some, waiting to see what he would do.

With him in front of her, she could see his features and attire better. A blue, red and black four-armed jester hat sat atop his head of baby blue short hair. Stunning dark blue eyes shone through his bangs while a painted blue heart decorated his left eye and a red tear lay under his right eye. His clothes consisted of a white button-up, light blue vest, with silver heart-shaped buttons, dark blue long coat, black pants and blue-heeled shoes. On his right side, a saber with a silver handle rested.

The strange man began to approach her, a gorgeous smile gracing his lips. Reaching her, he bowed before her and continued to smile at her confused expression. He grabbed her left hand and brought it to his lips, kissing it in the process. "A pleasure to meet you, my dear lady. You may call me Heart," he mentioned smoothly, rising to his full height of about 5'9. Blushing at his gentlemanly introduction, she stood frozen not knowing what to do. Nix tried to bring words to her mouth but only stuttered in the process. "I see that I left you speechless. That makes my job all the easier."

Before she could react, he removed the saber from his side and swiped it across her face in a quick movement. She could feel warm blood trailing down her right cheek and moved her right hand to touch it. Removing her hand a few moments later, she stared at the crimson substance before she returned her gaze towards the male in front of her. His eyes gleamed as he came closer to her. Nix tried to back away, but she couldn't get away fast enough.

Heart had his hand gripped around her left wrist, keeping her in place. "That looks like a nasty cut. Perhaps, I should fix it for you," he breathily spoke. She couldn't do much but watch as he brought his tongue across the wound, licking the blood away. Pulling away, he licked his lips and appeared satisfied. "There all better!"

Staring in shock, she soon heard movement all around her as the entire forest took on an utterly terrifying atmosphere. The movement only increased while Heart raised his arms into the air in a grand manner. "Now, let the show begin! Do well to entertain me, my dear lady. Or else, the next time we meet face to face; well, you'll see if it comes to that. Goodbye for now!"

With another bow, he vanished, but she became more focused on her surroundings due to the approaching movement. Suddenly, she felt a cold presence on her right arm. Terrified, she slowly turned her head, coming face to face with one of the shadows from before. She pulled her arm back and started to walk away from it, only to see herself surrounded. Why were they attracted to her all of a sudden? Was it possibly because of her blood?

She looked for a way to escape, and when she found an opening, she headed straight for it. Her feet propelled her forward as an earsliptting scream swept across the forest. Curiousity grabbing ahold of her, she looked over her shoulder to see the shadows suddenly on all fours. Their once human-like hands were now sharp claws.

Panick and fear washed over her as she began to dart through the trees. She heard many shadows chasing after her, their knife-like hands scraping across the ground and splashing through the small stream. Birds shrieked above her, seeming to laugh at her current predicament. Among these horrible noises, she heard the chuckling of a certain male. She wished that she had never encountered him. Her wish may have granted her access to this twisted world, but this world now seemed to control her.

As she ran away from the shadows, she avoided the stream as much as possible so that she would not slip. A shadow, however, jumped in front of her current course, sending her into the water. Upon contact, she slid down the stream as water and mud began to cover her figure. She could feel the mud sticking to her dark brown hair, and she had to close her dark brown eyes in order to avoid getting anything in them.

Trying to get up, she slipped back down as she felt the cold hands grasp her. The knive-like hands cut into her arms and legs as tears threatened to come out of her eyes. She had to get up, or she would die. That was the last thing that she wanted. Using all of her strength, she pried the shadows off of her and received some cuts upon her hands in the process. With the shadows off of her, she swiftly picked herself up and made a run for it. Blood ran down her arms and legs as she proceeded through the forest.

Soon, she would need to find a place to rest and tend to her wounds, or she would potentially die from blood loss. As her feet pounded against the forest floor, she began to feel a little dizzy. "Don't die on me now, my dear lady! I'm cheering for you! Run! Run! Your time is only ticking away!"

So, he was still watching her every move. He was right about her time of consiousness fading, and she needed to find a way out of this forest. Taking a quick look behind her, she saw the shadows closing in: their shrieks climbing in intensity. She hurriedly looked for a way out. As if another wish of hers was granted, a wooden door lay straight ahead of her.

Being her life line, she pushed herself to run faster towards it. Ten more steps, eight more steps, six, four, two, zero left. Her hand gripped the doorknob, and she turned it in a panic. Opening slowly, the door creaked as its ancient hinges protested against being used. Safety, presumably, waited past the threshhold, and she made her way through. Her ankles were swiftly grabbed, however, and she was pulled to the ground. Shadow hands gripped her, trying to bring her back into the forest.

Gripping the doorframe, she pulled herself into the other room. She managed to kick her ankles free from the shadows' grasp, and, in an instant, she slammed the door shut. Before the door fully closed, though, she caught sight of the amused smile of Heart before he disappeared once more.

Exhausted, she collapsed onto her back, breathing heavily and catching her breath from the chase. Glancing around the new room, she looked for anything that could bandage her wounds, but nothing of the sort stood out. Turning back over on her stomach, she was about to close her eyes before seeing a hand with long fingernails painted in red, black and gold extend out towards her. Too tired to refuse the hand, she clasped it. She hoped that the owner of the hand would help her and give her some insight into this strange world.

Chapter Three: The Red Diamond

When Nix came to stand on her legs, she gazed into fire-red eyes that seemed to only possess kindness. Tired still, she found herself not caring too much about the individual's appearance and merely noticed a figure clothed in hues of gold, blue, red and black. She saw the person guiding her over to a black round table with matching chairs. They placed her down in one of the chairs and disappeared from her field of vision. Feeling her body giving out, she laid her right arm on the table and rested her head on her arm. Soon, she heard something being set on the table.

"Don't go unconsiousness on me. I just summoned the bandages and medical supplies for you."

Despite the person's words, she had no energy left and just continued to rest her head on her arm. The person sighed before she felt a sudden sting. Shooting right up, she tried to pull her left arm back, but the person kept a firm grip on her.

"Hold still. This will go quicker that way. I need to clean your wounds before I put the bandages on. I can't have you dying on me."

When they had finished tending to her wounds, she placed her head back down and heard a chair move across the floor. With her wounds now tended to, she could finally relax after that encounter with Heart and the shadows. She had a feeling, though, that she would be seeing more of him.

Lifting her head up some and bringing her left hand up to her face, she gently glided her fingers across the cut on her cheek. Hopefully, it would heal soon. She didn't wish to be reminded of that jester's grin every time that she accidentally brushed the cut with one of her hands.

Hearing something else being set on the table, she found a black and white checkered teacup and saucer with gold trimming in front of her. The delicious scent of a cappucino filled her nose. Not being able to help herself, she wrapped her hands around the teacup and instantly felt the warmth of the coffee. Grateful for the comforting drink, she brought the beverage to her lips and took a careful sip so as to not burn herself. As the liquid touched her tongue, she seemed to awaken a little while the warmth spread throughout her body.

Analyzing her surroundings more, she noted the tiled floor followed the same pattern as the other room: a black and white checkered pattern. Red crimson walls surrounded her as the only significant piece of furniture was the table and its matching chairs. The rest of the room stretched on into a poorly lit hallway. Past a certain point, she could see nothing but a sea of darkness. So, where did the bandages and teacup with the coffee come from? This person did mention summoning the bandages and medical supplies.

Presently, though, it was hard not to focus on the man sitting across from her. Just like Heart, he was dressed like a jester. He wore a red, blue and black four-armed jester hat, which sat on a head of blood red locks. A painted red diamond decorated his right eye while a blue tear was under his left eye. A red button-up, with gold diamond-shaped buttons, red and black diamond-patterned vest, black pokcetwatch, black pants and red-heeled shoes covered his form. On his left side, a gold-handled saber rested.

Fully taking in his appearance, she tensed and hoped that he didn't have a personality like Heart. He seemed to notice her action and a smile fell upon his lips. "Don't worry. I'm not going to hurt you. I did mend your wounds, did I not? No matter, introductions are in order. I'm Diamond, but I do already know your name, Miss Nix."

Keeping her hands around the warm teacup, she froze. How did he know her name? Apparently, he understood her confusion and answered, "I have my means. Don't trouble yourself over it. Now, how's the coffee?"

"It's delicous. Thank you." Already, her warning signs were going off, though, and she probably should've been more careful about drinking the coffee. Her exhausted state, however, had caused her judgement on that to be less than sharp. "By the way, do you have any relation to Heart? I met him in the woods, and he was dressed kind of like you."

His smile widened slightly before he rested his head in the palm of his left hand. "Yes, he is my younger twin brother, but I assure you that I'm not like him. I just wanted to chat with you since you're our first guest in quite awhile."

Pushing the coffee away, she tried to remain calm after hearing his words. She had to keep reminding herself that he had tended to her wounds so in essence he had saved her life. "If you just want to chat, can you tell me more about this world. Anything would be fine. I just want to understand it a little."

A silence hovered in the air before Diamond started to laugh lightly. His eyes beamed in amusement at her question. She clearly didn't understand what was so funny and just waited for him to answer. "Miss Nix, that's not a question that I can just answer. There's many things for you to understand about this world. Would you please be more specific?"

"Well, you mentioned that you summoned the bandages and medical supplies here. What did you mean by that?"

He only continued to smile before adjusting himself a little in his seat. "I meant what I said. I can summon whatever I wish at will. Here in this world, individuals possess certain magical abilities. It varies with each individual, however. You came to this world by magical means as well."

"Magic? That seems far-fetched, yet this whole world is bizarre. So, I suppose that magic is the least of my worries."

"Magic is a normalcy here, and there are indeed things much worse than it in this world, but it seems that we have company. I had hoped to have more alone time with you, but we'll have more time in the future."

"I'm sorry to interrupt your time with our new plaything, my dear brother, but I couldn't stand being quiet any longer. Her wounds have been tended to. Surely, we can have some more fun with her now. Talking can wait," came a familiar voice to her ears.

Only staring at the coffee in front of her, she hoped that if she stared at it long enough, she would be transported away from the room that she was in, but no such effect took place. Slowly looking behind her, she saw Heart approaching her chair and grinning wickedly at her. Instantly, she went to dart out of her chair. Diamond, however, snapped his fingers, and restraints appeared on her arms and legs, securing her to the chair. "I thought that you weren't like your brother!" she shouted out at Diamond.

"I'm not with regards to appearances. See, he has mostly blue on, and I have mostly red on. Also, the color of our sabers is different. You just need to listen better, Miss Nix. Regardless, it's a shame that you couldn't finish your coffee; I don't want it to go to waste. Ah, I know; I will merely give you the rest myself."

"Just hurry up, Diamond. I want to play another game," whined the blue-haired male.

Diamond simply shook his head at his brother's impatience as he got closer to her. Picking up the teacup with the coffee, he brought it up to her lips, but she no longer desired to drink it and pulled her head back as far as possible from him. Sighing, Diamond pressed his right hand on her injured left arm, which sent a shock of pain through her.

Gasping, she becamse vulnerable as Diamond tilted the cup at her lips and poured some of the coffee into her mouth. Glaring at him, she spat the coffee back at him and caused coffee to run down the lower part of his face. Heart broke into a roaring laugh as the blue-haired jester gazed at his brother's unamused expression. "Looks like you'll have to punish her, Diamond," he managed out through his fit of laughs.

"Yes, it would appear that way, wouldn't it, Heart?"

A menacing look came over Diamond's face as he set down the coffee. "It would seem that my brother has already left a mark on you. I wish to place a mark as well. Please hold still, Miss Nix."

Her eyes followed his fingers as they glided over the cut on her cheek. His long painted fingernails trailed across her lips and traveled down her neck until they stopped on her left shoulder. Within a moment's notice, he dug the nail of his thumb into her skin. Biting the inside of her cheek, she tried her best not to cry out in pain as he dug his nail deeper. Dragging his nail across her skin, he formed the design of a diamond as blood trickled down her shoulder. Still glaring at him, she watched while he pulled away from her with a satisfied look on his face.

Blood dripped from his hand, falling onto the tiles below. The sound echoed throughout the room before Diamond pulled a cloth from one of his vest pockets and wiped the blood off. When he finished, the cloth vanished afterwards. "Miss Nix, would you like to try some coffee now? I really don't want it to go to waste."

"If you love it so much, why don't you drink it?" She didn't want to become their plaything. How dare they call her by such a name! A part of her knew, though, that she couldn't do much against them. Diamond could summon anything at will, and Heart might very well have the same ability if not some other magic trick up his sleeve.

"That is quite a good idea, Miss Nix." Taking the cup in his hands, he took a sip of the drink. Walking towards her, he lifted her chin up and pressed his lips to hers. He bit her lower lip harshly, causing her to gasp slightly, and coffee proceeded to flow from his mouth into hers.

Warmth swept across her cheeks in embarrassment, but she only felt disgust. She wanted to spit the coffee out, but Diamond kept his lips on hers, forcing her to swallow the liquid. Some droplets trailed down from her mouth and onto the floor below, creating an echo in the room like the blood had done. Diamond smiled upon breaking the forced kiss before she noted that there was still some coffee left in the teacup and hoped that he wouldn't do that again.

"I think that she enjoyed that brother," Heart mentioned with a wide grin.

Narrowing her eyes at Heart, she wanted to slap him on the spot, but the restraints held her back. "Like I would enjoy that, you sick monster!"

"I guess that I should try that again then," voiced the red-haired jester.

"What don't you ..." She was cut off by Diamond's lips crashing agasint hers. This time he was more aggressive, and when he bit down on her bottom lip, he sucked at it as he transferred the coffee. An almost inaudible moan escaped her lips, and when she realized this, her cheeks burned.

"I'm glad that you enjoyed it," Diamond breatheed out before he returned back to his chair and looked over at his brother. "Well, what fun did you have in mind?"

"I was thinking that we let her go into Remorse Forest and let her search for two doors that we summoned into the area. Whoever's door she finds first is the winner. The winner then gets alone time with her."

"It sounds fair. She'll definetely be mine. Prepare to lose, Heart."

"That's where you're wrong my dear brother, for I will claim her, not you."

Not being able to look at the brothers, she stared down at her lap. She wouldn't let them break her, but they were currently in control of her movements. What could she do to fight against them; she was currently only recovering from her injuries which she received from the shadows. In her weakened condition, she couldn't do much. Maybe, this forest would give her the chance to get away from them. It would be unlikely, but it was worth a try even if the name of the forest was somewhat discouraging. With determination now coursing through her, she awaited their game, ready to win against them.

Chapter Four: Running For Safety

The brothers, having decided on the game that they wanted to play, smiled at her as their eyes twinkled in delight. Heart walked over to Nix, grabbing the top of her chair with one of his hands. He began to drag her over to a golden door with a silver doorknob. Silver hearts and diamonds were engraved in the metal door, giving recognition to the two brothers. Diamond stood up from his chair and opened the door, allowing Heart to push her chair and her into the forest. Diamond proceeded into the new terrain afterwards, closing the door behind him. They must have used another magic ability to connect the forest to the room.

Looking over the forest, she was thankful that she could see no shadows roaming around the trees. Instead, dark green leaves grew on thick branches, which connected to a thicker tree base. Green grass littered the base of the forest and accompanied the seemingly endless trees. It was completeley silent except for the breathing of the three of them, which gave it an overly creepy atmosphere. She almost wanted the creatures with the glowing eyes to become apparent so as to give the forest a little more activity. Both brothers walked in front of her chair and stopped a few paces in front of her.

"Well, I am ready to start, Diamond."

"As am I, Heart."

They bowed in front of her, each with an excited grin planted on their faces.

"Please do try to have some fun, Miss Nix."

"Yes, do well to please us, my dear lady."

Diamond snapped his fingers and the restraints on her chair vanished. Feeling nothing holding her back, she stood out of her chair and grasped it. Despite her injured state, she threw the chair at the two twins, but before the chair could make impact, they disappeared. Colliding with the ground, the chair broke into several pieces.

Walking up to the broken chair, she picked up one of the larger pieces. At the current moment, she could see nothing ahead in the woods but the trees. Even if that was the case, she still felt that she needed to arm herself. A piece of wood would probably not do much, but it was better than nothing.

Making her way into the sea of trees, the grass crunched under her feet and gave away her position to anything that roamed in the forest. At one point, she became irritated to the point where she wanted to take off her shoes but decided against it in case she needed to run in the future.

What felt like twenty minutes had passed, and nothing had happened. She knew that the brothers wanted her to find one of their doors, but how could one find anything in these woods? Still, she was glad that she hadn't found a door yet. This gave her more time away from them. Nix was slightly delighted with the uneventful forest because she guessed that the two brothers were extremely bored at the moment.

When what felt like another ten minutes passed, still nothing had happened, nor did she see anything new. Frustrated and tired, she halted her movement and glanced around her, trying to catch sight of anything interesting in the forest; there was nothing. Her tired legs and injuries were only making this worse. Sure, they had bandages around them, but that didn't mean that they were healed. Not being able to stand anymore, she collapsed to the ground. She couldn't see anything new, but she suddenly felt something come across her legs.

Looking down, she saw mist beginning to form in the forest while the sound of crying resonated throughout it. A chill ran up her spine at the piercing sound. That crying sounded more of a warning than anything else and only grew louder. Deciding that it was time to get up, she got to her feet slowly and headed away from it.

"It would seem that the Crier has finally awakened," Diamond remarked from atop a tree branch close to their plaything.

"About time, it will surely speed things up. She'll find one of our doors in no time now," remarked the other brother.

"Indeed, but let's make sure that she doesn't die. I have too many plans for her."

"You worry too much, my dear brother. Let's just enjoy the show."

"I suppose that you're right."

Nix tried to quicken her pace, but her injuries refused to give in. This frustrated her as she could tell that the crying sound was only getting nearer. Sighing, she pressed forward until she reached two paths in the forest. One probably led to Heart's door and the other to Diamond's door. From where she was standing, she could tell that the paths made turns up ahead, one leading west and the other east. In between the paths, though, rested only more trees. She desired to get rid of the crying that was following her, but, at the same time, she didn't want to enter one of the brothers' doors. Gathering up her courage, she didn't take either path but went head first towards the area that separated the paths.

"Ah, it looks like she's avoiding the paths. What should we do?" Diamond asked, in a hushed voice as they followed after her quietly.

"Let's continue watching. She'll realize her mistake in avoiding the paths soon enough and will go back towards one of them," Heart murmured back.

Heading into that area, the mist at her feet grew and reached up to her knees. These trees allowed almost no light in, making the space almost pitch black. She had to slow down her already steady pace in order to navigate her way around the trees. Nix wouldn't go down one of the paths. A downside, though, was that she had no idea if the forest ended up ahead or if she was heading deeper into the possibly endless woods. Hopefully, it would be the first case and not the second.

As she continued, the crying finally stopped. The new silence only terrified her more, and she could hear her heartbeat quicken. Stopping, she turned around and looked through the trees behind her to see if the creature was still following her. To her utter horror, her eyes landed on a creature which was about her height of 5'3.

It had nothing covering its body except its own pale skin, with various small rips in the skin as though the skin wasn't made for its wearer. Its fingers were long and pointed. There were no eyes on the creature's face but only a circular mouth with skin stretching from one lip to the other. Inside the creature's mouth, there were no teeth or a tongue; it was just a pit of void.

Backing away slowly, she watched to see if it made any movements. Cocking its head to the side, it moved one foot forward before halting. Bringing both of its hands up to its face, it dragged its pointed fingers downwards. The creature's action seemed to happen in slow motion before it let out a horrifying cry, which was filled with sadness and hunger. Blood dripped down its face as it stared at her with its eyeless face.

There was only one thing left to do, run. The piece of wood in her hand would do nothing against that creature she reasoned. So, she dropped it and pushed her legs as hard as she could. Pain shot through them as the wounds on her legs protested against the action. Blood trickled down her legs and into her shoes, making her want to rip her shoes and socks off. In the current situation, however, such a thing wasn't possible. Her running was starting to die down as her legs couldn't carry on with the strain, but she could hear the creature trailing behind her.

A minute passed, then another, but hope came into her vision as light flooded into the forest. She could see a deserted village in the distance. Pushing her legs past their healthy limit, she bounded towards it. Cries carried on behind her, but she didn't turn around. Only ten more steps and she would be within the village. The creature let out another loud cry, and she could hear it increase its pace.

On her last step, she leaped forward and landed on the cobblestone road, collapsing to the path upon contact. Peering behind her, she saw that the creature couldn't step outside of the forest. It banged its hands against an invisible wall as it cried out loudly. Turning back around, she let out a sigh of relief and picked herself up. The creature lay behind her, and the deserted village lay in front of her; she had avoided the brothers' doors.

"She made it to the village. That's quite frustrating. We allowed our dear lady a loophole."

"Are you giving up, Heart? We can always change the game, or I can just take her for myself."

"I'm not giving up, Diamond; I will win. Like you said, we just have to change the game. I know. How about a game of hide and seek? First one to find and catch her wins. What do you say?"

"Yes, that will work. We'll leave her alone for ten minutes and then begin the game."

Both brothers agreed on the terms and disappeared until their game began, leaving her alone in the village. She knew nothing of their new game, though, and she was still a piece on their chessboard.

<u>Chapter Five: Hide and Seek Part One</u>

Gazing into the village, her eyes fell upon an abandoned cart which rested in the center of it. Not too far from the wagon was a fountain filled with stale water and dark green grass. Pointed houses outlined the walkway and led to the tallest building in the village, which looked to be a church. Only the moon in the sky illuminated the chilling place.

A cold breeze began to rise throughout the village, leaving her shivering in her pathetic excuse for clothes. Her shoes and socks were soaked with her own blood while her tan cargo pants were in shreds up to her knees; her black v-neck and hoodie were torn in many places. Mud was caked on parts of her hair and on her clothes. Even the silver hoops, which she had been wearing, had fallen off along the way.

Going further into the area, she began to explore. Nix hoped to find something to mend her now reopened wounds. She doubted that there would be bandages, but, maybe, there would be some cloth, in a decent condition, lying around somewhere.

Examining each house to see if she could enter, a loud bell began to ring from the top of the church. The sudden noise startled her, and she had the urge to look around her. Terrified, she watched as the once cold breeze began to swirl around itself. It started to form the shapes of people. They had no face, just a featurless head and an upper body while the bottom was entirely composed of the wind. Seeing the transformation of the breeze, she began pounding on all of the village doors and attempted to find one that would open. Sadly, her panic drew the forms' attention.

The bell rang a second time, and that's when they started to move towards her. Cursing to herself, she tried each door in a mad rush. At last, she found a door that opened. Swiftly, she raced into the house and slammed the door behind her right before one of the forms reached her. She locked the door, ripped the tattered curtains from the dusty window and shoved them underneath door, preventing the forms from entering through the tiny space.

Hearing their raspy breath against the door, she waited to see if they would attempt to enter. Her heart pounding, she stood close to the door until they finally left to somewhere else in the village. When the last one passed the window, she went over to dusty old couch and collasped upon it. Dust came up in a cloud, making her cough in reply.

Once the dust left her alone, she examined the house for any form of a decent cloth. Only an old wooden table with broken chairs lay in front of her while a kitchen accompanied a peeling wall. Drawers were removed from the kitchen counters, and broken dishes were scattered on the ground. Sighing, she turned her field of vision to the left side of her and saw stairs heading up to the second floor. She might find something in a bedroom. Getting up slowly from the faded pink couch, she made her way up the stairs but had to stop a few times due to the pain in her legs. Having run around and searching for a door hadn't exactly aided her condition.

When she reached the upstairs, she saw all the doors to the rooms removed, and her eyes landed on the master bedroom. Making her way to the room, she peered into the other rooms as she passed. Two more bedrooms were in the house: one on the right and one on the left. In the right one, the bed was torn into pieces, scattering wood shards and fabric throughout the room. There was nothing else distinguishable in the room. The left room remained emtpy except for a barren bedframe and blank papers that were spread on the floor. Beyond the two rooms was a single bathroom with a broken mirror and only pipes remaining instead of a sink, toilet and shower. She shuddered to think what happened to the village given what she was seeing so far.

Entering the master bedroom, she was surprised to view it in perfect condition expect for the dust that covered everything. A king size bed lay in the middle of the room while rich purple sheets covered it, and cozy pillows rested at the head of the bed. Rich mahogany furniture outlined the room, extending from a dresser, to a vanity and a writing desk. A door was on the left side of the room, which probably led to the bathroom.

Making her way over to the dresser, she opened the first drawer and found it stuffed with scarves and socks. Smiling to herself, she grabbed several scarves, which looked brand new, and decided to use them as her new bandages. Nix grabbed a pair of grey socks, which were a little big for her as well. Opening the second drawer, she found a couple pair of pants, two belts and some shirts within. Picking out a pair of cotton grey pants and a long-sleeved, black and cotton shirt along with a brown leather belt, she made her way into the bathroom.

Entering the bathroom, she set everything on the sink counter. A shower with no shower curtains lay to her side while a toilet sat in between the sink and shower. Dust covered the bathroom mirror as well. Locking the door behind her, she began to change her bandages. Ten minutes had passed, however, and a game unknown to her began.

~ ~ ~ ~ ~ ~ ~ ~ ~ ~

Sitting in a round room in their seaside manor, the twins sat on polished silver chairs with gold cushions. A silver square table separated the two while a bone china teapot with gold hearts and diamonds painted on it rested on top. Fresh earl grey tea sat within the teapot as well as in the brothers' teacups. Cream and four cubes of sugar were in Heart's cup while no sugar or cream rested in Diamond's tea. Each brother sipped their beverage, waiting for the ten minutes to be over. A large grandfather clock ticked away in the back of the small room, the pendulum swinging back and forth. Heart tapped his foot against the blue and red checkered tiled floor as Diamond stared at the black and white walls, hoping that the time would somehow go faster by doing so.

"Is it time yet brother?" the blue-haired male whined, popping a sugar cube into his mouth.

"Not yet, we still have four minutes to go. I only hope that the spirits have not gotten her yet. I heard the bell ring. I really wouldn't want to find her harmed by them."

"You wouldn't have to worry if you hadn't set such a long waiting time."

"I set that time because it gives our plaything a chance to hide. In her current condition, it was only fair to do so. Now, we're almost down to three minutes."

Heart continued to tap his foot against the floor impatiently while pouring some more tea into his cup and adding two more sugar cubes to the mixture. Stirring the additional sugar into the tea, Heart stared at Diamond with a bored expression. "You know, brother, the condition of our plaything's clothes is quite horrendous. Whoever wins will have to change that, don't you think?"

"Yes, I agree, but I think that she will put up quite a struggle."

"I know; I'm hoping that she does. It will be all the more fun to break her and make her ours."

Diamond shook his head a little at his brother's comment, but he knew that he too would enjoy her struggle against them. He was still surprised at how much she resisted them. He had expected her to give in after entering through the first door and to beg not to go through another round. The red-haired jester, however, remebered her eager look to go into the forest.

It was a shock that she had decided upon neither path but ran head first towards the area that could have led nowhere. He certaintly didn't think that she would make it out of the trees before the Crier got her, but she had surprised him on that point too. Her performance so far was greatly entertaining to him, and he looked forward to seeing more of it.

Time pressed on, and, soon, the grandfather clock rung loudly, indicating to the brothers that the ten minutes were up. Heart jumped out of his seat happily, his teacup disappearing and preventing it from crashing against the tiled floor. Diamond gently set his own teacup down before it vanished as well. Soon, they both transported themselves to the village. Their game had begun and no sooner were they walking the cobblestone streets of the village.

By the time the brothers had arrived, most of the spirits had retreated either to the church at the back of the village, which was also the village's meeting area, or the underground passages. This gave the brothers nearly trouble free access to the village, and both would be able to mostly avoid drawing their sabers. Heart took one side of the street while Diamond took the other.

~ ~ ~ ~ ~ ~ ~ ~ ~ ~

After she took off the old bandages, she found that the sink still functioned, and the water that came was clear and clean. Grabbing one of the dusty towels that lay on the door hook, she drenched it in water and began to clean her wounds once all the dust was washed off of the towel. During this, she had no idea how close Heart and Diamond were to finding her hiding spot. To be honest, she had forgotten about the twins for a moment. She was just relieved to be rid of the monster back in the forest and the forms which were outside.

With her new bandages on, she took off her damaged clothing; glad to be rid of the blood soaked socks. Picking up a new towel, she wet it as well and began to wipe the rest of her skin off. Rubbing the mud, blood and filth off of her body felt great, even more so when she ran hair under the water in the sink.

Once satisified, she put on the new set of clothes and laughed a little at the pants. They were two sizes too large, but the belt held them up. They did keep her warm, though. The shirt was huge as well and hung loosely on her, going down almost to her knees while the sleeves hid her hands. Looking in the mirror, she saw her appearance and shook her head in disapproval, but, at the same time, she had never been so thankful for new clothes.

Glancing down at her shoes, she looked at them in disgust. They were covered in blood and mud, giving them a horrible appearance. Pushing their appearance aside and walking back into the bedroom, she looked around for any usable shoes. When she saw none, she sighed in annoyance. Her irritation evaporated, however, due to hearing the front door open. Soon, the front door closed again while humming resonated throughout the house.

Focusing back on the room, she looked around her but found no good hiding place. She could hide under the bed, but that was too obvious, and she knew that she would be found within seconds of the newcomer entering the room. Nix was certain that the newcomer was either Heart or Diamond, though.

Peering to the the small window in the bedroom, she bolted to it. It was shut tight, unfortunately, and she couldn't get it to budge. Speedily, she ran over to the writing desk, grabbed a large metal paperweight and threw it at the window, shattering it into the pieces. She heard the newcomer quicken their pace as the sound resonated throughout the building.

Just as she was climbing out of the window and avoiding the glass, she saw Heart enter the room. His eyes met hers, but for no more than second because she soon jumped down below, landing on the roof of another house. Making her way down it, she gripped the edges of the roof and let herself drop to the street below. Luckily for her, Heart couldn't fit through the window. This gave her time to run into one of the alleyways. Pressing herself against the wall, she waited for Heart to exit the house and pass her by. The front door slammed shut as she heard him yell out, "You can't hide forever, my dear lady. I'm sure that you're quite tired and hungry at the moment. Wherever do you plan to get your food, my dear lady? Surely, you don't intend to find some in this abandoned village? So, come out, come out!"

Nix heard another set of footsteps appraoching the area and assumed it to be Diamond. "I see that you had found Miss Nix, but you didn't catch her. I must say that I'm amused at your failure, brother."

"Tch, I'll find her again and catch her before you. I'll definitely have that alone time with her!"

"That waits to be seen, Heart. I will take your failure and claim my victory."

After their conversation, she could hear footsteps coming closer to her. Panicking, she looked for a way out of the situation. Two doors lay in the alley and finding one of them unlocked, she quickly went inside.

Chapter Six: Hide and Seek Part Two

When she shut the door quietly behind her and locked it, what she saw terrified her; she almost wanted to go back into the alley and take her chances with Diamond. Moonlight shone through the small window and illuminated two demonic looking masks, which decorated the wall just above a fireplace. Each mask bore dried blood on it. Next to the masks was an oil painting , depicting many shadowy figures attacking some sort of creature. To make matters worse, a dried pool of blood lay by the fireplace.

Drawing her attention away from the strange objects, she noticed ancient looking texts piled on the floor by the fireplace while to her right side rested aisles of books, which had the same ancient appearance. Dark grey painted walls and spider webs were common among the old room.

Thinking that she would search the building some, she progressed down the first aisle of books. Besides, she wished to get away from the horrifying masks that stared back at her with hollow eyes. As she made her way down the aisle, she continually listened to see if anyone would enter the room. So far that did not happen, and she continued to glance at the books' titles to the best of her ability. She had limited light to work with after all. Still, she hoped that maybe she could find something on this world or the sunhat girl.

Her fingers glided over the books and wiped some of the dust off to give her a better view of their titles. The first aisle provided not a single text that would enlighten her curious mind, and she pressed onto the second aisle. About to proceed down the second aisle, a wispy hand slowly emerged from around the corner of the next aisle. Quickly and quietly, she went in the other direction. She could hear a slight breeze still from the other aisle. Trying to breathe as softly as she could, she went into the first aisle that she had entered and went back down its dusty shelves. Accidentally, however, she knocked off a book from one of the shelves. In that moment, a quick swoosing sound resonated throughout the room.

Not being able to move quick enough, she was faced with one of the featureless forms from outside. It stared at her, seeming to determine what to do with her. Backing away slowly, the form followed her, its arms draped casually at its sides. Reaching the end of the aisle, she saw a mass of books coming straight for her. Having no time to dodge, she raised her arms and placed them in front of her face. To her surprise, they never came into contact with her. Instead, they were slashed into pieces.

"Found you, Miss Nix."

Making eye contact with Diamond, she didn't know whether to fill happy or extremely concerned or both. He just protected her, but she didn't want to discover his future plans for her. She stared at him wide eyed, not knowing what to do. Diamond just smiled kindly at her before he turned his attention to the approaching form. With saber in hand, Diamond neared the form, giving Nix the slight opportunity to get away from both Diamond and the form.

Getting her legs to work, she bolted for the door that was opposite from the aisles. She heard a high pitched scream behind her before slow footsteps followed. There were only a few seconds probably left before Diamond would reach her. With that small window of time, she twisted the doorknob, leaving the room and the jester behind.

Back on the cobblestone street, she headed further into the town. Glancing around for any hiding place, she saw out of the corner of her eye Heart, whose back was currently turned towards her. She needed a place to hide fast, and, not having many options presented to her, she ran for a broken window. When she jumped through the window, Heart turned around and noticed her vanishing form. Smirking, he made his way over to her new hiding place.

Knowing that time was not in her favor, she quickly examined her surroundings, only to find a giant hole in front of her. There was nothing else in the house, but, looking down the hole, she could see nothing: just darkness. Hearing Heart's footsteps nearing her, she edged her way over to the gaping hole.

"I wouldn't go down there, my dear lady. Only nasty spirits live in that pit. Honestly, just let me win. It will be better for the both of us."

Just seeing Heart's smiling face made her want to gag in disgust. His left hand extended out towards her, but she wouldn't give up. Besides, he could just be lying to her. So, she jumped into the abyss below.

~ ~ ~ ~ ~ ~ ~ ~ ~ ~

"This isn't good, and I was hoping that I wouldn't have to fight any spirits," Heart sighed out, rubbing the back of his head, with his left hand, in vexation.

"So, she went into the underground of the village. Looks like we'll have to go after her. Of course, brother, if you want to avoid fighting spirits, you can always stay behind," came the voice of the other twin as he came into the building.

Heart glared at his brother before he began smirking. There was no way that he was going to lose to his twin. If fighting countless spirits meant winning and claiming her, he would go head first into the fight that was waiting below. "I don't think so, my dear brother. Let's see who can find her first!" With no further hesitation, Heart jumped into the hole, letting the darkness engulf him. Diamond followed soon after, determined to win as well.

~ ~ ~ ~ ~ ~ ~ ~ ~ ~

As she fell down the hole, air pushed her hair back, and she waited to make impact with the floor below. At last, she hit something soft while a giant cloud of dust arose around her. Waving the dust away, she found an illuminated tunnel in front of her. Lanterns' grey light, probably lit by magic, cast shadows all along the stone tunnel and allowed her to see that she had landed on a pile of sacks filled with hay. Knowing that Heart would soon come down, she hopped off of the sacks and went down the tunnel. She could see that it broke off into two separate paths up ahead, and, upon reaching the break, she went down the left path.

Behind her, she could hear another person land on the sacks, which she was certain was Heart. Another person soon landed afterwards, indicating that probably Diamond was down in the tunnels as well. As she traveled down the tunnel, it made several turns, which hid her well in case either or both brothers took her path. On the seventh turn, a breeze shot through the tunnel. Several spirits soon appeared in front of her. They swayed in the light breeze as they blocked her path.

Not knowing what to do, she grabbed one of the lanterns from the wall and opened it. Holding it in front of her and with the flame to them, she waited to see if the spirits would react. To her relief, they moved to the side, allowing her passage. With caution, she proceeded past them and quickened her pace as she heard footsteps coming closer to her. Cursing, she pressed on and desired to make it out of the tunnels soon.

Sadly, only more spirits blocked her path, but these ones were much more aggressive than the last ones. One of them quickly flew at her, making her lantern go out as it swept past her. When she tried to grab another lantern, the spirits formed a circle around her. They began to spin rapidly around her, not stopping for even a second. Getting quite dizzy, she closed her eyes and wanted it to be over. Within a few seconds, a numbness started to wash over her arms and legs. Opening her eyes, she saw ghost-like hands clasped around her limbs.

The energy in her body seemed to decrease as the numbness spread throughout her body. Collasping, she lay on her left side as all feeling in her body vanished. Her consciousness started to fade, and her heart slowed down. Before losing consiousness, she saw heeled shoes approaching her. One of the brothers had found her. There was nothing that she could do against them; her vision was vanishing, and her body was numb. With her eyes now closed, she heard metal ringing and multiple high pitched screams echoing down the long tunnel until she went unconsious.

Chapter Seven: A Dinner of the Heart

The brother carrying her finally reached the other tunnel and made his way down, catching up to his twin. High pitched screams could be heard further down the tunnel as the distance between the two brothers decreased rapidly. Soon, blood red hair made itself apparent. Heart smirked, seeing his brother's back turned towards him.

"Oh brother, look what I found. It appears that I won."

Diamond turned around and noticed their plaything's unconsious form in his brother's arms. A frown crept onto his face as he realized that he had lost the game. Sighing, he walked up to his smirking brother and looked down at her. Running his fingers through her soft dark brown hair, he brought his lips down to her forehead and kissed it gently. "Next time, you'll be mine, Miss Nix,"he whispered softly and possessively.

Now stepping away from his brother, the red-haired jester smiled before bowing and disappearing. After Diamond had vanished, Heart formed a portal in one of the nearby walls and walked through with her. When they entered their new destination, Heart set her down on a mahogany chair with a velvet blue cushion and pushed the chair closer to the dark blue painted fireplace. He summoned a match box to his hands and lit the wood inside.

After tossing the match into the fire, Heart sat across from her and waited for her to wake up. When about five minutes ticked away, Heart began to grow quite impatient. He snapped his fingers and summoned a bucket full of warm water. He didn't want to douse her in cold water since her body was just recovering from the spirits and was still rather cold. With no further hesistation, he threw the water on her. The bucket disappearing, he watched amused as she sprung up from her chair.

"Finally, I've been waiting five minutes already, and I want as much time as possible with you, my dear lady."

Rubbing the water from her eyes, she glared at him in vexation and found that she wasn't bound to the chair. Not thinking, she quickly got up and went to dart out the blue door to her right. A blade, however, rested threateningly on her left shoulder. Scowling at the male, she pushed the blade aside and took a seat again. Her eyes did a quick scan of the new location.

Royal purple walls outlined the room while blue carpet covered the floor. Silver chandeliers hung from a blue ceiling. A dining table sat in the middle of the room, bearing multiple crystal glasses and glass plates.

"I suggest that you behave, or I will bind you to the chair. I believe that you wouldn't want that."

He was right; she didn't want to experience that again. "Fine, I'll sit here, but you didn't have to throw a bucket of water on me."

"Actually, I did because otherwise you wouldn't have awoken. Be thankful that it wasn't ice cold water. Besides, I was going to have you change clothes. Those clothes simply don't suit you."

"Excuse me, how do you expect me to change clothes when these are the only ones I have? Where would I even change? And, don't say in front of you."

"My dear lady, I would never disrespect your privacy that much, at least not yet anyway; I was going to have you change in that armoir over there. As for the clothes, they're in the armoir all ready for you. Now, go change," he ordered, signaling for her to get moving.

Knowing that she really had no choice in the matter, she went over to armoir. Her clothes were soaking wet, so a change of clothes wouldn't be bad. Opening the armoir door, she walked in, flipped on a light switch and closed the door behind her. A blue light came on, which illuminated a short black lolita dress with a blue and red ribbon around the waist. Crystal blue hearts and red diamonds were around the collar of the dress and the ends of the sleeves. Black over-the-knee socks were resting on top of over-the-knee black lace-up boots, which had red and blue shoe laces.

Out of all the things that she had to wear, it was a dress. The boots looked comfortable but a dress? It was pretty, but it was impractical for her current predicament. How could she hope to make it through another one of the brothers' games in a dress? It could easily get caught on something, which could mean death for her. Just imagining the dress getting caught on a tree back in the forest before the village gave her chills.

Still, it was either put on the dress or remain in oversized wet clothes. She really didn't want to be soaking wet anymore. So, she removed her wet clothes and put on the new ones. Nix didn't know how the brothers knew her clothing size, but, right now, she decided not to worry about it. When finished, she walked out, turned off the light and carried the wet clothes. "What should I do with these?"

"You can dispose of those wet clothes by throwing them in the fire. I certainly don't want them," he responded, looking at them with disgust.

Once she tossed them in, she returned to the chair and ignored his stares. "You know; I'm curious about something. What happened to that village? You didn't exactly seem bothered by the condition of it."

"So, you finally wish to strike up a conversation with me, my dear lady. How interesting," he voiced, leaning a bit forward in his chair with a grin. "Regardless, to put it simply, the villagers were obssessed with gaining more power. One day, they found that their obssession was too great. They wanted power so badly that they decided to summon a demon into their village. Of course, their summoning went horribly wrong. It was quite an interesting show to watch. Diamond and I knew that they were too weak for the summoning, but they pressed on with it. We watched as their foolishness destroyed them.

"At the time, we were courteous enough to give them a warning, but they tried to kill us for it. So, when the summoning occurred, all of them had their lives taken from them and were turned into spirits that forever haunt the village. This failed summoning also managed to leave parts of the village in quite a ruined state. Does that satisfy your curiousity, my dear lady?"

"Yes, I'm surprised that you gave me such a straight answer, though. You don't give off the perception of a helpful individual," she remarked, crossing her arms over her chest.

"I do try to be helpful at times," he answered with a smirk and casual shrug. "Now, for something that I've been looking forward to," he continued, getting up from his seat and coming over to her. Swiftly, he took both of her hands and pulled her up out of the chair. He spun her around and held her back to his chest.

"Let go," she warned, trying to wriggle out of his grasp.

"Why would I do such a thing? Right now, you're mine, and I want you close to me," he whispered into her left ear.

She tried to get out of his grasp, but his grip was too strong, and her body froze when he began to nibble on her right ear. Her cheeks warmed up as she tried even harder to get out of his hold. He proceeded to move his lips from her ear down to her neck slowly. "Get off of me," she managed to say through her embarrassment.

"You know that dress looks stunning on you, my dear lady" he responded between passionate kisses, which he planted all along her neck.

Noting that he had ignored her demand and not being able to take anymore, she was able to shift her left arm some and elbow him in the gut. The action caused him to release his grip on her. She instantly created distance between the two of them. Trying to steady her breathing, she looked back at Heart and found him looking to her with amusement in his dark blue eyes.

"I compliment you, and you injure me; you really are entertaining. I'm afraid, however, that cannot go unpunished."

A terrifying smile graced his lips as his eyes darkened. He quickly closed the distance and grabbed her right arm. He dragged her back to her chair, acting as if she wasn't struggling in the slightest. Once she was forcibly seated, he snapped his right fingers. Straps appeared and secured her arms and legs to the chair. Heart snapped his fingers again, and food appeared on the dining table. She would've been impressed by the spread, which ranged from lobster to eggplant parmesian to vegetable soup, if she weren't in her current condition.

"I was going to let you feed yourself, but I'm afraid that's not possible anymore. Now, I suggest that you don't resist me any further; it will make things easier. Besides, I can tell that you're hungry. What should I give you first, though? You're welcome to pick if you want."

Nix only turned her head away from him, not wanting to look at him. His fingers were soon under her chin, however, making her look at him. "Don't be that way, my dear lady. Don't you want to have a satisfied stomach?"

Seeing his left hand on the hilt of his saber, she didn't want to know what he would do if she didn't comply. So, she agreed to his command; she needed no more injuries. Smiling, he relaxed and retrieved a spoonful of vegetable soup before he placed it in her mouth. To her surprise, it tasted delicous, but she kept a straight face, not wanting to show that she liked the food. Continuing to keep up her mask, she let him feed her more of the soup along with some of the lobster and eggplant parmesian. These dishes tasted extraordinary as well.

Once he finished feeding her, he tilted a cup with the sparkling grape juice against her lips, letting the drink flow into her mouth. Like before, she was surprised at how delicous it tasted. Not being able to restrain herself any longer, a small smile tugged at her lips. To her disappointment, Heart noticed, and his smile widened.

"So, you did like the food, my dear lady?"

Turning away from him, she muttered to herself and desired to wipe the smile off of his face.

"Tell me, did you enjoy me feeding you?"

Not expecting the question, her cheeks warmed up again. "Of course not, you ..."

Before she could finish, she found his lips on hers. Due to her restraints, she couldn't do anything, especially since he held her head steady by keeping her chin in place with his fingers. His kiss was hungry and passionate as he begged for entrance. When he didn't receive it, he bit her lip, causing her to gasp at the slight pain. His demanding kiss came to a close, though, when someone began coughing at the other side of the room. Heart stepped away from her and looked over. She breathed a sigh of relief and followed his gaze to see Diamond standing there.

"I believe an hour is long enough, Heart."

Merely ignoring his brother's statement, Heart kissed her once more, much to her shock and annoyance. When he seemed to be satisfied, he pulled away and glanced back at his brother. "Sounds fair, I believe that we should start the next game, then. Our plaything is now well fed after all."

"Yes, I do want to start. After all, I wish to gain some alone time with her."

Both brothers now stared at her, their eyes gleaming with delight. She glared back, but, inside, she was worried. What did they have in store for her next?

Chapter Eight: A Sunny Ride

"We're going to the carnival, correct?" Diamond questioned, leaning against the table now.

"Yes. I was thinking that we could lock the door on the other side of the carnival. We'll then hide two keys. One key will lead her to one of my rooms and the other to one of yours."

"Well, let's start, then."

The two brothers, agreeing on the terms of the game, walked over to her and began pushing her towards the blue door. Heart opened the door before proceeding to push her out into the carnival. Gazing out in front of her, she looked through the doorway to a bright carnival under a night sky.

Nix was soon distracted by her chair collasping under her or rather disappearing completely. Now, on the wet stone pavement, she noticed that the two brothers were gone once again. Her mind relaxed a little at their lack of presence. They were probably watching her, but at least she couldn't see them.

Picking herself up from the pavement, she noticed a ticket stand, a manager's office and what looked like a fortune telling booth. An orange-lighted carnival sign greeted all its visitors to the colorful place. Neon orange ballons were tied down to the ticket booth, bouncing lightly against eachother. Numerous rides were in the distance as well as a circus tent and multiple funhouses.

Upon all of the bright lights and exciting rides, a statue of a man stood right in front of the manager's office. His unmoving form was clad in a grey suit and fedora. In his hands was a grey umbrella. He looked out of place among all of the colors. She decided that it was best not to near the weird statue.

Going over to the ticket booth and peering inside, she saw that it was devoid of life, which she had expected. After all, she hadn't seen any other visitors around. She thought that it was silly to retrieve a ticket, but she figured that it was probably better to attain one before entering the park. Who knows what would happen if she entered without a ticket in hand, especially with that statue seeming to watch her every move.

Reaching her right arm into the ticket booth, she grabbed a ticket from one of the shelves. With the ticket in hand, she quickly proceeded to go past the entrance and the statue. As she was walking by the statue, however, she noted that it was turning its head. Blank glass eyes followed her until she was no longer in the statue's field of vision. She breathed a sigh of relief and looked around the carnival more.

How was she supposed to find a key in this place? It would take hours to find one of the keys. She wasn't eager to get back to the one of the brothers, but that statue had really concerned her, especially after it had moved its head. Running her fingers through her dark brown hair, she decided to head off in the direction of one of the funhouses.

On her way there, she saw a miniature carousel and mutliple food stands. The miniature carousel creaked slowly as it went in constant circles, each horse rusted beyond repair. All the food stands were empty and stood abandoned. She couldn't help but wonder what had happened to the place. Did the brothers have something to do with this? Or, was it something else? Whatever the case, she understood that she needed to keep moving. From her previous 'games' with the brothers, she figured that every area in this world had some dreaded monster lurking around the corner.

In the distance, she could see a larger carousel in the distance. This carousel was in prime condition while a fitting tune played along. Bright lights illuminated the many colorful horses. She could even see an occasional kelpie among them. Nix wasn't sure if she was delighted to see the mythical creature or greatly disturbed by its presence. What intrigued her most, though, was that a little girl was on the ride, who happened to have short golden blonde hair, an orange dress and a sunhat.

Not losing another minute, she forgot her current objective and headed over to the carousel. She even found herself sprinting over to it at one point. By the time that she got to the carousel, she needed to catch her breath. Resting her hands on the ride's fence, she glanced up and saw that the ride started to slow down until it stopped entirely. The sunhat girl now smiled at her. This time, there was no trace of any ill intent. Instead, her smile was the defintion of childhood innocence.

"It's nice to see you again, Nix. Why don't you join me on the ride?"

She stared at the open gate, hesitating to ride the carousel.

"There's no need to worry, Nix. Just don't go near one of the kelpies, and you'll be fine."

"I don't really want to ride. I just want to talk to you about what happened when I first came to this world," Nix responded, still remembering how the child had locked her in the house.

Smiling, the girl shook her head before replying, "I'll tell you if you get on the ride. It's so much fun."

Something bad was bound to happen on the ride, but she wanted some answers. So, she entered through the gate and hoisted herself up onto a purple horse with a purple and turqoise saddle. Next to her sat the sunhat girl, who was on grey horse with an orange saddle. A few moments passed, and the carousel began to move again, the horses going up and down in a smooth motion. The sunhat girl seemed to be thoroughly enjoying herself while a childish smile plastered itself on her face.

"So, tell me why you had locked me in the house," Nix inquired.

"Why to protect you from your violent aunt."

"You could've unlocked it and let me out after she went away."

Her smile now twisted into that wicked one of hers before she began giggling to herself. "Oh, Nix, you're funny. Your aunt completely destroyed the music box beyond repair. There's no going back. You're stuck here forever."

Eyes widening, the words seemed to echo in her mind as the prospect of never returning to her previous world made itself apparent. Sure, she didn't desire to return to her aunt and uncle, but, now, she was trapped in a world where she was constantly toyed with. Her few minutes of silence seemed to amuse the sunhat girl.

"You know; it's not that bad. Remember, you're the one who wished to enter this world. Besides, aren't you having fun?" she questioned, grinning.

Having fun was a weird way of putting her predicament. She wouldn't called almost being killed multiple times by strange creatures fun. Nor, would she call being tormented by two twisted brothers fun. That's when it occurred to her. Did the sunhat girl even know of the brothers? "Tell me, have you met Heart and Diamond. Did you know that they would find me?" she inquired, her gaze fixed on the girl.

Giggling some more, she answered, "Why of course I know of them. They don't know much about me, however. And, yes, I knew that they would find you. I figured that they needed something to entertain them. You happened to fit the role splendidly. I must say that you've even been entertaining me as well."

"Wait, you have been watching me also? Why?"

Only smiling her twisted grin, she remained quiet and vanished into thin air. Now alone on the carousel, a dangerous air hovered around the ride. She heard something fall onto the base of the ride. Turning her head a little, she now saw multiple kelpies staring at her with an evil glint in their eyes. Nix wanted to run away, but the ride kept moving. The song in the background now felt sickenly dreadful.

Moving towards her, the kelpies contiued to stare at her hungrily. Generally, they drowned their victims, but there was no water in sight. At least that's what she thought before looking down at the base of the ride. The solid base was now a pool of greenish-blue water. There was no floor below the water, only an endless pit of death. How would she get off of the ride? Her mind struggled to think of a solution, but nothing came to her. With her heartbeat quickening, she stared back at the approaching kelpies. Death gazed at her, and she had no way to fight back.

Chapter Nine: Mirror Image

One of the kelpies was now only a few inches from her. Jumping and hoping for the best seemed to be her only available option. Carefully, standing up on the carousel horse and using the pole as support, she glanced at the next horse over. Gripping the pole hard, she began to place her right leg onto the other horse. Once her foot was secure on it, she reached her right hand out and grabbed the pole attached to the other horse. Luckily, for her, the two horses were going up and down in the same rhythm. This made the switching of horses slightly easier.

Part of the way onto the other horse, she managed to pull the rest of her body onto it right before the kelpie behind her lunged at the cream colored horse. Now, the last step was to jump off of the carousel. As the kelpie now lunged at her new horse, she threw herself off of the horse and landed flat on the pavement below, hearing multiple parts of her dress tearing as she slightly slid across the ground.

Raising herself up, her limbs cried out in protest, but, thankfully, none of her wounds reopened. There were a few scrape marks, however, on her exposed skin. Standing, she quickly made way for the fence, which was still open. Passing through the entrance to the carousel, she looked behind her to see that the carousel had returned back to its original state. She glanced down at her dress and found the fabric torn in multiple places, which was to be expected.

Leaving the carousel behind and not planning on returning any time soon, she felt even more worried than she was before. After all, she now knew that the sunhat girl was watching her every move. She had a gut feeling that the small girl had other reasons for watching her rather than just for entertainment.

Remembering her original reason for being in the carnival, she continued further into it. She searched game stands and rides but not daring to actually go on the rides. Still finding nothing, she pressed onward and arrived at a house of mirrors. The plain cement building just had *House of Mirrors* etched sloppily onto its front while there was a doorway with no door. There was only a bright hallway, leading further into the building. Nix really had no desire to enter the building, but there was a chance that one of the keys could be in it. Mustering up her courage, she headed inside.

The hallway didn't last long as she was met with a descending staricase. She walked down the stairs, each step bringing her further underground. When she reached the bottom, she saw countless white rimed mirrors in front of her. The carpeted floor had the pattern of repeating circles while the ceiling was covered in lights in the shapes of spheres.

Wishing to be done with this mirror house quickly, she advanced and hoped that the key was on the other side of these mirrors. As she made her way through the maze, she cast quick glances at the mirrors, refusing to peer into them for too long; she was afraid to see something else looking back at her. At one point, though, she almost ran into one of the mirrors and ended up staring into it. Looking into it, she blinked a couple of times. There was now another figure in the mirrors besides her own. That figure was none other than the statue of the manager. He had his grey umbrella opened, seeming to just stare back at her. She moved a step forward and so did he. His blank glass eyes watched her every move.

She wanted to move but was afraid to, knowing that the statue would move as well. Standing still, she waited to see if it would do anything. A minute of eternity passed before the statue started to twitch, its limbs contorting and popping until the statue was now on all fours. Its umbrella lying on the floor, it cocked its head to the side before returning its head back to its original position. Thinking flight the best option, she darted off, and the thing charged after her.

Due to all of the mirrors, she could only run so fast. She didn't need to run into a mirror, or she could meet death at the hands of that statue. If she took too long trying to find the right path, though, the same fate might still occur. To her disappointment, the mirrors kept showing the disturbing statue. Frankly, she didn't need a constant reminder of its appearance. Annoyance swept through her as one of the brothers' keys was looking pretty nice at the moment. "I hate carnivals," she kept muttering to herself, wanting to be rid of the entire place.

When she made the next turn, she saw the statue now on the ceiling, crawling rapidly towards her. "Why can't you run like a normal person!" she screamed at the statue as if it was actually listening to her. The rows of mirrors continued, but she could only bolt ahead in order to escape that thing. She had no weapon to defend herself with. Making another turn, she finally saw the exit up ahead. She wanted to shout in glee; however, she had no idea how long that statue was going to chase her.

Her legs pounding, she sprinted towards a passage that read *exit*, and, upon reaching it, she saw an object glimmering in the distance. To her amazement, it was one of the keys. When she reached it, she snatched it up into her hands and held onto it tightly. She could still hear the statue chasing her, though.

Not looking behind her, she hauled herself up the stairs. She needed to catch her breath, but the statue was still chasing after her. So, she exerted her body more and kept her legs moving.

Exiting the mirror house, she quickly glanced around her and looked for the door that the key would open. Ahead of her, she could see a castle door that was painted red and blue. Recognizing the colors, she assumed that was the door that she needed. She ran for it, still hearing the statue's popping limbs. To her astonishment, though, the terrible sound stopped. The silence only made her nerves go on alert, and that's when she heard footsteps coming towards her.

The wet pavement reflected her scared face. She wanted to keep running for the door, but she found that she couldn't move; she was frozen in place. The door lay right in front of her, and she couldn't reach it! In fact, looking back down at the pavement, she saw two shadowy hands holding her ankles in place. Turning her head, she noted that the statue was nearing her.

It was standing upright once more while the carnival lights cast the statue's shadow across the pavement in the very same fashion that the shadow was holding her in place. Blank glass eyes gazed into hers as the grey umbrella rested against the statue's right shoulder. Somehow, the statue had called the umbrella back to it, which only made the statue more horrifying.

Two sets of eyes looked upon the situation from above: one set dark blue and the other fire-red. Both sat atop the highest point of the wooden roller coaster. Presently, the roller coaster wasn't turned on, leaving them to sit safely upon it. A pitcher of iced green tea, bowl of sugar, teacups and saucers rested between the two.

Diamond picked up his red teacup and saucer after pouring some tea into it. He took a sip and looked at the situation with displeasure. Heart kicked his legs back and forth, excitement wild in his eyes yet a hint of distaste was also present. The blue-haired male poured himself some tea and added seven sugar cubes to it. Since the tea was cold, the cubes didn't dissolve quickly, leaving the male to drink the cubes. So, in reality, he was eating green tea flavored sugar cubes.

Both brothers were at first enjoying their twisted entertainment. They were quickly becoming displeased with the situation, however. Their plaything was right in front of the door that would lead to another one of their rooms, yet the statue was holding her in place. The statue, or rather the manager, was always a severe nuisance to them, and he obviously hadn't learned his lesson yet. The brothers glanced at eachother, nodding their heads in unison.

They summoned their beverages away and back to their manor kitchen before they transported themselves to their plaything's location. Soon, the loud sound of their heeled shoes hitting the pavement caused the statue to fix its gaze on them while its shadow still held Nix in place.

Drawing their sabers, metal glinted under the lights of the carnival. The two brothers wore unamused expressions as they narrowed their eyes at the statue. As for the statue, it seemed unfazed by their stare and regarded them as easy prey. With the shadow of the statue continuing to hold her in place, the statue walked towards the brothers and tapped the umbrella against its shoulder.

Stuck, Nix watched the brothers remain motionless as the statue approached them. When the statue finally reached them, both brothers disappeared from sight while the statue swung the umbrella down where they were previously standing. The statue, missing its targets, turned around confused. As it turned, two sabers pierced the statue. Both brothers retracted their blades, but the statue still stood standing. The statue's jaw dropped open, emitting an earsplitting shriek.

Covering her ears, she continued to watch the fight as both brothers appeared unfazed by the terrible scream. In one swift movement, the two sliced their blades through the statue's neck, severing the head from the body. The head tumbled across the floor, but the eyes still seemed present with life while the body crashed to the ground. Both brothers now faced her as the shadow disappeared, releasing her from its tight hold.

Her legs gave way under her, and she now sat on the wet pavement. The brothers stood over her, smiles having returned to their faces. They looked at her expectantly. She was confused by their action, still in shock from the previous situation. Heart kept glancing behind him, looking over at the statue until he held her gaze once again. "Well, I assume that you found one of the keys, my dear lady."

"May we see it, Miss Nix?" Realizing that she had the key still clutched tightly in her hand, she turned her palm upwards and unclenched her fingers. Revealing the key that she had found, one of the brothers smiled in delight.

Chapter Ten: An Evening of Red

An elegant gold key with a red velvet string attached to it lay in her hand. Diamond's eyes gleamed while a delighted smile graced his lips. Placing the saber back in its scabbard, he held his right hand out to her. Refusing his hand, she looked away since she wasn't willing to accept help from him so openly. Instead, she focused on her appearance in order to avoid his gaze.

The scarves on her arms, which were meant to serve as her bandages, were coming apart while the scarves on her legs were no longer present due to the long socks and boots that were there. Both socks weren't the most comfortable against her healing wounds. Beads of sweat were on her forehead, and her dress was torn in places. Her dark brown hair was in tangles while she had multiple scratches due to her fall from the carousel. Bruises would most likely be covering her body in the near future. All in all, she currently felt terrible. Even with her enery lacking, she managed to stand on her two feet and headed for the blue and red door with the key in hand.

"Looks like you won Diamond. It seems, however, that you're the only one happy about it," Heart remarked.

"Yes, well, I'm sure that Miss Nix just needs some rest. Hopefully, she'll soon realize that we're the right ones for her."

"I think that she's too stubborn to make that realization. Anyway, I'll leave you. Tomorrow, though, I expect for you to share our plaything."

Heart gave one last glance at his brother before looking at their plaything possessively until he vanished, leaving Diamond alone with her. Diamond wasn't too inclined to share her tomorrow, but his brother and him had a special plan for her. Sadly, that meant that he wouldn't get alone time with her. He soon swept that thought out of his mind and approached her, looking forward to the evening ahead.

By this point, she was inserting the key into the lock and was hearing the lock click open. The door opened on its own, and she soon leaned against the doorframe. Her body was just too exhausted at this point. Closing her eyes, she desired to just sleep where she was, but she felt someone's hand rest on her left shoulder.

"You know, Miss Nix; I don't think that's the best place to sleep," Diamond whispered into her left ear.

She didn't really listen to him but decided to just keep her eyes closed. Nix heard, however, a familiar popping sound behind her. Immediately, she opened her eyes and turned her head slighty. Diamond's fire-red eyes were looking at her kindly, but, glancing around him, she saw the statue repairing itself. Words couldn't escape her lips, and she could only stutter, fear evident in her eyes.

On the other hand, Diamond didn't seem concerned by the statue fixing itself; he just continued to smile at her. Behind him, the statue was now on all fours before it began to charge at the two of them. Fully facing the statue, she covered her face with her hands and peeked out between her fingers. Diamond continued to remain calm.

Jumping into the air, the statue lunged at the two of them. With one swift movement of his hand, Diamond drew his saber and removed the statue's head from its body once again. Putting the saber back in its scabbard, Diamond grabbed her hands in his and removed them from her face. "Miss Nix, why don't we proceed forward before the statue repairs itself once again?"

Nix only nodded and removed her hands from Diamond's grasp, heading into the new room. Diamond closed the door behind the two of them, shutting out the carnival. Walking into the new room, she realized that it was pretty barren.

An unlit stone fireplace rested against a red flower-like patterned wall. Crimson drapes hung over paned windows, which revealed a starry sky outside. A simple gold chandelier hung over a red and gold carpet, which lay on the wooden floor. Near the windows was a luxurious looking leather armchair, which had a wooden side table next to it.

Overall, the room looked cozy and made her barely functioning legs want to collapse on the chair. Before they could, though, she was lifted off the ground. With her in his arms bridal style, Diamond carried her across the room until he set her down on the armchair. "I could've walked you know," she mumbled.

After those words left her mouth, she felt something squeeze her leg tightly, sending a shock of pain up her body as a cry of pain escaped her lips. Diamond removed his right hand from her leg, standing up in a triumphant way. "You were saying, Miss Nix?"

Looking away, she silently cursed him in her head as she heard him snap his fingers. Instantly, a large fire filled the once lifeless fireplace. A wave of warmth spread throughout the room, making her even more tired. She refused to close her eyes while Diamond was still in the room, though. Her tired eyes began to follow his every move. He summoned clean bandages, lifted up her left arm and began unwrapping the disgusting scarf.

"I can change my own bandages," she grumbled, trying to move her arm away from his hands.

"You'll find it easier if you hold still unless you want one of my fingernails to reopen one of your wounds," he suggested, with his focus still on her arm.

Not wanting to feel anymore pain, she muttered a few curses under her breath but allowed him to change the bandages on her arms. She had to admit that the new coverings felt nicer against her skin. When he finished, he stepped away from her and eyed her closely.

"Would you like anything to drink, Miss Nix? Surely, that run in with the statue has tired you out."

Diamond was quite right; her throat was sore and called for something to soothe it. Reluctantly, she nodded her head in reply, staring into the crackling fire. Diamond smiled before disappearing from the room, leaving just her and the fire. The fire danced in her eyes as she let her mind drift. No thoughts entered her mind. At the current moment, she didn't want to think; she just wished to enjoy the brief peace and let the warmth wrap itself around her.

A few minutes passed before Diamond returned, with a purple and black checkered teacup cup and saucer. He set it down on the round table, allowing her to see that hot chocolate rested inside. She could smell the delicious chocolate drink that was topped off with whipped cream and chocolate sprinkles.

"Hopefully, you like the drink. It's my own recipe, and I felt like you would deserve such a treat after today. My brother has told me that it's quite delicious," the red-haired jester voiced, standing close to her.

Picking up the glass, she took a careful sip. Like the food and drink back in the dining room, it tasted amazing. "Thanks for not letting the statue kill me," she muttered, not making eye contact with him.

Hearing this, a wide smile spread across his face. "You're quite welcome. I never would have expected thanks from you. Are you warming up to me?"

"Not at all. Me thanking you means nothing except for the intent of the words. You saved my life, and I'm glad that I'm not dead. That's all there is to it," she answered, taking another sip of the hot chocolate.

"Well, that's a shame."

With no warning, Diamond knelt in front of her and began untying one of her boots. At the time, she had hot chocolate in her mouth, and she almost choked on the drink. Coughing a little, she managed to exclaim, "What are you doing? Stop!"

"No, I won't stop, and I don't appreciate you ordering me around. Besides, I thought that the socks would be scratching against your healing wounds. Am I wrong on that assumption?"

"I suppose that they're uncomfortable," she mumbled in an irritated voice.

"Then, stop trying to pry your leg from my hands and drink your hot chocolate. Remember, I can easily restrain you."

"Whatever," she voiced, bringing the hot chocolate back up to her lips and taking some more sips.

Taking her silence as a surrender, he continued to remove her boots from her legs. Once her boots were removed, Diamond went on to her socks. As he started to remove the first sock, she felt his long fingernails gliding over her skin ever so lightly. This simple action sent chills up her spine as she bit the inside of her right cheek, trying to calm down her warming cheeks. When he had the first sock off, he stared at her right barren leg. He gently brought his fingers over the cuts that were on her leg, causing her to wince slightly.

"My brother was so careless. He should've given you new bandages. I'll make sure to remedy that," he said more to himself than to her.

With that, he began to wrap bandages around her leg before moving onto her other leg. What he did next utterly surprised her, however. As he started to remove her sock, he brought his lips to her leg, kissing it as he slid the sock off. She tried to pull her leg away from him, but he held firmly onto it. By now, her face felt like it was on fire, and the feeling didn't go away even after he stopped. In the next moments, new bandages were on both her legs, yet Diamond still kept his gaze on them.

"You have very smooth skin, Miss Nix. It's very tempting," he breathed out.

Bringing her drink to her lips and taking a sip, she tried to ignore his comment and her burning cheeks before drawing both her legs up onto the chair. With the hot chocolate now gone, she set the teacup back on the table, feeling her eyelids grow heavy. Diamond standing up, brought his right hand up to her face, resting it on her left cheek. Rubbing his thumb gently across her skin, she found her head tilting against it. She quickly realized her action and moved her head away.

"You must be tired," he mentioned, smiling softly at her. "I'll prepare some comfortable sleeping arrangements for you." Diamond removed his hand from her face as the sound of two snaps resonated throughout the warm room. The first one caused the chair beneath her to disappear and be replaced by a couch. When the second snap sounded throughout the room, she felt a soft blanket resting on top of her.

Seeing his work accomplished, he sat down on the couch next to her and drew her over to him. He placed her head on his lap and made sure that her feet were now resting on the couch. As Diamond combed his fingers through her hair, she felt herself too tired to protest. Her eyes closed as sleep claimed her.

Chapter Eleven: A Flight of Wings

When she opened her eyes, morning light was spread throughout the room. The fire in the fireplace had been extinguished, and Diamond was gone. In his place was a luxurious crimson colored pillow. Rubbing the sleep out of her eyes, she sat up. The blanket, which was once covering her, fell to the floor. Her boots and socks lay next to the couch as her bandaged legs hung over the couch. Blinking a couple of times, she examined the room and expected to see Diamond somewhere within the vicininty, but she couldn't find him anywhere.

Part of her was happy about his current lack of presence, but, to her utter terror, another part of her was slightly saddened. She couldn't deny that last night Diamond was quite kind to her despite her stubborn nature. Granted, he had overstepped his bounds when it came to those kisses on her leg. When this thought came across her mind, she felt her cheeks burn up ever so slightly.

Still, she refused to consider those thoughts more. He may have been tolerable last night, but that didn't excuse the games which he kept playing with her, which constantly put her in life threatening situations. Besides, she had only known him for a day. Her mind was probably just trying to wrap itself around the predicament before her. "I refuse to let last night excuse his past actions," she muttered.

"Why is that?" asked a high pitched voice.

"That's obvious, isn't it?" she answered until her eyes widened as she wondered who just spoke to her.

She scanned the room, looking for the source of the voice before finding a rectangular wooden table in front of her. On top of the table sat a pixie with tinted green skin and long flowing green hair. She wore a green dress while delicate wings beat back and forth on her back. Her eyes were entirely a dark green.

Without realizing, her mouth hung open in surprise. She had to blink a couple of times, making sure that she was seeing the pixie in front of her. The pixie smiled in delight at noticing her shocked expression. "What ... how ..." Nix stuttered, still staring at her.

Laughing a little, the pixie stared up at her before remarking, "I'm sure that you have a lot of questions right now, but first let me introduce myself. My name is Woodlily, and Diamond left me here as both a messenger and assistant while he went to his room in their seaside manor. The message being that you have one hour to get ready before Diamond and his brother retrieve you, so I suggest that you don't go over that hour because the two of them aren't going to wait. Oh yeah, ten minutes of that time have already passed."

Leaning back against the couch, Nix crossed her arms over her chest and thought about what Woodlily had just told her. "Wait, what do I need assistance for?"

"Well, mainly Diamond asked me to prepare your breakfast for you while you get a shower."

"A shower?" she questioned before looking over her appearance and being reminded of her roughed up condition.

"Yeah, you need to bathe at some point, you know. Anyway, the bathroom is through that door. I'll go prepare that breakfast for you. Oh yeah, I picked out your clothes for you. I hope that you like them."

With that, the pixie vanished into thin air. Getting off of the couch, Nix made her way over to the door and came to the conclusion that a shower would feel quite nice. Opening the door, she found the familiar black and white tiled floor while a dark crimson paint was spread over the walls. A simple black sink stood next to a toilet, and a shower with red and black checkered shower curtains rested against the far wall. A small red table rested against the opposite wall of the sink. On top of it was a black and red checkered towel while a set of clothes lay next to the towel.

The set of clothes was comprised of a dark purple lolita dress that hung just above the knees. Red and blue buttons went down the front of the dress while a gold chain belt was placed around the waist. There were new socks as well, one had blue and black stripes while the other had red and black stripes. She assumed that she was wearing the same pair of boots. A set of black undergarments rested among the pile of clothes as well. Seeing those, she was quite thankful that it was Woodlily who picked out her clothes and not one of the brothers. New bandages accompanied the outfit also.

On a shelf over the table was a multitude of various shampoos, conditioners and bath gels. Picking out a matching set of milk and honey scented shower supplies, she undressed herself and went into the shower. To her relief, the water was warm and soothing. She rested her head against the shower wall, letting the water wash over her as each droplet of water calmed her nerves and cleaned her healing wounds.

When she finished with her shower, she dried off and got dressed. Before putting on the socks, she wrapped new bandages on her legs and arms. Afterwards, she finished up her usual bathroom routine. Walking out of the bathroom, she found a tray of food on the rectangular table. Woodlily sat beside the food, hanging her legs over the table's edge and kicking them back and forth while she hummed a light tune.

Woodlily stood up on the table and waved her over, upon noticing her. Walking over to the couch, Nix sat down and observed the food before her as Woodlily examined the clothes on her. "Those look really nice on you. Do like them, Nix?"

"I would prefer something a little bit more practical, but thanks for them anyway," Nix responded, eyeing the french toast covered in strawberries and whipped cream, which lay on a black and purple checkered plate. Picking up a golden fork, she dug into the food while Woodlily continued to watch her.

"How's the food?" she asked, now laying on the table on her stomach.

"Good, thanks. How did you bring the tray in anyway? Isn't it a little heavy for you?"

"Nope. I'm quite strong. Well, I use magic," she grinned, revealing a set of sharp pointed teeth.

Nix swallowed her next bite of food and nodded, eyeing her deadly teeth. She seemed to notice, but her smile only grew wider. "Don't worry, Nix; I won't kill you, but I really hope that the brothers bring me something to eat," she commented, trailing off while Nix could see the pixie's mouth starting to water at the prospect of food.

Ignoring her far off gaze, Nix took a sip of the earl grey tea in the matching checkered teacup. "Hey Woodlily, can you tell me more about the brothers?"

Her trance-like state broke, and she stared at Nix, tapping her right index finger against the side of her face. "I guess that I could tell you something. Well, Heart likes his drinks to be sweet while Diamond prefers them bitter," she answered before going back into a trance.

Hearing the pixie's answer gave her a mental sweatdrop. Sighing, she took another sip of tea and figured that she wasn't going to get anything useful out of Woodlily. A few more minutes passed before she heard the windows behind her open, letting in a harsh wind. Her hair blew all over the place, making her set down the tea, so she wouldn't get her dark brown hair in the drink. Woodlily looked up in excitement, flying right over to the window.

Two forms emerged from the open windows and came into the room. She wasn't surprised to see that it was the brothers, but she was shocked that they weren't holding their hats down due to the strong wind. In fact, their hats stayed stable on both of their heads, making her think that they had pinned them to their hair.

Closing the window behind them, she noticed that Woodlily was now tugging on Diamond's left shirt sleeve. Diamond peered down at her before looking over at Heart. Heart sighed and snapped his fingers. A piece of meat was dangling from Heart's fingers. Woodlily stared at it intensely before swooping over to it and snatching it between her teeth. She flew to the other side of room, eating her meal.

"With that taken care of, Miss Nix, will you please come with us?"

"Sure, it's not like I have much of a choice," she murmured, standing up.

"Woodlily, we'll be leaving now," the red-haired jester annouced to her.

Woodlily didn't even look up but nodded in reply. Shaking her head, Nix went over to the two brothers and reopened one of the windows as the strong wind almost knocked her backwards.

"Do you need some assistance, my dear lady" Heart asked, smirking at her.

Ignoring him, she looked out the window and saw nothing below except for a sea of blue. She stood at the window confused before stepping back. "Is this another one of your sick games?" she inquired, looking between the two brothers. Diamond looked amused at her comment while Heart began to laugh.

"My dear lady, it would seem that you do need our assistance."

"It would seem that is the only way. Well shall we, Heart?" asked Diamond with a smile.

"I think that we shall."

The two brothers nodded at eachother before each took one of her arms in theirs, linking the three of them together. Before she could protest, they walked out of the window. At first, she closed her eyes, expecting to fall, but no fall came. Only the harsh wind blew against her. In fact, she felt something hard under her feet. Looking down, she now saw red and blue steps, which descended down into the sea below. They led her down, and the water below neared the three of them.

Chapter Twelve: Games on the Water

Reaching the bottom of the steps, she could see the water splashing up against the last step. By this point, the harsh wind had stopped and was replaced by a gentle sea breeze. The breeze caused light specks of water to splash up onto her face, cooling her in the process.

Focusing her attention back on the view in front of her, she heard a snap, and a ship appeared in the water. She was getting used to the brothers' ability to summon objects out of thin air, but to see a ship form right before her eyes was still a little shocking.

It was a magnificent vessel, though. The natural red color of the wood gleamed under the sun as it was freshly polished with something probably water resistant. Dark blue masts waved in the breeze, and gold and silver rails outlined the decks of the ship. They obviously took care of it.

Without another moment's hesitation, though, the two brothers led her onto the ship, by stepping onto a wooden plank that appeared out of thin air. When aboard the deck, Heart asked, "Well, my dear lady, are you ready to see the inside of the ship?"

"I'm curious to see it, but, at the same time, I don't wish to see what you two have planned."

"Oh, it won't be that terrible," Diamond reassured with one of his characteristic smiles.

"That's not helping," she commented and rolled her eyes.

Both of them chuckled before keeping her linked to them and entering the hold of the ship. Once down the stairs, the brothers released their hold on her and began to light the lanterns in the area. She noticed, though, that they only moved around the perimeter of the hold, but she could soon see why.

In the middle of the ship was a massive maze. Nix could see what looked to be the towers of a miniature castle in the center of it. Right in front of her was a metal door with a lock on it. She couldn't see over the door even when stepping on her tippy toes. Just how was the ship supporting this weight? Her guess was most likely magic of some sort. At some point in the future, she would need to figure out how magic exactly worked in this world.

When the twins finished with illuminating the place, they came back over to her. Diamond went over to the lock and summoned a key to his right hand. Heart stood behind her and rested his hands on her shoulders. "Ready to play the next game, my dear lady?"

"Let's just get this over with."

He chuckled some before signaling for his brother to unlock the metal door. "I look forward to winning you in this next game," he whispered into her right ear.

His brother overheard him and remarked, "How about we play and see who wins, brother? I don't easily lose."

"Nor do I, Diamond."

Nix, judging the game off of their smiles, wasn't looking forward to what was ahead. Then again, she already knew, based off of past experiences, that their games were never beneficiary to her. Once Diamond had the lock off and the door open, Heart began to push her forward. "So, do I get an explanation of what I'm exactly heading into?" she inquired, pushing against Heart some to stall her entry into the game.

To her surprise when she asked this question, he did stop shoving her forward. "I suppose that's a reasonable request. Well, to start off, you're the objective of the game for us. Diamond and I will have our own pieces that will be sent into the maze from other door locations. If one of us catches you, we win. If you reach the castle in the center, you win, and we'll leave you alone for some time."

Adding to his brother's explanation, Diamond commented, "In other words, Miss Nix, my brother and I draw cards, following their instructions and moving along the board accordingly, in order to reach you. Of course, you're free to move along the board, which makes it harder for us."

"See we even gave you an advantage, my dear lady. Beware of what waits in the castle maze, however. We aren't going to give you an easy ride, so do be careful. Then again, the creatures will only activate once we place our pieces on the board. Well, Diamond should we start?"

"Of course, let us head to our proper positions, brother."

Before either of them left, Heart gave her a final shove, and she entered the maze. They closed and locked the door behind her before she could hear their footsteps getting quieter and quieter. Regardless, the game had begun, and she had to face whatever horrors awaited her. Staying in one place would just result in the brothers reaching her. She did wonder, however, how they could see her.

Glancing up, she now saw each brother standing on a balcony. Both of these looked over the maze, allowing them a clear view of her. She was slightly hoping that such a view wouldn't exist to them, but it was lucky that they could only move by the draw of cards. So, she could get pretty far from them and reach her objective. Of course, she had to avoid getting lost in the maze before her.

Going forward, she glanced between the right and left path. She decided on the left and walked slowly. Nix wanted to get far out of the brothers' reach, but she also didn't wish to run right into a monster. The wood creaked under her steps, however, and she wondered if it was loud enough for some monster to hear.

As if a monster was answering her call, footsteps approached her, and the scent of peppermint filled her nose. Squinting ahead, she saw a form about equal height to her own. A top hat was perched on its head while curled horns protruded out of the hat. It stood upright on its two hoofed feet as a horse tail swished back and forth behind it. In fact, the figure was a chestnut colored horse, wearing pants, a dress shirt and a tailcoat. A candycane cane rested in its hoofed hands.

Her senses finally cutting in, she darted down a path to her right and crawled through a small hole which was at the end of the path. There was no way that the horse creature could follow her through the tiny opening. So, she backed away from the hole and waited for the creature to pass.

Soon, she saw the hoofed feet walk by, but the sound of its hooves against the wood floor stopped. The hooves reappeared as a cane was thrust through the hole. Instantly, she sprung farther back from the hole; the cane missed her by about a centimeter. After the creature withdrew the cane, it brought its head down to the hole and peered inside, spotting her terrified form in the process. Its beady eyes stared backed at her while it unveiled rows of gold sharp teeth within its mouth. Neighing in frustration, the creature got back up and walked away.

Her heartbeat slowed back to normal before she got up and went down the next path. So far, she had not spotted the brothers' pieces. She realized, though, that she had no idea what they looked like. Could that creature have been one of their pieces or just one of the obstacles. Her thought was soon interrupted by something moving around her feet. Looking to it, she saw chains twisting all around. Seeing them near her ankles, she broke out into a run as the chains chased after her.

When she was just about to round a corner, the chains shot out towards her, wrapping tightly around her wrists and ankles. They pulled her back, securing her to the wall behind her. The chains started to turn to a forest green color as spikes appeared on the chains. Each of the spikes dug into her skin, but this shockingly didn't hurt. Instead, she noticed that they sent some strange substance into her body. Her vision began to darken, yet she felt fully awake. In a state between consiousness and unconsiousness, she watched the chains slowly retract from her body.

Chapter Thirteen: The Killer and the Trap

When at last her vision was restored to her, all she could see was green. Rubbing her eyes, she saw that in fact she was behind a tinted green window. Standing up, she noticed that there were three white and black checkered walls that mirrored the pattern on the floor while the sheet of green glass replaced the fourth wall. Walking over to the glass wall, she rested the palms of her hands on it as she peered through the window.

What she saw confused her greatly. On the other side of the window was darkness except for two holes that gave her a view to the maze that she was supposed to be in. Backing away from the glass wall, she began to rub her forehead with her right hand. "What's going on? Have I finally lost it?"

"No, you're quite alright. You're just trapped inside your own mind," stated a voice behind her.

Turning on her heel, she saw an alligator in a black suit with a green tie wrapped around the collar of his white dress shirt. A top hat rested on his head, which was adorned with a green bow that had two decorative skulls on it. Its eyes looked drawn on due to them being in the shape of swirls. In its hands was a cane that had a skull on top. It stood at a height of about two feet.

"Who are you, and what do you mean that I'm trapped within my own mind?"

"Why, I'm currently just a guide; someone to explain the situation to you. I have no name. As for your second question, I meant exactly what I said. You're currently in your mind. This room and the one beyond are merely creations of your mind. My presence is aiding you in upholding these rooms."

"If that's the case, why can I still see the maze outside? Why is my body seemingly moving through the maze of its own accord?"

"The poison, which the chains injected you with, is currently controlling you."

"Well, can I get my body back?"

"Certainly, follow me."

The alligator turned around while a doorway appeared, leading into a hallway filled with darkness. His cane struck the floor in harmony with his movements as he trailed on ahead of her. Figuring that she might as well, she went down the hallway.

~~~~~~~~~~~

Leaning forward on the railing of the balcony some, Heart raised an eyebrow. "Diamond, I thought that you had removed that trap from the game."

"Heart, you know very well that I asked you to repair that problem. You were supposed to use that vanishing spell that I showed you."

"Well, I got distracted by the cake which I was making that day. You know how sweets draw my attention away from such things."

Diamond sighed and rubbed the bridge of his nose. "For right now, we'll continue to play and pull our pieces out if it gets out of hand. We can't remove it now since it's already infected her. We'll just have to wait until we finish the game, or she beats it on her own."

"The game should be over soon. After all, my piece is nearing hers."

"Don't rule out my chance to win just yet brother."

~ ~ ~ ~ ~ ~ ~ ~ ~ ~ ~

As she went down the hallway, paintings began to appear on the wall. The first had a multicolored checkered teacup surrounded by a black background. Next came the same teacup, but there was a crack in it. When the third painting popped up, it showed the teacup but with several cracks in it. This process continued, each new painting displaying the teacup more ruined than the previous. Reaching the end of the hallway, she gazed upon the last painting and noted that the teacup was shattered beyond repair.

The alligator went into the next room, turning around to face her and signaling her to enter. Upon walking into the room, loud bangs sounded behind her. Looking over her left shoulder, she saw the hallway exploding behind her. Pieces of the hallway went left and right, up and down, leaving nothing left behind. When the explosions reached the doorway, which she just entered through, a large purple door appeared and shut itself immediately. Going up to the door, she tried to open it only to find it locked. There was no going back.

"Why did the path explode, and why is the door locked?" she questioned, facing the alligator now.

"You said that you wanted out. Going back would serve no purpose to you so that option vanished. The only way out is to continue forward. Now, shall I explain the room to you. Please listen closely as you will only get one chance to reclaim your body."

Hearing these words, she nodded and took in her surroundings. The usual black and white tiled floor greeted her eyes until she focused her attention on the walls. A dark purple paint covered them while eight black shelves lined the circular room. On each shelf was a teacup, each a different color. These eight colors being red, blue, purple, black, white, green, orange and yellow. In the center of the room was a black table in the shape of hexagon. Six chairs, which were painted black and had white cushions, sat around the table. There were no doors in the room, except for the one behind her.

"As you can see, eight teacups are in this room, but only six chairs are around the table. On each chair is engraved a title. You must match the teacups with the right chair. The titles on the chairs are clues meant to help you match the right teacup with the right seating. Each teacup has a small note, which is meant to aid you as well. If you're able to arrange the table correctly, you're free to leave. If you fail, you're stuck in your mind forever."

At the mention of her possible failure, the alligator's eyes gleamed for a moment before returning to normal. He obviously was keeping something from her, but, for now, all she could do was play this game and hope to win. She was just worried about what her body was doing on the outside. Sure, she was away from the brothers, which is what she wanted, but it was at the cost of her body. If she were to be free, she wanted to be free with her body not just her mind.

She proceeded to walk up to the chairs and examined the writing on each of them. The six titles were *Jester, Joker, Queen, Puppeteer, Observer,* and *Shadow.* In the shadow chair sat the alligator, who smiled up at her. "I take it that this is your chair then," she remarked.

"Quite right, just make sure that you give me the right teacup."

Inspecting all of the titles, she knew that *Joker* and *Jester* meant the brothers, but which was which? As for the other titles, she had no idea. Well, except for the alligator of course. One of them probably meant her, and if that were the case, she was definetly not the *Observer*. This only left *Queen* and *Puppeteer*, both not representing her at all. So, maybe, she was the *Observer* after all. Who were the other two, though. Could they mean the sunhat girl and possibly Woodlily? They were the only other two beings in this world which she had spoken to. If that were the case, the sunhat girl was most likely *Queen* or *Puppeteer*. As for Woodlily, she might be *Observer* or *Queen*, since *Puppeteer* didn't fit her in the slightest.

She couldn't decide, and, so, she went over to the teacups. Before reading the messages, she knew who some of the colors belonged to. The blue represented Heart while the red symbolized Diamond. Looking at the other colors, she guessed that green meant Woodlily and purple meant her due to the color popping up a lot recently. The sunhat girl was either orange or yellow, meaning that white or black corresponded with the alligator. Having the colors in order, she began to the read the messages tied to the teacups.

Blue: I joke and I jest, but I am the one with two e's in my title, but only one in the name.

Red: Like a mirror I reflect the other, but backwards is my game.

Purple: Struggle is my calling, but I can still conquer.

Orange: I love to giggle and smile, for I control my entertainment.

Yellow: Laughing and smiling is my job as I sit on my work.

Green: Three vowels is what I am, but I cannot be purple.

Black: Absorbing what is around me, I never watch nor wait.

White: I may reflect, but I also follow green's lead.

After reading the messages, she only hoped that she would be able to solve the puzzle.

Chapter Fourteen: Song of the Servant

"It seems that she is continuing to come towards my piece. Your attempts to reach her are failing marveously, Diamond."

"Ah, you think so? Just wait, I have a plan that will work quite splendidly."

The brothers watched her moving form, which was advancing towards Heart's blue knight. Heart's eyes gleamed in delight as he saw her nearing his piece while Diamond watched the scene, his eyes etched with frustration. Granted, both were concerned about how the chain trap affected their plaything. So, they were on the ready should she act out of control.

Despite having knowledge that she was under the poison's influence, they didn't understand how severe that influence was. Right now, her body followed the orders of the poison; the current order being to kill. The notion to kill kept racing through her body, and nothing else concerned it. As a matter of fact, her body's first victim was determined to be Heart's piece. It pressed on through the maze, so far not encountering any obstacles.

"One more move, and I'll reach her," Heart annouced with a grin.

"You forget brother that she is approaching the Keeper of Spades. If you want her, you'll have to get through the Keeper first. Can you accomplish that before I reach her?"

Heart only shook his head in response before another grin spread across his lips. "Of course, she'll be mine," the blue-haired jester voiced as his mad smile stayed plastered on his face.

Before Heart could make his next move, Nix's body did indeed encounter the Keeper of Spades. The Keeper was well over six feet and didn't appear to have any skin. In place of skin was a sort of shadowy substance. His arms and long legs swayed with his movement, making him seem drunk with madness. There was no face on the Keeper; there was only a large spade stuck to the front of his face. A full set of spade cards were stabbed into his arms and legs, but no blood came from these wounds.

When it caught sight of her, no sound came from the creature. Just the sound of Diamond's piece dealing with a trap echoed down the maze. As the Keeper neared her, it became Heart's turn. His blue knight now stood behind the Keeper. The knight drew his sword while she stared emotionless at the two forms in front of her as the poison demanded bloodshed. Before her body could act, Heart drew and played an attack card, causing the blue knight to charge at the Keeper while the Keeper drew a card from his arm. Once the card was pulled out, it transformed into a dagger with the handle being the shape of a spade.

This was a formidable weapon, but it stood no chance against the sword of the blue knight. In one attack, the Keeper now lay on the ground as blood formed a pool underneath the Keeper. The poison seeing the fresh blood celebrated at the sight of it.

"It would seem that I have won," Heart declared triumphantly, but his smile began to fade. Her body was now approaching the fallen Keeper and was staring down at the blood. Reaching the crimson substance, her body swirled its right index finger around in the liquid and enjoyed every moment of it. Heart's inner alarms started going off as did Diamond's.

"Heart, I suggest that you pull your piece out of the maze now. We can't attack her, or we risk killing her," Diamond recommended, though; in truth, he was demanding his brother to get out of the maze.

"Yes, I'm doing so now," the other twin responded.

Before his piece was fully out, her poison filled body now withdrew one of the cards from the Keeper, allowing the card to transform into a dagger. The blue knight couldn't react in time as her body charged at the knight and brought the blade down on his face. Upon contact, the blade slashed through the knight's face, causing the knight to fall to the ground.

At the same moment, Heart let out a deafening scream as he took a few steps back and held his hands to his face. Diamond immediately teleported himself over to his twin, concern written all over his face. Blood ran down Heart's face as curse words resonated throughout the hold. Being careful, Diamond took Heart's hands away from his face and noticed a large slash mark there. The blue-haired jester told his brother that he would be fine as he finished retracting his piece from the maze.

Once the blue knight was out of the game, Diamond told his brother to go take care of his wound while he would watch over their plaything. As his brother teleported out of the hold, Diamond observed her. All he could do was hope that she would fight off the poison or reach the castle. If she managed to get there, the game would end, and he could deal with the chain trap.

Some curse words left his lips as he knew that their carelessness might cost them their plaything's life. She still had to face the rest of the monster pieces if she ran into them, and she could die easily by their hands. Right now, he would move his red knight around the maze and try to defeat as many of the monsters as possible while avoiding her.

~ ~ ~ ~ ~ ~ ~ ~ ~ ~

After reading all of the messages, Nix glanced back at the table before returning her attention to the cups. Looking at the blue message, she said the words in her head and analyzed the phrase. The title must be referring to the title on the chair, which means it has to be *Jester*, since there is only one e in Heart's name. If Heart is the *Jester*, Diamond is the *Joker*. Besides, the riddle says that the red teacup reflects the other, which probably refers to the blue teacup's message. Addiotionally, there is only one e in *Joker*; however, there are no es in Diamond's name. Maybe, though, the clue still fits *Joker* because it did say *backwards*, so it might mean that the red message doesn't necessarily follow the blue's message. That had to be it. Having confidence in her decision, she placed the red teacup in the *Joker's* place and the blue in the *Jester's* place.

Now, she only had four titles left to work with. Her eyes landed on the green teacup's message, and she read it over as the alligator watched her closely. He only hoped that she would get the puzzle wrong, for he didn't want to let her go. He may have had a smile on his face, but his eyes showed only a look of concern.

She knew that the green didn't match *Shadow*, so there were only three titles left. Nix already got rid of *Puppeteer*, however, since the title didn't fit Woodlily. Both *Queen* and *Observer* had three vowels in the name. The second part of the clue stated that they cannot be purple, meaning most likely that the two titles were the purple and green teacups.

So, she couldn't be *Puppeteer*, but she had to be *Queen* or *Observer*. Reading the purple teacup's message again, the word *conquer* echoed in her head. Could her title really be *Queen*? The clue certainly didn't fit the title of *Observer*. With that in mind, she decided that she had to be *Queen*. With the green and purple teacups in hand, she placed the purple in the *Queen's* chair and the green in the *Observer's* chair.

Two titles were left, and worry was only increasing in the alligator's eyes. He kept his grin on his face, though, giving her no hint as to whether she was so far right or wrong. Nix now examined the remaining four teacups. Yellow or orange belonged to the sunhat girl but which one? The first part to yellow and orange clue fit the sunhat girl, so she needed to examine the second part more closely.

Between the two, the orange clue described a puppeteer's actions the best. She placed the orange teacup in the *Puppeteer's* place. That left the white and black teacup, one of them describing the shadow. Reading the last two clues, she knew instantly that it was the white teacup due to the second part of the clue. Like the *Observer*, the *Shadow* also watches. Grabbing the cup, she placed it in front of the alligator.

The moment the teacup touched the table, the chairs and table vanished as the teacups crashed against the ground and shattered into multiple pieces. At first, she was worried that she got the combination wrong, but soon a black and white door appeared on the wall facing her.

"It would seem that you solved the puzzle correctly. You're free to go," stated the alligator as he stepped aside, allowing her to pass. When she reached the door, she turned the crystal doorknob as a bright light greeted her eyes.

Chapter Fifteen: Poisoned River

Diamond was still strategically moving his knight around the maze and was keeping the monster pieces from their plaything. Heart soon appeared next to him. Bandages were wrapped around the left side of his face, but his wound was already healing itself. "How are things going?" Heart asked, leaning on the balcony railing.

Gazing over at his brother, Diamond saw bandages and frowned upon seeing them, but he knew that his brother's wound would soon be healed. The red-haired male looked back out to the maze. "I've been managing to keep the monster pieces from her, but she hasn't reached the castle. Also, she's still immensely fascinated with blood. So, the poison is still affecting her."

"Then, it's still a waiting game for us," Heart breathed out, resting his chin in the palm of his right hand.

"Unfortunately. We'll get her back, though, brother. We've waited for her too long to lose her."

"I can't argue with that, nor would I wish to."
~~~~~~~~~~~

When the light vanished, she gazed upon no maze. Instead, she stood on a grassy hill that led down to a sapphire blue river. On the other side of the river was an assortment of different trees, which swayed in the peaceful wind. She had to admit that the scenery was beautiful and serene, but where was she? Nix had gained her freedom, and she had solved the puzzle. So, why was she here?

Taking in her strange surroundings, she heard footsteps in the grass next to her. Looking over to her right side, she saw the alligator standing next her. He rested the palms of his alligator hands on the skull head of his cane, staring down at the river. "Where am I?" she questioned as she narrowed her eyes at the creature.

"Do you not like it here? I thought that you would."

"You didn't answer my question."

"I suppose that it can't be helped. You're still trapped in your mind. However, wouldn't you agree that this place is much more agreeable than being back with the brothers?"

"I don't care if its more agreeable. I want my body back. I solved the puzzle correctly, so why am I not back in the maze? And, who are you really? You stated that you were my guide, but obviously that isn't really the case."

"Well, I suppose that there is no further need in hiding my true identity. I'm the poison that has infected you. I'm able to assume this form because the strength of your body permits me to. As for solving the puzzle, that no longer applies. I thought that you would fail it, but you didn't. So, I'm using another method. Did you honestly think that I would let you obtain your body back so easily? I finally have a chance to escape the confines of the maze. I can live in the world outside. I was hoping, however, that you wouldn't want to fight. Instead, you can live in peace in your mind. Here, you can be free of the brothers, be free to enjoy life."

She turned away from the alligator and looked out at the scenery. The water flowed gently down its destined path while the wind continued to the blow through the distant trees. Clouds rolled by, blocking the sun every now and then. In truth, the alligator was partially right. Here the brothers could never torment her. Endless joy filled days could consume her life.

The poison watched her and knew that she was almost in its grasp. Tapping its cane against the grassy field, a beautiful mansion now appeared on her left side. Her attention turned towards it before gazing back to the river. "It truly is magnificent here," she commented, closing her eyes some and enjoying the relaxing breeze.

"Of course, it is. You'll have a mansion to live in, any food you desire; anything you want will come to you."

Rocking back and forth on her feet, she let a genuine smile grace her lips. Still smiling, she looked over at the poison. It smiled back until it heard her words. "Thank you for offering me such a wonderful option, but you said anything that I wanted would come to me. That isn't true. My body wouldn't come. In a certain respect, I would indeed be free, but, at the same time, I would be a prisoner: a prisoner of my own mind. Can I really call that freedom? Sure, the brothers would no longer bother me but at what cost? I'll tell you. In exchange for this false sense of freedom, I would lose my body, and I would give up my existence in the world. I can't accept your offer for those reasons. So, I guess that we will have to fight one another."

"I guess that there is no persuading you," the poison responded regretfully.

The poison looked down at his cane before twisting the top of it. Soon, she heard a pop sound and saw the poison withdrawing a blade from inside of the cane. It glinted in the bright sunlight as the poison stared at her.

A harsh breeze swept over the grassy field while the poison charged at her. Before the blade could reach her, the sound of metal against metal resonated throughout the field. In her hands rested a sword of her own. The blade shined in the sunlight as she blocked the poison's attack. Seeing the blade, the poison wore an expression of pure shock. "How is that possible? How could you summon that?"

"Didn't you say that I could summon anything that I wanted. This is my mind after all. Don't underestimate me!" she yelled as determination burned in her eyes.

Looking annoyed, yet slightly impressed, the poison held back no longer. Each blade clashed against the other, sending sparks in the air. Both of them wanted her body. It was live or die; no other option existed for them.

Nix had no conception of time; she just understood that her body was becoming tired. This battle would have to end soon, or she would surely die. The next blow would have to be her last, her winning move. The poison stood quite a distance from her, recovering its breath. Holding the blade in both hands, she closed her eyes.

This was her mind, and she would summon everything that she had. Concentrating, she thought of her blade and her strength becoming stronger. She channeled her energy into the blade as she heard the poison charging at her. Nix just needed another moment. Hearing the poison running at her, she could tell that it was now only a few feet from her. Feeling ready, she raised her blade above her head before bringing it down hard. It impacted the ground so harshly that it cracked the earth, sending both the poison and her flying.

Grass scraped agaisnt her back and arms. Raising herself up a little, she saw blood running down her arms while her back ached in pain. Her injuries, though, were nothing in comparison to the poison's. Across from her, she saw the poison's alligator body scattered on the grassy field. The poison was no longer alive, and she had won. A bright light shot throughout the area, and she collasped on the grassy field.

Chapter Sixteen: Sailing to the Edge

As the two brothers watched, time ticked away in the room. At first, her body continued on its search for spilling blood, slicing down any obstacle or trap in its way, while a wide smile painted her lips. This seemed to last forever until at last the brothers witnessed her form suddenly collaspe on the stairs to the castle. The spade dagger tumbled down the steps, and its sound was the only noise in the maze.

Both brothers peered closer, trying to notice anymore changes in her behavior. Currently, her body could easily be mistaken for a doll or mannequin as she showed no signs of life. The brothers had no idea of the fight that was occuring in her mind, and they continued to wait.

One minute passed, then two, then five before something happened. Once the fifth minute concluded, she threw her head back as a soundless scream left her lips. Poisonous liquid dripped from her eyes, and the same green substance trickled down the sides of her mouth, falling onto the stone steps below. Concern flickered in the brothers' eyes, but they dared not remove her from the maze yet. Diamond, just in case, kept his piece stationary in the maze.

When her mouth closed and the green liquid disappeared as well, she closed her eyes and entered a state of unconsciousness. The brothers found it time to release her from the game. While Heart teleported to inside of the maze, Diamond retracted his knight. Heart picked up their plaything bridal style and opened a portal within in the maze. Walking through, he now appeared by the hold stairs while the portal closed quickly after he had exited.

Heart's brother soon appeared next to him, looking over to the girl in the blue-haired male's arms. "Diamond, what should we do? The poison has seemed to have left her, but we should make sure."

"We'll head up on the main deck and tie her to the main mast just in case."

"Sounds good to me. Let's just hope that the poison truly is out of her."

Nodding in agreement to that, Diamond headed up the stairs first. After opening the hatch, both of them headed out. Heart positioned her against the mast as Diamond summoned some rope and began to tie it around her. As they were working on her restraints, she started to stir.

Opening her dark brown eyes slowly and blinking a couple of times, she took in her surroundings and let out a sigh of relief. No longer was she in the poison's hold. She had her body back; however, her momentary relief soon vanished as she realized that she was being tied up. "Hey! What do you two think you're doing!" she shouted out, struggling in her binds.

Both of the twins stared at her before they glanced to the other. "Hmm, she seems to be acting like her normal self, Diamond. Maybe, we should stop wrapping her up."

"The element of bloodlust is definitely gone from her eyes, and she has that stubbornness back in her gaze. We should do another test, though," he voiced as they stepped back from the ropes. Swiftly, he swiped his right index fingernail across the palm of his left hand. Blood started to trickle out from the wound, and he held it up to her face.

She looked at him puzzled and drew her face away as best as she could. A relieved sigh left his lips after he had stared into her eyes for time. "There's no excitement in her gaze at the sight of my blood. The poison is gone," he stated, summoning a cloth and dabbing his hand with it. The wound itself appeared to be healing quite quickly.

Soon, Heart came over to her and started to undo the knots, allowing the ropes to drop. Nix, happy to be free from the bindings, stretched her limbs some. Her gaze turned to the blue-haired jester and to the bandages. "What happened to your face?" she asked, making sure to keep some distance between the brothers and her.

"My dear lady, it was you who injured me. While the poison had control over you, you attacked me suddenly. I had little time to react, and it resulted in you slashing my face. Not to fret, though, the wound is healing. In fact, it should be done by now," he answered, starting to unwrap the bandages.

"I wasn't fretting," she responded, rolling her eyes and watching him remove the bandages. When he finally had them off, his face bore no marks of ever being wounded. Granted, she hadn't seen the wound previously. She was amazed by the fact, though, that his face paint was still on. If there had been blood running down his face, why hadn't the paint come off? "So, two questions," she started, glancing between the two males. "One, why are you two acting so worried about the poison when you clearly know about it? Two, what's up with your face paint?"

Answering first, Diamond voiced, "The chain trap was supposed to be removed from the maze since it was an unstable trap. You see, we had built the maze on this boat using a magic text meant for enchanted games. When we had completed the spell, we did a test run since the spell highlighted the various monsters and traps that came with the game.

"We discovered its instability when a monster walked by it. The chains attacked, and after the monster was released, it went berserk on the board, killing off other monsters. At the time, the objective was just for one of us to reach the castle. In order to keep ourselves safe, we cheated, and I summoned my piece to the castle. The game ended, and everything returned to its previous state. From there, we made a mental note to remove the chains. That never happened, though, since we became distracted with other things."

"So, you just thought to throw me in there without checking your game first for issues?" she asked, her voice becoming slightly heated.

"We apologize, my dear lady. This fault does lie on us, and we realize that you could've died."

"Well, no sh*t," she answered, rolling her eyes. "I could've died in any of your other games too. Seriously, you two seemed worried about my health at times, yet you keep putting me in these life threatening conditions. Can you even grasp at how frustrating and confusing that is?!"

"Miss Nix, do calm down. In those past games, we wouldn't have permitted you to die. We don't want you to die, but we do desire our amusement. Perhaps, it doesn't make sense to you, but you need to learn to accept it. You're ours, and we're treating you in the way we know best. If we had wanted to seriously harm you, we would've done so already, and you wouldn't be standing before us.

"Regarding the matter of this game, we were foolish to overlook that detail. We didn't have full control of the situation like usual, and like my brother mentioned, we apologize greatly for that. We'll do our best to prevent such a situation from happening again."

"Or, maybe, you should just stop playing twisted games, but I doubt that's going to change," she grumbled before combing her right fingers through her hair. "Whatever, just answer my next question."

Filling in for his brother, Heart replied, "Our face paint is infused with a durability spell. Like Diamond's nails, we cast such a spell over things that might be ruined easily. Once this spell is cast, the item in question lasts longer and can withstand a good variety of things that might ruin it."

Figuring this made sense, she nodded and walked past them over to the one of the railings. She looked out over the water. "So, we're are we heading next?"

"Over the falls and to the repeating playground," Diamond answered, stepping up next to her on her right side. "Right now, that doesn't matter, though. We answered your inquiries, and, now, we want you to tell us of what you experienced with the poison. It may be dead, but it would be best to still learn of how it affected its victims."

A scoff left her lips. "You apologize, but you then treat this as though I'm some guinea pig. I bet that was your plan all along. Put a person in there and see how the poison reacts to them. Aren't you lucky that I survived, you sick jester, but I'll fulfill your curiosity." She was only doing so because she could already see that Diamond was withholding anger. Then again, she didn't regret how she spoke to them. They had mistreated her, and they deserved her ill temper.

As she recounted the events that occurred in her mind, she noted the brothers' expressions. Diamond remained generally expressionless, listening to every detail, but, occasionally, shock and admiration highlighted his facial features. Heart listened as well, but he continually wore a smirk across his face that she couldn't decipher.

When she finished her account, she waited for the brothers' reactions. Diamond tapped his long nails on the wood of the railing as if in deep thought. Heart, on the other hand, broke out into laughter. "My dear lady, I'm impressed. Who knew that you could handle a sword so well. Maybe, we should increase the restraints on you." A glare crossed her face as she wished to push the male overboard.

"He is only joking, Miss Nix. I'm quite honored, however, that you wanted to come back to us so badly. Giving up an eternity of peace in order to return back to us. How charming, especially since you seem so hateful towards us now."

"You're wrong. I didn't come back for either of you. I came back for my body," she countered, but the two of them seemed to ignore her comment. Annoyed, she looked back to the water and thought back to what Diamond said was their next location. "So, this repeating playground, what's it like? Am I playing another game there?"

Stepping up next to her on her left, Heart nodded. "Yes, you're going to have to find your way out and back to us. We'll set up a time limit for you. Find a way out within the time limit, you win. If the time limit expires and we have to come get you, we win."

"Oh, the joy," she remarked, sarcastically. "Now, what's this about a waterfall?" she questioned, looking to Diamond.

"To get to the repeating playground, we must go down a waterfall. It's quite simple, Miss Nix. Should I expand on my answer, though?" he inquired with a small smile.

Wanting to punch the smile off of his face, she clenched her fists and glanced back out over the water. "Both of you are such a**holes," she mumbled under her breath.

Evidently, Diamond had heard her because she felt a hand rest on her right shoulder. Seeing the painted nails, she knew that it was him. He squeezed her shoulder slightly before bending down to her height. "Keep in mind, Miss Nix, that we're only tolerating your rudeness right now because of our mistake with the maze. That courtesy won't be extended for the entire future," he whispered into her ear.

It wasn't hard to detect his threatening tone, and his actions only exemplified it. Deciding to keep her comments quiet for the moment, she nodded and waited for him to remove his hand. When he did so, she mentally sighed in relief. She glanced over to his brother, though, and saw him just peering out at the light waves. If he had heard any of what had just transpired, he certainly didn't show it.

Silence remained among the three of them until she heard the sound of rushing water. She noticed how the boat now sped faster through the bright blue liquid. Looking ahead, she saw the ocean seemingly drop off. Suddenly, she wanted to be tied again so that she wouldn't risk falling off of the boat.

Directing her gaze to the once forgotten ropes, she headed over to them. Both twins grabbed her and pulled her back. "Just hang onto the railing, my dear lady. You'll be fine," Heart tried to reassure as he wrapped his right arm around her waist. "Look, I'll even hold onto you as well."

To her, that wasn't exactly comforting. She felt another arm wrap aroudn her waist, though, and she glanced over to Diamond. He merely gave her a small smile, but she could tell that he was still peeved at her past behavior some. Regardless of how he felt, she turned her attention to the approaching falls and braced herself. Soon, the ship and the three of them flew over the edge of the water and descended downwards.

Chapter Seventeen: Nighttime Playground

Water splashed against her face, and wind rushed past her. Every second made her feel like she was going to fall off of the boat. So, she kept her eyes closed, not wanting to witness the fall. The brothers' grip on her tightened as gravity tried to knock her off of the deck. It seemed like the descent lasted for forever, but, soon, she heard a loud splashing sound around her.

Hesitantly, she opened her eyes and saw calm waters around her. Nothing stirred in the waters below, and a mysterious and deadly atmosphere filled the air. The brothers released their grip on her, and she was glad to be rid of it. Granted, it did keep her on the deck during the fall. Regardless, she was now more concerned with the game ahead of her.

Peering into the waters below, she noticed sickly green grass, which remained completely still. There was nothing else that she could see in the water. Nix noticed, however, that the water wasn't very deep unless the grass itself was just very tall. She moved her gaze from the water to the playground that was nearing them.

Nix saw a fence surrounding the island while a lifeless tree with a tire swing stood crooked. In front of the tree were two slides with one being higher than the other. Both slides appeared old as the paint was faded and peeling. Grey-blue mushrooms grew around the perimeter of the playground. A sense of utter dread washed over her as she gazed at the area. Sighing, she seated herself on the railing and awaited for the boat to reach the terrible destination.

Upon arriving at the island, she asked, "Have you two decided upon a time limit for me to find the exit?"

"You have an hour to discover a way out of there, Miss Nix."

She was quite surprised by the time limit since the playground was pretty small. Then again, she knew that something was wrong with it, and she would probably soon discover why it bore its name. Hearing this, she merely nodded and jumped off of the boat. Despite the unnerving atmosphere of the place, she was tempted to swing on the tire swing some and go down the slides a couple of times. After all, she had rarely gone to a playground after her parents had passed. With this in mind, it would be fun to enjoy the equipment some. Once her feet hit the dirt ground below, she went over to the fence, opened it and headed inside the tiny playground.

"My dear lady, we haven't even told you to start yet," Heart called out after her. She just shrugged her shoulders and closed the playground fence. Afterwards, she turned her back on them and explored the small area.

~ ~ ~ ~ ~ ~ ~ ~ ~ ~

The twins watched her walk off and enter the playground. Heart leaned forward some more on the railing so that his feet weren't touching the deck. "She really isn't thinking about her situation. I thought that you had warned her, Diamond. Did she not get the message?" Heart asked, chuckling some.

Diamond stepped away from the railing some and crossed his arms over his chest. "It would seem that she's choosing to ignore it. Just walking off like that, how rude. I thought that she would behave more today since I treated her so kindly last night." The red-haired jester narrowed his eyes as he observed her walking around the playground. Tapping his long nails against his arms, a small smile graced his mouth. "Heart, I believe that we need to give our plaything some space."

"What do you mean, Diamond?"

"Simple, the next time that she is near death, we'll leave her like that for awhile. I'm sure that will cause her to be more agreeable with us."

"Interesting, I'm fine with that plan as long as she doesn't die."

"Of course, I would never dream of letting her die on us."

Both brothers nodded at each other, their wicked grins highlighting their lips.

~ ~ ~ ~ ~ ~ ~ ~ ~ ~

Dried leaves, on the playground floor, crunched under her feet as she approached the higher slide. Its metal stairs were rusted and creaked under her ascending form, and one of the stairs nearly collapsed under her. Reaching the top of the slide, she sat down and just stared out at the still sea. She decided not to go down the slide. Instead, she began to count the stars. Of course, she was working with a time limit, but she figured that it would be best to rest her mind some.

This didn't last long since she felt something push her forward. Instantly, she slid down. Once at the bottom of the slide, she glanced back and up but saw nothing. Looking forward again, she found that the scenery in the playground had changed. The higher slide disappeared completely, and only the lower slide remained. Additionally, the brothers' ship was now gone.

Hearing movement behind her, she noticed that the tire swing rocked back and forth despite there being no wind. Hesitantly, she got up and approached the swing. Grabbing it, she halted its movement. She examined it and attempted to find something that was causing its movement, but there was nothing. Beginning to become worried, she glanced around her. To her horror, she saw two yellow eyes staring at her. They hovered in midair as they began to near her. Not really having anywhere to run, she ran for the playground gate but found it jammed shut.

Cursing, she looked back but saw no more floating eyes. Confused but grateful, she went to take a cautious step forward, but she was knocked over by a sudden gust of wind. When she got back to her feet, she noted that the higher slide had returned to its proper place, but the tire swing was gone. She turned her attention back to the fence, but it still couldn't be opened anymore.

This left her no choice but to climb the fence. As soon as she placed her foot on the fence, however, she was thrown backward, hitting the lower slide. Recovering herself, she rubbed her back as she checked to see if her surroundings had changed again. Annoyingly, they did.

Now in the playground, there was only the lower slide. Everything else had vanished. A few feet away from her lay a piece of yellowed paper. Walking over to it, she picked it up and gazed down at it. Across the old paper was a single written line: *Let's play together.*

She tensed and wondered who had written the note. Holding the note in her hands, she glanced around to see if there was anyone around her. Once again, there was nothing. She could soon feel someone breathing down her neck, however.

Jumping, she turned around and came face to face with a shadow being. Unlike the one from the forest, this one had four arms. It rubbed its knive like hands together as it moved closer to her backing away form. She neared the fence behind her and stood still, waiting for it to attack. When it raised two of its arms towards her, she made a run for it. Not really having a plan, she climbed up the slide. Just as she reached the top, the shadow swung two more of its arms at her. Luckily for her, she had just slid down the small slide.

Checking behind her, the shadow was now gone as was the lower slide. Sitting on the leaf covered ground, she noticed that the higher slide was back as was the tree and tire swing. She heard whispers, however, coming from all around her. Her eyes couldn't pinpoint anyone, though. Maybe, her mind had finally broke, and this was the result of it. Getting to her feet, she hesitantly moved forward some.

Chapter Eighteen: Mushroom Dance

The whispers continued to sound around her, and she glanced back behind her sometimes. Still, nothing greeted her, so she stood her ground and crossed her arms. She tapped her right fingers against her left elbow and wondered what was going on. Her eyes glanced out to the waters surrounding the area, and she still couldn't see the brothers' boat or the brothers.

Frustrated, she seated herself on the leaf covered ground and rested her chin in the palms of her hands. Her dark brown eyes gazed out over the area in front of her. Upon doing so, she noticed something peculiar about the grey-blue mushrooms. There seemed to be three slits on the stems of them. Curious, she scooted closer but not too close.

She noted that the whispering had stopped, but she saw one of the slits on the mushroom nearest to her twitch some. Hesitantly, she murmured, "Hello?" All three slits now moved some. Other slits on other mushrooms did the same. Whispering started up again behind her.

Swiftly, she turned back, but it stopped upon her doing so. She looked back to the front of her only to jump back some. The mushrooms had positioned themselves closer to her. When they moved towards her again, she backed up some more. This process continued between them until she went to put her hand back and heard a quiet shout. "Stop!"

Peering back and down, she now saw that the slits on a particular mushroom had opened. Tiny blue eyes and a small mouth were on the stem. She quickly retracted her hand and turned to face the mushroom. Nix went to speak, but the mushroom beat her to it.

"Why have you come to our playground, human?" it asked in its quiet voice. A collective whispering went around, voicing the same curiosity.

Nix noticed that by now all of the mushrooms had their eyes open, and their mouths moved as soft murmurs came from them. Focusing back on the mushroom in front of her, she answered, "The brothers forced me to come here. It's one of their games. Do you know of Heart and Diamond?"

"Of course, we know of the twins. They're quite troublesome. It's a pity that you have to deal with them. Still, do you have proof of this? We don't see them around."

"I ... well, we came on a ship, but the ship and them seemed to have vanished. They teleport themselves around after all, but they're probably watching from somewhere nearby."

"I suppose that we can believe you. You do know their names and that they can transport. You even mentioned their ship. Well, what game did they put you to? Perhaps, we can help. They give us trouble from time to time, so we should return the favor."

"Wait, really?! Any help would be appreciated."

"Yes, yes, we can aid you. Still, we need to know the details of the game. We should also know the name of the individual that we're going to help." Another collective whisper went through the crowd of mushrooms, and they all agreed on this.

"I suppose that is a fair request. My name is Nix," she started, not finding a reason to not disclose information to the mushrooms. She had encountered weirder things during her time in this world. If the mushrooms were a trap, she was stalling. After all, she was surrounded by them, and she didn't know how to escape the playground. So, she might as well go with their offer of help. "As for their game, it concerns me finding a way out of here within a time limit of an hour. I don't have a clock on me, so I have no idea how long I've been in here."

"Well, that's simple enough, Nix. If all you have to do is escape this place, we can easily get you out. Besides, this is our island, so we know all of its tricks. We'll perform a dance that will erase the shroud over your eyes and help you to see the exit."

"If you know where the exit is, though, why can't you just show it to me?"

"Even if we presented the exit to you, you wouldn't see it. It would seem like we were pointing to a dead end. We must clear your vision to show you the way," the mushroom explained as the other mushrooms nodded in agreement.

This seemed incredibly fishy to her, but it might be her only way out. She wasn't exactly making any progress on her own, and she would probably still be wondering around the playground if it weren't for the mushrooms deciding to speak. There was also the fact that she wished to beat one of the brothers' games. She desired to show them that she shouldn't be underestimated. "Alright, I look forward to seeing this dance of yours."

An excited whisper raced across the mushrooms as the one in front of her nodded. "Everyone get to your places!" After the mushroom's quiet shout, they all spread out into four rows. The back row had the most, and the front had the least. The mushroom that she had been talking to stood at the very front of the four rows and whisper-yelled, "Begin!"

Upon this command, the ones in the back started to move their mushroom caps down and up. Those in the middle split, moving to the right and left. This allowed those in the back to be better seen while the middle ones began to jump up and down. Concerning those at the front, they laid down and began to roll side to side. The leader, on the other hand, began to sing.

Bob, bob, jump, jump, roll, roll, this is the mushroom dance. Bob, bob, jump, jump, roll, roll, mushrooms open the gate. Bob, bob, jump, jump, roll, roll, this is the mushroom dance. Bob, bob, jump, jump, roll, roll, mushrooms let them out.

The song continued on like this, and she began to clap along. Granted, she did hope that the gate would open soon, though. She didn't want the brothers to come in and have to get her out.

~ ~ ~ ~ ~ ~ ~ ~ ~ ~ ~

"It looks like we'll be winning this game," Heart commented, chuckling some, while he continued to lean on the railing.

"Yes, I doubt that she will find the exit. Then again, it's the same way that she came in. How unfortunate for her," Diamond mentioned as a small smile tugged on his lips.

"Well, who knew that we would get this amusing result. I didn't think that the mushrooms would affect her so quickly. Still, it's quite funny to watch her run around the playground like that."

"It would seem that she is quite sensitive to their hallucinogenic vapors. Oh look, she is now talking to nothing. I wonder what our plaything is seeing at the moment, Heart."

"Agreed, though, at least she brought us up. Now if only she could compliment us while she was at it."

They continued to watch and were quite entertained. Heart chuckled some more, and Diamond laughed a little when they saw her began to clap along to something. Both of them continued to enjoy the performance thoroughly.

~ ~ ~ ~ ~ ~ ~ ~ ~ ~

Steadily, the song began to slow down, but she still didn't see any gate opening. Instead, she heard the crunching of leaves to her left. Glancing that way, she saw a shadow advancing towards her. It was only a few feet away, but the mushrooms weren't bothered by it. They just continued to sing, and she listened to their song more carefully.

Eyes widening, she realized that they could be referring to any gate and that *them* didn't necessarily refer back to her. Instead of creating an exit for her, they were summoning one of the shadows to her location. She didn't have time to deal with the mushrooms, though. Hastily, she rose to her feet and backed away from the large shadow.

Swiping its four knife-like hands at her, she continued to step backwards. She was nearing the fence and wouldn't have anywhere to go soon. If only she had a weapon of some kind. Nix scanned over the area to find anything that could be of use. Maybe if she could push the slide onto it, she might have a chance.

Dashing over to the said object, she waited for the creature to follow. It turned around and scraped some of its fingers together. She rested her hands on the slide and wondered if she could even push the thing over. If she couldn't, she would have to find some other method. The mushroom song in the background wasn't helping, though. Now, it sounded like a disturbing chant more than a song.

Keeping her focus on the shadow, though, she noted that it had stopped. It was most likely getting ready to charge at her. She stared at it intensely, and it soon bolted towards her. Putting as much force as she could muster into the push, she began to tilt the slide some. Seeing that she was being sucessful, she smiled to herself and continued to press against the slide. With another shove, the slide tipped over onto the oncoming shadow.

Unfortunately, it didn't crush the shadow. The shadow crashed against the slide at such a speed that both began to topple her way. Cursing loudly, she ran out of the way and headed for the fence again. She decreased her pace dramatically and nearly fell forward, however, when she noticed a boy standing a few feet from her. Wondering how a child came to be in the playground, she guessed that perhaps he had an ability like Heart and Diamond.

Frankly, though, she wanted to shout for the child to run. Speedily, she turned around to see where the shadow was, but it was gone. The mushrooms were now back in their original places. Everything else had disappeared. It was just the child and her.

With her life not in immediate danger, she looked over the child to see if he was a threat. Then again, something innocent in this world could actually turn into a nightmare. So, she kept her guard up as she observed the boy. Their face was hidden under a blue mask, but their bright yellow eyes shone. He had on a simple blue shirt and a long sleeve black shirt on underneath it. A pair of black shorts matched his shirts while blue knee-high lace-up boots rested on his feet. Messy black hair framed his face.

When he held out a hand, she questioned what he was doing and took a step back. He just motioned for her to take it. "Do you know a way out of here?" she inquired, keeping the distance between them. He nodded in reply before reaching forward and grabbing her right hand. The action startled her, but for such a young kid, he had a strong grip on her. She tried to pull away, but he kept tugging and wouldn't let go.

Reaching the gate, he opened it with ease and a portal formed. Despite her continued struggling, the strange child dragged her through with him. The playground and surrounding ocean disappeared from her sight as new scenery formed before her.

Chapter Nineteen: Painting the Crown

"Diamond, she went with the circus leader. It would seem that he still hasn't learned his lesson," Heart practically growled out, his eyes glaring at the spot where their plaything disappeared with him.

"We do need to pay Cirsis a visit. It's been so long since we had a nice chat with him," Diamond laughed out some as his fire-red eyes gleamed with ill intent.

Glancing to his brother, Heart smirked some. "It has been awhile since he called on us to perform in one of his lovely shows. We do know how to make the audience's hearts race."

"Indeed. So, why don't we go change into some of their circus clothes. Cirsis would really love that."

With their plan in mind, the twins vanished from their boat and headed to the carnival. They would change when the show first started and before their plaything could be seriously injured since they assumed that their plaything would be changed into a performer's clothing. Technically, they could both stop the show before it started, but they desired to have a little fun with Cirsis; they would make sure to ruin his next show.

~ ~ ~ ~ ~ ~ ~ ~ ~ ~

Nix found herself in a dark room which was surrounded by blue fabric. The child released her hand and gazed up at her. His yellow eyes glowed before he started to clap his hands. She was confused by his action. That confusion was soon replaced with worry as four people appeared out of the darkness.

One of them was a female child who seemed to be about seven. This girl had long, mint green hair and golden eyes. A green clover was painted under each of her eyes. Another was a man who appeared to be in his thirties. He had combed back purple hair and blue eyes that shone through a green half-mask. The third was another man who looked no older than nineteen. Messy mint green hair decorated his head while his right eye was covered with an eyepatch, and his other eye was a stunning green. As for the last person, it was a woman who looked to be in her twenties. She had curly brown locks and brown eyes. Orange lipstick covered her lips.

The male teenager grabbed Nix's left arm while the man in his thirties took hold of her right arm. Tugging at her dress, the girl gazed up at Nix. As for the woman, she sat on a nearby crate, merely watching the scene unfold. Looking at the boy, Nix asked, "Why are you doing this?"

"I thought that we should have some fun with the brothers' new plaything. The manager told us about you after you had escaped. He was quite saddened that you didn't stay long enough for him to kill you. Regardless, we told him that we would look for you and have some fun. I'm sure that he'll be quite pleased as will we. The brothers do need to pay for their crimes after all.

"So, I began looking for you. Of course since I don't have the magic capabilities of the brothers, my range of portals is limited to a few places. One of those places happens to be the playground since its hallucinogenic mushrooms create quite an interesting show for an audience to watch. And, I knew that the brothers liked that place, so I figured that I would give it a shot and see if I could find you there. Turns out that I made a lucky guess. Regardless, I've talked enough. Em, Wat, take her to the dressing room. Leaf, Daisy, you two will prepare her for the show," he commanded before walking off behind the curtain to her right.

"You're going to be a great performance piece," chirped the little girl by her.

"Leaf, leave her alone for the moment and let Em and Wat take her to the room," voiced the woman on the crate, who was presumably Daisy.

Dread coursed through her veins, and she wondered what crimes the boy had been talking about. Just what was his relationship to the brothers? Not only that but also the manager fit into all of this as well. Clearly, the brothers had left out some vital information about the carnival. Then again, she really didn't know much about the two, except that they were powerful and loved twisted games. They also seemed to have some weird affection for her.

Her thoughts, though, were disturbed when the two males began to drag her across the dirt floor. She considered struggling, but she could already tell that she had little chance to break out of their grip. It would serve her better to conserve her energy for whatever performance they had planned for her.

Both men moved her into a room with rows of costumes. Red fabric outlined the walls of the room. Tiny lamps illuminated the area, highlighting the costumes perfectly. The little girl walked over to a wooden chair, drawing her attention to an old vanity, which sat in front of the chair and had lightbulbs surrounding the frame of the mirror. The two men pushed her into the space before leaving.

She heard their footsteps fade until she heard nothing. Both the woman and the girl now took her arms. The woman's grip was as tight as the males' grip, but the girl's was much looser. Nix could easily break free of her hold and attempt to injure the woman with her free arm. If she could avoid her awaiting performance that would be all the better.

Carrying out this plan, she wrenched her left arm from Leaf and swung her arm around to punch Daisy in the face. Before her fist could reach Daisy, she cried out in pain as she felt something stab her left leg. Her legs still hadn't recovered from the shadows back in those woods. She collapsed to the floor as Daisy continued to hold onto her right arm.

Glancing to where Leaf was, she saw that the girl had vines sprouting from her right hand. Those vines were jabbed into her leg. "You really shouldn't try to escape. It will only end in increasing your chances of death during your performance," the little girl mentioned in her high-pitched voice. Leaf proceeded to pull out her vines as Daisy hoisted Nix back up. The small girl held onto her left arm again, and the two circus performers guided her over to the vanity.

On the way there, Nix didn't try another attempt at escape. She didn't need any more vines piercing her already wounded skin. So, she let them seat her in the vanity chair and take off her boots, socks and bandages. Leaf stood guard while Daisy went to retrieve some new bandages. When the woman returned, she began to bandage Nix's legs back up as Leaf picked out clothes.

Once the bandages were on, Daisy stood up and grabbed a towel from the topmost left vanity drawer. The woman drew water from the air and wet the towel before she wiped her hands of the blood that had got on them. "Now, we need to do something about your face. You don't need makeup but some face paint will do. You can be just like your twin lovers."

Heat erupted in her cheeks. "I'm not their lover! I don't even like them! How on earth did you come up with that assumption?!" Nix shouted, almost shooting up from her chair in the process and from embarrassment.

Daisy raised one of her eyebrows before brushing Nix's response aside. "Whatever you think. I'll still add some face paint after you've changed. Do you have the outfit ready, Leaf?"

"Yep, she'll look perfect in it!" called the young child, running over to the vanity with clothes in her arms.

Looking over the clothes, Nix saw a pair of black and purple checkered over-the-knee socks. Along with them were a pair of purple shorts and a long-sleeve black blouse. A purple and black vest and black ankle boots accompanied the outfit as well. Thankfully, there was no dress involved.

"You have five minutes to change before we'll return," Daisy mentioned as she took Leaf's right hand. "If you try to escape while we're gone, you'll be left to crawl during your performance." With that, they both left the room.

Understanding that the threat wasn't to be taken lightly, Nix sighed and got up from the chair. She grabbed the pile of clothes, which Leaf had left on the vanity. Standing up, she limped a little ways away from the chair and slipped out of her old clothes. Carefully, she put on the new ones, doing her best not to put pressure on her left leg. Nix finished just in time as the two females returned to the room and headed over to her.

Seating herself back in the chair, she tried not to focus on Leaf, who was playing with some of her vines. Instead, she paid attention to Daisy, who pulled out some face paint from the middle right drawer. She grabbed a brush and dipped it in the paint before proceeding to paint Nix's face. Nix closed her eyes and allowed the woman to work.

It felt cold against her skin, but Nix tried to figure out what Daisy was painting on her face by paying attention to the brush strokes. She could tell that she was painting the same design below both of her dark brown eyes. The brush was also brought down on her bottom lip.

When the woman finished, Nix opened her eyes and turned to look in the mirror. Under both of her eyes were two small purple crowns while on her bottom lip was a single purple line going down the middle. Daisy, though, started to tap her right index finger against her lips. "There's something missing, but what? Ah, I know."

Before Nix knew what the woman was doing, Daisy opened the top drawer on the right. She pulled out a circular tin, which rattled in her hand. Opening the lid, she pulled out tiny purple and black gems. With the gems in hand, she put the tin back in the drawer. Daisy proceeded to pull out a tiny glue bottle, and started to add the gems on Nix's face. The gems only decorated the tips of the crowns. After the older circus performer finished, Leaf exclaimed, "You'll look so pretty when you perform on stage! Now, let's get you to your performance!"

Leaf grabbed her left hand and led Nix out of the room. Daisy followed behind the two of them. Eventually, the three of them reached a cushioned golden chair. The two circus performers seated Nix before metal clasped around her wrists and ankles. Nix was seriously getting tired of everyone securing her to chairs. Granted, the two soon left her alone, and she was grateful for them to be gone. Her attention, however, turned to the light which shone through the curtain in front of her.

"Welcome everyone to tonight's exquisite show! We have a real treat for this evening! So, hold onto your seats, ladies and gentlemen!" she heard being yelled. She recognized the voice as the boy's.

When the annoucement ended, she waited in the chair and readied herself for whatever lay ahead of her. Of course, she was going to fight back with everything she had, but, no doubt, the task ahead of her was going to be a tough one. Would she face more shadows, something like the manager or perhaps worse? Knowing her luck in this world, it was probably the last one. As the blue curtain in front of her was raised, she gripped the arms of the chair and gazed out ahead of her.

Chapter Twenty: Applaud of Misfortune

Out in front of her were rows and rows of red cushioned chairs. The domed ceiling above was decorated in bright lights, which were in the shapes of stars. A ball cage hung in the center of the stage, but it was high enough so that it wouldn't interfere with other performances. There were only about ten people in the seats, and all of them looked to be a part of the circus. It would make sense since she had seen no others roaming around the carnival.

These people whispered, "I wonder how long she'll last," over and over again. Nix blocked these words from her mind, trying to ignore the crowd. All that mattered was passing her performance and finding a way out of the tent. She wondered, though, if the brothers were coming after her, but it seemed like a vein popped in her head.

Back in that playground, she had been imagining the whole thing. At least, she assumed that she had been since the boy mentioned that the mushrooms there are hallucenogenic. Those two twins were probably laughing in amusement at what she had been doing. Regardless, she would get back at them once her stupid performance was over.

The restraints on her chair became undone as the chair was pulled out from under her. She crashed to the ground with a loud thud as those in the crowd began to laugh. A scowl set on her face as she looked back and up. Leaf stood behind her with an innocent smile before she motioned for Nix to head out on stage. Muttering some curses under her breath, Nix headed out as the curtain closed behind her.

To her right was the boy, who was now grinning over at her. "And, here she is! The star of the show, the lady of the hour, the brothers' latest plaything!" he called out, pointing to her with his left index finger. Her fists clenched as she made sure to put more weight onto her right leg. "Now, to give the details of her performance!"

She would've listened more intently to what the boy was saying if it weren't for the individual that just walked through the tent opening. The sunhat on the girl's head of golden locks gave her away. Catching Nix's gaze, the small girl sent her a sickly sweet smile as the boy pointed to her. "Ah, and here's the one who arranged this performance! Thanks to her, we were able to pinpoint the location of their plaything and bring her here to have another fight with the manager!"

Nix's blood went cold at the mention of her fighting him again. Once was enough for her, but she couldn't help but glare at the girl. Last time, she had barely escaped those kelpies, and, now, the small child was purposefully sending the manager on her. Doing her best to keep her voice steady, she turned to the boy again. "I thought that you said that you had found me by making a lucky guess. What happened to that?"

A grin spread across the boy's lips, and he shrugged. "I lied on that bit. She told me to keep her part in it a secret until the show began. Now, no more questions, you need to entertain us all. Bring out the manager!"

Dread started to creep up on Nix, but her gaze focused back on the sunhat girl for a moment. Rage filled her dark brown eyes as she watched the sunhat girl take a seat in the crowd. That stupid grin of hers remained plastered on her seemingly innocent looking face. She forced herself to look away and focus on the task at hand while the boy called for the manager to come out again. When the manager didn't come, murmurs went throughout the small crowd. The boy and the sunhat girl shared a glance before the sunhat girl raised her left hand up and summoned something onto the stage.

Hurriedly, the boy stepped off of the round stage and announced, "While we wait for the manager, we'll have the brothers' plaything fight off some aciflo. As you all know, these creatures come from the Berrytree Woods. They like to sit at the bases of the blue strawberry trees there and act like flowers until prey comes along. Let us see how the plaything handles them!"

Each of the monsters were identical in appearance. They had the body of a mannequin and stood at a height of most likely over six feet. None of them had feet; they only had hands. In place of a head was a flower in the shape of a purple pansy. She limped back some and scanned the area for anything to use. There was little to be found. All she could think of was getting them to somehow accidentally attack each other.

There was no time left to think as one of the monsters launched itself at her, making her jump out of the way. She landed flat on her stomach, having used her arms to protect her face. When she looked up, she saw that she was at the hands of another one. It stared down at her as she heard movement behind her. Nix wanted to look back, but she didn't wish to glance away from the creature in front of her.

Knowing that she didn't have much time left to act, she pushed herself up and reached her hands out. She gripped the ankles of the aciflo and tugged towards her hard. To her surprise, this worked, and the creature lost its balance and crashed back onto the stage. Sitting up as quickly as she could manage, Nix saw the other approaching.

Remembering how light the one aciflo was, she grabbed its ankles again and swung it around. This knocked the oncoming one over, but the other two were now closing in. One of them opened the center of its petal face. A long purple tongue came out while an acidic looking purple substance dripped from it.

When she went to move away, the one to the right of her leaped forward. Instantly, she forced herself to push herself backwards. She managed to dodge the creature but barely. That one, though, had opened its mouth as well and, in the process of its jump, had flung the purple substance around some. Some of it happened to land on her right hand, and she could already feel it burning her skin. Swiftly, she ripped off part of her shirt and wiped the substance from her hand before casting the fabric away from her.

The two, which had previously been knocked down, were walking towards her again while the other two were coming near as well. She could try to make a run for it, but, on her nearly injured leg, she wouldn't make it far. Plus, any of the individuals might stop her with some magic that they possesed. In other words, she had little hope to make it past these things. Nix didn't desire to give up on the fight, but she didn't see anything in sight that would help her. Its not like her audience would lend a hand.

All four of them surrounded her, but she would give it her all until the end even if the situation seemed hopeless. She went to reach for the legs of the one in front of her, but its head came flying off before she reached it. Nix backed away from the falling body, which oozed out the purple substance, and she thought that she would back into another aciflo. Instead, she heard a crash to her left and saw one of them tossed into the blue curtains.

Trying to grasp at what was going on, she stared ahead and noticed Heart leading the other two away from her. When she turned around and glanced up, she noticed Diamond standing there. A smile was on his lips before he grabbed both of her upper arms and hoisted her upwards. "Sorry, that we took some time to get here, but we had to make ourselves look presentable for the circus, Miss Nix."

"Of course, you had to do such a thing. The two of you were already dressed for a circus," she remarked, wriggling out of his grip and looking over to Heart, who had just finished off the two aciflo as well as the one that had been thrown to the curtains.

"Well, we wished to taunt Cirsis. Taking you from us was a very poor choice on his part," the red-haired male responded as his gaze turned towards the small boy. A menacing smile coated Diamond's lips while he took steps towards the boy. "Ah, Cirsis, it's been such a long time. I see that you still harbor hate towards us for ruining that face of yours. My brother and I, though, can always add a few more scars if you would like. You seem to be asking for some more after all."

The boy seemed to be glued to his spot as he looked over to where the sunhat girl had been sitting, but she was there no more. His attention instantly turned back to Diamond, and Nix noticed that those in the audience had grown tense as well. Apparently, they weren't expecting the brothers to arrive so soon. Or, they had been anticipating her to die before they came. Thank goodness, the manager hadn't shown up.

Still, she wondered what history had occurred between the circus and the brothers. Obviously, there was bad blood between the two. She looked over to Heart, who sent a grin her way. "Not to worry, my dear lady, we'll take care of things from here. Just take a seat on the stage and watch us perform a show for you."

Sitting down did sound nice, especially due to her left leg. She glanced around, however, just in case there were any monsters still hiding away. When she saw none, she did take a seat. Nix thought that maybe she should try to stop the twins since the look of bloodlust in their eyes was unsettling, but those in the circus really didn't deserve her sympathy. A few moments ago, they had been trying to kill her to get revenge against the brothers and to amuse themselves.

So, she looked away from their concerned faces and focused on what the two brothers were doing. Granted, their new attire was also fitting for a circus. Both had on black ruffled button-ups, red and blue striped pants, black pirate hats with red and blue feathers and black-heeled shoes. A blue half-mask rested on Heart's face while a red one was on Diamond's. She could just see their face paint peeking out from the bottoms of the masks.

"Please, Diamond, we were only having a little fun. You know how performances are here. They always appear to put one's life on the line, but we always step in to prevent someone from dying," the boy argued. "When you two served here, neither of you ever were allowed to die," he explained nervously.

Hearing this, though, she peered back over to the boy. He was taking some steps away from the red-haired male until he backed into a chair. Diamond continued to approach him, his left fingernails tapping the handle of his saber. She became puzzled, though, as to how the brothers could've served the circus under the boy. He was clearly younger than them, so how was that possible? Did people age differently here, perhaps?

"Cirsis," Heart called out, chuckling some. "We may not have died, but we were treated oh so terribly. Having us fight monsters when we were starving, having us eat only the scraps left by your audience when we were finished, giving us one pair of clothes for a half a year, I could go on and on, but you know all of that as well. Not to mention how your lovely circus troupe abused us as well, and only because we were two boys who could turn nowhere else for shelter and food.

"There are other forms of death than just physically dying. You were trying to kill our spirits and turn us into little helpers who would follow your every command with no hesistation," Heart annouced, looking out to the audience as well. "Now, onto more important matters, where are the other four? We have a show to begin for all of you. Don't make us teleport them to us, or some more punishment will be served."

Scanning the crowd for Leaf, Daisy, Em and Wat, she didn't see them. Until Heart had mentioned that the four were missing, she had completely forgotten about them. She went to turn around but felt something cold and sharp press to her neck. An arm wrapped around her waist as a water bubble covered her mouth. When she went to elbow her captor, the water moved over her nose. "If you try to attack me again, I'll drown you," came the familiar voice of Daisy.

Not wishing to die, Nix remained silent while Daisy dragged her backstage. Nix could see that the boy had noticed Daisy's action, but he averted his gaze quickly enough so that presumably neither of the brothers had noticed. The water moved back down only to her mouth as the two of them went out of sight.

Chapter Twenty One: Sharpened Hold

As she was being dragged away, she kept opening her mouth and eating at the water bubble. To her luck, it started to diminish, but Daisy caught on quickly and created a new one. Soon enough, she was restrained back to the golden chair. Granted, the chair had been moved to one of the performers' tents. No longer could she hear either of the brothers' voices or the boy's voice.

Daisy turned on a lantern in the small tent and illuminated the room. There was a simple bed, chest and desk in the room. A vase of orange daisies was on the desk, and Nix presumed that this was Daisy's room. The woman left the tent for awhile afterwards but returned shortly after with Em. He pulled out a piece of fabric from his right pants' pocket. Nodding, Daisy popped the water bubble as Em quickly tied the fabric around Nix's mouth.

He took a few steps back and glanced to his fellow performer. "So, what did you want me to do to her while we wait?"

"Cirsis wanted the manager to fight her, but she escaped that fate. So, we'll remedy that. He'll be pleased if we give her a treatment that the manager would've given her. I'm sure that you can arrange that, Em."

"Certainly, I'll have some fun with her. Has Wat found the manager yet, though?"

"No, I haven't heard any word back from him. Let's hope that he does, though. Anyway, I'll be heading back to Leaf. It will be better for two of us to deal with the twins," she commented before taking her leave of the tent.

Em focused his attention on Nix now while a smirk played at his lips. "You know, this is the first time that I've gotten to play with something precious to the brothers. I wonder why they find you so fascinating," he mused as vines sprouted from his right hand and wrapped around his fingers. His fingers seemed to be more like claws when the vines were finished.

Her hands clenched the chair, and she desperately wanted to yell or something. Personally, she didn't like the brothers, but, right now, it would be nice to have their help. In cases where she could defend herself, she would, but she kept finding herself in positions where aid was required. She hated how she needed to rely on those two at times, but she would push back her pride if it meant she would live.

Still if they had never started these games with her, if she hadn't grabbed their attention, she wouldn't be in this mess. The sunhat girl was also to blame, though. Perhaps, she was really the only one to blame. After all, the girl had mentioned that she had basically delivered her to the brothers. At the same time, however, she desired to just scream at all of the inhabitants of this world since all of them seemed to want to harm her in one fashion or another.

Then again, she had wished to enter the music box, and this was the cost of it. Even so, she didn't desire to return back to her aunt. That place may have not put her life on the line, but she hated the idea of ever going back there. She had made that wish for a reason, and she would do her best to turn that wish into something positive. Maybe, it wouldn't happen immediately, but she still had more of this world to explore. Back at her aunt's, she would've never had a chance of exploration. The world would've been kept closed off to her, and she would only have the sanctuary of her room.

When she felt sharp vines brush against her left shoulder, she jolted out of her thoughts. Em leaned down some in front of her and smirked as he trailed his sharp fingers up her neck steadily. They eventually stopped under her chin as he met her gaze. "The feeling of your skin is quite soft, plaything. I wonder if the brothers have made any marks in it. They were always wanting to keep people away from their things; they're just so possessive."

Heat rose to her cheeks slightly in embarassment, but she wished to shout at him. She was getting tired of being called a plaything; she was person, not some item to be toyed around with! Despite her warm cheeks, she managed to narrow her eyes at him in a threatening manner.

"Oh, are you desiring to hurt me, plaything? That's pretty cute, but you can't free yourself from this situation. It will just be you and me until negotiations are worked out. Now, about those marks, I can already see one on your right cheek. Then again, that could've been from something else. Let's see if I can find something more obvious," he breathed out, bringing his clawed hand down from her chin.

In an instant, he ripped through her vest and threw it to the side. She tried to move back into the chair more out of instinct as she struggled against the restraints. "Now, plaything, you need to hold still, or I might cut into you too much. I can't have you dying on me." Her eyes widened as he brought down his hand again.

This time, he used only his right index finger and drew it down slowly. She could feel it cut into her skin some as the buttons broke while he went down. A trickle of blood slid down her torso, but he stopped upon reaching her bra. Withdrawing his hand back, he now reached to her shoulders and slid the sleeves of the shirt down. Soon, a smile broke loose on his lips. "Ah, so it was Diamond that left one. I wonder how he would feel if I ruined the design."

She wasn't able to help herself and gulped in the process. His sharpened fingers came closer to her skin, and he pulled her bra strap down to get a better area to work with. He rested the tips of his fingers against the carved diamond as he moved himself to sit on the chair with her. Straddling her hips, he pressed his left hand into her right shoulder as he brought down his right fingers.

A cry of pain exited her lips but was muffled by the cloth. She could hear her skin tearing under his fingers, and she couldn't do a d*mn thing about it. Tears threatened to cascade down her face while he only dug slightly deeper. When she tried to draw her left shoulder back some, she felt something stab her right shoulder. Another cry left her mouth as she noticed that he had stabbed a vine through her flesh there.

His right hand was about to reach her bra, but he stopped and smirked. "Shall I check for other marks, plaything?" Rage clouded her eyes as her mind became consumed with knocking this man out of his senses. "Oh, I love that look in your eyes. I guess that I'll take that as a yes," he chuckled out while his fingers trailed down.

~~~~~~~~~~

Heart and Diamond stood still when they went to glance back at their plaything and found her to be gone. In her place was Leaf. A grin rested on the girl's lips as she rocked back and forth on her heels. "You two look quite shocked. Maybe, you should keep a better eye on your things," she laughed out.

In a second, Heart was on her. His right hand secured itself around the collar of her green dress and lifted her up into the air. The male saw a vine shoot towards him, but he stopped it with his left hand with ease. Crushing the vine in his grip, he growled out, "Where is she?!"

"Oh, somewhere, but you won't find her without my help. For all you know, she could be leaving the carnival as we speak. I know that you can't summon her here, or you would've done so already. Now, set me down, or you'll find your plaything in quite terrible condition."

The blue-haired jester tightened his grip for a moment before tossing the girl to his right. A satisfied smirk touched his lips when she slid across the ground with a loud crack. Diamond, just as angered, had advanced on Cirsis and held the tip of his saber to the boy's neck.

Both twins saw the blue curtain move and watched as Daisy came out. She accessed the situation and remained where she was while Leaf picked herself back up steadily. "Shall I tell them of the offer?" the older woman asked the younger. Leaf nodded but winced when she touched her left arm. The young girl hung her arm limply by her side, for it had broken when impacting the floor.

Looking to both brothers, Daisy proposed, "Here's the deal before you two. You comply to our demands, and we'll tell you the location of your plaything and allow you to leave with her. Our demands are that you two suffer some of the pain that you have dealt us. One, you will step away from Cirsis and hand him your saber, Diamond. From there, you will allow him to cut the marks which he bears on his face onto your brother's face. He will then cut them into your face.

"Afterwards, the two of you will fight each other. You don't have to kill each other, but we want to see a real fight for fifteen minutes. Once your fight is over, Diamond you will go with Pina. Heart you will go with Saxia. I'm sure that you two recall how much they adored you when you were children. So, you can accept this offer, or you will forgo your plaything."

The twins glanced at each other before Heart burst out laughing, and Diamond merely smiled some more. "That's the worst offer I have ever heard of," Heart chuckled out. "We're not giving her up, nor are we following that dumb plan. We may not be able to summon her here, but we can summon Em and Wat here. They're the only two missing, and one of them is bound to be with her unless you left her all alone. That will end the threat on her."

Leaf, becoming annoyed by their laughing, exclaimed, "She'll bleed to death by the time you two find her! You'll need our help! And, you're wasting precious time now!"

"No need to lose your head, Leaf," Diamond commented, pushing the tip of the saber closer to Cirsis's neck. "Once we summon those two here, we'll leave all of you alone and search the back of this tent and your rooms. Once we find her, we'll kill whoever adminsitered her wounds, and it sounds like it's Em since Wat is so sensitive to blood. And, I doubt that she'll die of blood loss. There's a reason why we have a healer at our castle."

"You won't find her in time!" the girl argued back.

"Leafy, there's another reason why she won't die of blood loss," Heart pointed out. "Whoever is with her right now will make sure not to kill her. After all if she's dead your whole plan goes to waste, and you'll have two very enraged jesters on your hands. There's also no means of communication between you two and the other two. So unless you intend to run back to her and inform your companion to kill her, she won't die. Of course, should you run to her location, we'll know where to go."

"Now, that your idiotic plan's flaws have been revealed, I suggest that you take us to her. Maybe, we'll consider not killing Em if you do so. Otherwise, his fate isn't looking too bright at the moment," Diamond voiced, his smile turning into a wicked grin.

Each of the females looked defeated before they glanced over to their leader. He sighed some and motioned for them to comply. Noting this, the brothers turned on the two females and demanded in unison, "Hurry up, then!"

Chapter Twenty Two: A Rest

How Nix desired to break the restraints on her chair and injure the man in front of her, but she couldn't even struggle at the moment. If she thrashed around, his sharpened fingers would only pierce her skin and make his next move worse. At the same time, she didn't want him to go any lower; she didn't wish for him to see her chest.

Making matters worse was her blood loss. Blood was running down both of her shoulders now, and it wasn't in small quantities. She figured that she only had a few more minutes before she lost consciousness. If she survived this, she would never go to a circus again.

When his hand was getting ready to tear through her bra, she heard him gasp as his hold on her loosened. The vine retracted from her right shoulder, and he fell back some before he was thrown off of her. Nix could see blood starting to soak through his shirt on the right side of him. Her eyes turned to look over at the nearby girl, though.

"And, this is why I have been keeping a close watch on you. I never know when someone is going to try and ruin my plans for you, Nix," the sunhat girl remarked, tossing what looked like a throwing knife up and down. She rested her left foot on the male's wound, eliciting a cry of pain from him.

"Why did you do that? I thought that you wanted me dead," Nix inquired, still remaining tense.

"Dead? Well, not at the moment, I need you alive for now. Calling the manager in was just for a bit of fun. I would've stepped in at a certain point. Like with those aciflo, I would've come onto stage if the brothers hadn't decided to show up. Anyway after I followed that Daisy here, I decided to go back to the tent for a bit but hidden this time. It seems that the brothers are figuring out the problems in the performers' plan and will be on their way shortly. I still wanted to check up on you, and it's a good thing that I decided to teleport inside of the tent," she explained, unlocking the restraints on the chair.

"Now, you should find some bandages in that desk over there. I'll be heading out but not without this young man," the girl continued, grabbing him by the back of his collar and lifting him up some. "I do need a gift from the circus after telling Cirsis your location. Anyway, until later Nix."

"Wait! You made a deal with Cirsis! You can't take me with you!" Em yelled out as utter terror entered his visible green eye.

An amused grin stretched across the girl's face. "Yes, I did make a deal with Cirsis, but I didn't make one with you. He never said anything about me not taking one of his workers along with me. And, you'll do nicely. Besides, I'm sure you want that wound fixed."

Nix observed the scene, and she couldn't help but notice how horror stricken Em appeared. It seemed like he was receiving a fate worse than a death sentence. There was no doubt now about how dangerous that little girl was. Then again, she wondered if the sunhat girl really was just a child since the brothers had apparently been children working for Cirsis.

"I'll see you in the future, Nix. Do take care of those wounds," the sunhat girl suggested before disappearing along with the male.

With both of them gone, she collasped somewhat in the chair and glanced over to the desk. She needed to stop the bleeding. So, she proceeded to force herself up and out of the chair. When she managed to get up, the flap of the tent was thrown back. Nix saw Daisy and Leaf standing there. Behind them were the brothers. Both of the females, though, looked shocked. Before they could voice their concern, the brothers shoved them aside and headed over to her.

Heart almost instantly picked her bridal style. "Don't worry, my dear lady, we'll have you fixed up in no time," he reassured, and she just nodded lightly. At this point, she wished to be rid of the circus. Plus, in her condition, she couldn't struggle against the male even if she wanted to. Thankfully, though, he wasn't trying to hurt her presently. Instead, she noted the genuine concern in his dark blue eyes.

"Heart, take her back to the castle and have Aberrous tend to her wounds immediately. I'll remain here for some time since we planned on giving the circus a performance, and I intend to give them one that they're deserving of," Diamond remarked, glancing over to the two females.

Daisy looked past the red-haired male, however, and into the tent. "Where's Em? What happened to him?"

"The sunhat girl took him," Nix answered, now not being able to resist resting her head against Heart's chest. She was beginning to get dizzy.

Nix heard the woman gasp as she heard mumbling follow. She could hear sobbing coming from another, and she assumed that it was from Leaf. Heart turned to face his brother, and Diamond nodded back. The blue-haired male formed a portal and walked through with her, leaving Diamond and the two females behind.

Only a few moments went by before she found herself in a comfortable looking room. Another figure appeared upon their arrival, but, by that point, Nix couldn't hold on any longer. Her world went dark, and she slipped into the arms of sleep.

~ ~ ~ ~ ~ ~ ~ ~ ~ ~

Bright morning light danced across her eyelids as she rolled over onto her left shoulder, only to be jolted awake by a sharp wave of pain. Immediately, she moved onto her back and pulled the covers over her eyes some. She desired to go back to sleep, but the sound of a door opening caught her attention. Carefully, she peeked out from the blankets and glanced to her right.

To her disbelief, she saw a frog dressed in a butler's suit. The amphibian was standing upright and was carrying a tray of food. Bronze eyes looked to her, and a soft smile touched the frog's lips. "It's good to see you awake, Mistress Nix. How are you feeling this morning?" he questioned in a low, smooth voice as the tray was set on the black wooden nightstand to her right.

"As fine as I could be given my state. Are you Aberrous, by any chance?" she inquired, remembering Diamond having mentioned that name.

Clasping his hands behind his back, he nodded. "Yes, the brothers instructed me to take care of your wounds and serve you breakfast. They presumed that you would be sleeping for some time due to your injuries. Is there anything else that you need, or shall I inform the brothers that you have woken up?"

Slowly, she managed to push herself up into a sitting position where she could rest her back against the plush purple pillow behind her. "Do you mind handing the tray to me? My shoulders are a bit sore."

He nodded and picked up the tray once more. After setting it on her lap, he bowed some and went to leave the room. "Wait!" she called after him, causing him to turn back around. "Can you not tell the brothers that I'm awake? I'd like some time by myself to think things over."

"I'm sorry, Mistress Nix, but I was ordered to inform them as soon as I saw that you were awake."

"Figures," she sighed out. "Well, at least just call me Nix, then. There's no need for the title, and thank you for taking care of my wounds."

"Of course, you're welcome and as you wish. Please, eat something now. You'll need it to recover your strength," the amphibian voiced before leaving the room and closing the door behind him.

Once he left, she took the time to examine her surroundings. The room that she was in was quite grand, and the bed was incredibly plush. Thick purple sheets and a puffy purple comforter offered her comfort on the black, wooden four-post bed. Metallic purple curtains were pulled aside to let in the morning light through the black-paned windows. A black ceiling and walls enclosed her in as a marble fireplace had wood in it, ready to be lit. Two purple and velvet cushioned chairs were in the room next to the fireplace, and a painting of the night sky hung over said fireplace. Besides the entrance door, there was another one, which presumably led to a bathroom.

Placing her attention on the food now, she peered down at the tray and found a simple breakfast. There was a glass of orange juice, sausage, hash browns and toast with butter and strawberry jam. Picking up her fork, she began to eat some of the sausage. When finished with it, she moved onto the hash browns. Two forms appearing in the room, however, caught her attention.

She saw a blue blur before Heart's face was close to hers. The proximity between them caused warmth to rise to her cheeks some as she backed her head away some. "I'm so glad to see you finally awake, my dear lady! I would hug you if you weren't eating!"

Swallowing her bite of food, she scooted on the bed some to create some distance between them. "Yeah, so am I. I would prefer it if you didn't hug me, though, even when I'm done eating." The male chuckled in response to this before heading over to one of the chairs. Diamond took the other chair for himself. Nix observed the two and saw that they were wearing quite ordinary clothes. Heart had on a blue peasant shirt, black pants and blue slippers. Diamond wore a red peasant shirt, grey pants and red slippers. Neither had a hat on like usual, but she thought that they looked better without them. At that thought, heat rose to her cheeks before she pushed it aside.

"As my brother already stated, we're glad to have you awake. Those shoulder wounds were quite horrendous, and we apologize that we didn't get to you sooner. That man didn't do anything else to you, did he?" questioned the red-haired jester.

After taking a sip of orange juice, she shook her head. "No. I can't believe that I'm about to say this, but if the sunhat girl hadn't come, he would've done something worse. Are you sure that you two don't have anymore information on her?"

"My dear lady, let me just say that we're keeping an eye out for her now. She's popping up too often for it not to be a cause for concern. We don't know what she wants from you, but we'll do our best to keep you safe."

"That's funny coming from you. Both of you say that you won't let me die, but I keep finding myself in situations where I could very well die. Your games are taking things too far, and, no matter how much either of you thinks that you can keep me from dying, I could die in a split second before either of you could intervene."

"Miss Nix, we're giving you luxury shelter, food and taking care of your wounds. Doesn't that show you that we care about your health?"

"Maybe, it does, but it doesn't forgive those games. I'm sick of finding myself facing off against some life threatening creature, getting injured, getting strapped to chairs and being considered a plaything. I'm a person, not some toy that the two of you can mess with."

"Well, my dear lady, we were going to stop the games for a week so that you could recover, and we'll try to take a calmer approach to them. We'll even keep them limited to this castle, especially with the sunhat girl appearing in places."

"Miss Nix, understand that we want to keep you alive and safe. The games are just a part of our nature. We can't help it. That's not a good explanation, but it's all we can offer. If we don't have the games, we lose ourselves and might end up hurting you."

"You two just don't get it. You've already hurt me. Maybe, it hasn't been directly, but it has been indirectly," she murmured, deciding to ignore them for a bit and return to her food.

Chapter Twenty Three: A Proposal

Both of the brothers watched her and realized that she was ignoring their presence. They glanced to the other before looking back to her. When she finished eating, they saw her put the tray on the nightstand to her right and look down at her hands afterwards. Now, she didn't even have a reason to ignore them.

Diamond sighed and shifted in his chair. "Miss Nix, we won't apologize for our games because it's something that we must do. You may not like that reason, but you'll have to deal with it. I will say, though, that my brother and I have revoked one of our previous plans. Before you entered the playground, you were incredibly rude to us and continued to be so right until you entered that area. Originally, we had planned to let you suffer a near dead state to punish you.

"Back at the circus, though, we found that we couldn't let those aciflo do anymore harm to you. When you were taken from us by those performers, we nearly lost ourselves with anger. That plan seemed to disappear before our very eyes as we only thought of getting you out of harm's way. That made us both realize how childish our plan had been.

"You have every right to be mad at us, especially since we thought of such a thing. Still, we ask that you look past our games this week. Can you try to see past our flaws and give us both a chance?"

Glancing over to the red-haired male, she noticed the slight desperation in his fire-red eyes. It was faint among the otherwise look of neutrality, but she couldn't look away from it. So, she closed her eyes and sighed heavily. Meeting his gaze once more, she responded, "You two already stated that the games won't be stopped in the future. Moreover, you just admitted that you had wanted me to suffer when all I had been doing was defending myself. And, I bet that even if I refuse, I'll be kept here by you two against my will. Is that a correct assumption?"

"Yes, my dear lady, that is correct. We consider you ours, and we don't intend to let you go. We won't shy away from that or our contradictory nature. We're just asking that despite all of this, you at least try to see the good in us."

"I'm not going to agree to that, but you can help me towards agreement by answering some questions."

"And, what would these inquires entail?" Diamond asked, resting his right cheek against his right knuckles.

"First off, you two held back the manager, I presume."

"That's correct, my dear lady. We couldn't have you fighting him again."

"Alright, and second, I want to know how you two worked for Cirsis, and, well, you two look to be in your early twenties while he's only a kid. How is that possible?"

"I suppose that we should inform you of how aging works here," Heart began, getting more comfortable in his chair. "On this world, people don't age past a certain point. Typically, the max age one stops aging at is twenty-six. There are multiple cases, though, where one stops aging when they're only a child. It varies for each person, but one cannot die of old age here since such a thing doesn't exist. Since you're here now, my dear lady, you'll stop aging as well. Who knows, you might've stopped already."

"If that's the case, how old is Cirsis, and how old are you two?" Nix was taken aback by this some, but she had suspected that the aging process was different. Still, to hear that one could technically live indefinitely on this world was mindblowing. Suddenly, she might have countless years ahead of her to explore and to live her life.

Even if this world had its obvious flaws, her life seemed more free than at her aunt's despite the brothers' hold. Their games were cruel, but she had to admit that they were giving her a chance to explore new places. Those places weren't exactly desirable, but she had seen more in two days here than she had seen back with her aunt and uncle.

"Cirsis is three hundred and ninety-two years old. As for my brother and me, we're three hundred and seventy years old," came the voice of Diamond.

This information broke her out of her thoughts, and she stared between the two. Her face was ridden with astonishment. They were that old?! Words became jumbled, but she knew that it made sense due to this world's aging process. It was just startling to meet someone of that age, let alone two people.

"People from your world must age differently, then," the red-haired jester mentioned, laughing some at her expression.

Finding her words, she nodded and answered, "Some have lived past a hundred but not far past it. Granted, people wear their age where I'm from. An hundred-year-old doesn't look like a twenty-six-year-old." She went to comb her left fingers through her hair but winced and stopped. Her shoulder did well to remind her of her healing wound there. Nix did notice, however, that both of the brothers looked ready to leap from their seats when they saw her brief show of pain.

"Should we bring you some more pain relieving tea?" Heart asked, looking just as worried as his brother.

"Right now, I'm fine. I still have some other questions. Now, that my curiosity about people's ages here is settled, I want to know more about your time in the circus. Heart, you mentioned that you two had nowhere else to turn to for food and shelter. How come?"

The twins visibly tensed at this. Neither of them liked to talk of their past that much, and memories of the circus were haunting at times. "Miss Nix, we'll not recount our experiences there. Heart gave enough information back at the circus tent. Just understand that those early years of our lives weren't pleasant. They were a living nightmare for us. As to how we came to be there, we were told that our parents died when we were still babies. We were taken there afterwards and given our names by Cirsis. That is all that we will say on the matter."

"Then, can you either of you tell me how the carnival came to be in that state?"

"We made it that way, my dear lady. When we grew older and understood our magic capabilities better, we gave them what they deserved. Like Cirsis and the circus performers, the manager and other workers at the carnival had been cruel to us. Before we had carried out our plan, the two of us studied various spells that we could use from our collection of texts. Once we had those learned, we evacuated the park of the visitors and told them that park was now closed.

"The manager tried to stop us, but while I was getting people out, Diamond took care of him. One of the spells was a combination spell. This allows the spell user to combine a person with various objects. Only the spell user can undo the combination. So, Diamond merged the manager with a mannequin, shadows and a knife. We gave him some defesnes so that he could have the illusion of beating us, but we defeat him every time, which is very satisfying. Plus since he's part mannequin, he doesn't die if his limbs are removed."

"After Heart and I took care of him, we moved onto some of the workers. The ones that were nice to us were allowed to escape with the visitors. From there, we traveled to the circus. Some of them were trying to escape, but we summoned everyone to the main tent. We spared the performers, but we had them watch while we administered Cirsis's facial wounds. His mask hides the scars to this day.

"Since the park was shut down, the circus had no audience but themselves.That was part of their punishment, and if they ever leave the carnival, they will be summoned and killed. Granted, the manager still takes care of his park, but we run the area. Of course, we also administer supplies from time to time, but we made sure to develop a small farm for them in the carnival. That way, they could and can provide for themselves. We were rather generous despite their treatment of us," Diamond answered as he finished the account for Heart. "Now, do you have anymore questions for us?"

"No, for now, I would like to explore this place since it seems like I'm going to be staying here for awhile. Is that acceptable, or am I confined to this room?"

"We'll have Woodlily give you a tour. We still have breakfast to eat since we came here right after Aberrous woke us up," Heart mentioned, getting up from his chair. He walked over to her, and she scooted away from him some. A smirk graced his lips at this action before he placed a soft kiss on top of her head. "We'll see you later in the day." With that, he vanished from the room.

Her gaze turned to Diamond, who was just standing up from his chair. He walked steadily over to her and took a seat on the bed. She watched him carefully, keeping her guard up. "Do you hate us, Miss Nix?" The simple question caught her of guard some, and she hesitated for a moment.

"No, I don't, but I don't like you two either. I appreciate that you two have given me food and shelter here in this world, but your games come into conflict with that. Until I can wrap my head around all of this more, I can't like either of you."

"I see," he breathed out, a bitter smile falling on his lips. "But, you don't hate us. I suppose that's a start," he laughed out some before locking his gaze with hers. An unreadable expression crossed his countenance before his eyes trailed down to her lips. "Do you mind if I kiss you, Miss Nix?"

She had no time to answer as his lips met hers gently. Her eyes widened in surprise while his crimson red locks, which were rather soft, tickled her face. Heat rose to her cheeks while both of his hands rested on the sides of her face delicately. When he pulled away, he rested his forehead on hers and whispered softly, "Thank you." He disappeared a second later.

Chapter Twenty Four: Unveil the Letter

Rubbing her cheeks furiously, she tried to rid the heat from them. Why had he thanked her? They were the type of people to just take what they wanted, and that was proven by him kissing her out of the blue. Then, he had thanked her. It didn't make sense to her. Those two confused her too much.

Mumbling some curses under her breath, she got out of the bed and looked over her banadaged legs and shoulders. She also noticed that she had been changed into a purple tank top and purple pajama shorts. Wait, who had changed her?! Panic rose up in her as more heat flooded her cheeks. If those two had done so, they would pay.

A blur of green caught her attention, however. She looked to her left and saw Woodlily now sitting on the bed. The pixie peered up to her and grinned. "Not to worry, I changed your outfit. The brothers didn't want you in those bloodied circus clothes any longer," she mentioned as if reading Nix's mind, but the pixie most likely saw her concerned countenance.

"That's good to hear. Before our tour, I think that I'm going to get a shower and change. Is there any other clothes for me to wear?"

"Yes, there's a closet attached to the bathroom. You'll have a wide selection. I'll wait here for you while you wash up, Nix!" she responded, still wearing her smile.

She was certainly a cheery pixie, and Nix couldn't help but smile back to her. With that, she turned on her heel and headed towards the bathroom door. After opening and closing it, she saw a bathroom with a purple-tiled floor and dark purple walls. A black trim outlined the walls while a white sink, toilet and shower rested on the tile. Black and purple checkered towels rested on the sink counter. To her right was an opened door, leading to the wardrobe.

Before getting a shower, she grabbed a pair of cream-colored shorts and a purple long-sleeve v-neck along with some new undergarments. With these items in hand, she headed back into the bathroom and got her desired shower. The water stung against her wounds, and she noted that she had stitches where the deeper wounds had been. Once done, she rewrapped her wounds with bandages, which she found in the cupboard below the sink, dressed herself and continued on with her usual morning routine.

When she was completed with everything, she exited the bathroom and saw Woodlily still on the bed. The little pixie looked over to her and asked, "What would you like to see first?"

"I'm not sure. Is there any place where the brothers keep spell books. It would be interesting to study them since I've never seen one before."

"Of course, they have a place like that. I'll take you to the study, Nix. Follow me!" she chirped out before flying into the air.

Leaving the room with her, Nix closed her room door behind her and trailed behind the pixie. Up ahead were multiple doors while there was a turn in the hallway up ahead. Traveling past the doors, both of them made the turn, and a double-doored entrance stared back at them. They went forward, and Woodlily turned the handles on the doors, revealing a magnificent study.

The room had everything that a study should have as well as a few extra items. There were two parts to the study: the main section and the area that was on a raised platform. In the main section was a piano, sofa, a floor lamp and a rectangular table with crystal glasses and decanters. On the raised section was an elaborate office desk and a plush desk chair. A lounge chair was next to the right window of the desk. Two bookcases were off to the side of the desk. Throughout the whole room were paned windows with velvet curtains. Everything sat on top of a wooden floor.

Entering the room, she made her way over to the piano, which had many picture frames on top. She picked up a gold frame and found the frame to be barren of a picture. Setting the picture frame down, she realized that all the frames lacked an image. So, she went onto the raised section while Woodlily closed the doors and sat atop the piano.

Stopping at the desk, she seated herself in the armchair. She had originally wanted to look at the spell books, but she was curious to see if the brothers were hiding anything in the desk. So, she began to open the drawers. Most of the drawers had nothing, except a collection of dust. In the last drawer, however, was a pile of papers and ripped envelopes.

Fresh tears trailed down her face, but, soon, boiling anger coursed through her. Reading the letters, she understood that both brothers had known about her well before she had ever met them, yet they had never revealed such a secret. Still, who wrote these letters to them? As soon as the question entered her mind, she had the answer. As she was about to get out of the armchair, Heart walked into the room. "So, this is where you decided to go, my dear lady."

Holding up one of the letters, she stated, "The three of us need to talk."

Heart's expression changed instantly upon seeing the letter in her hand. He sighed as his brother walked in. Diamond noted the letter in her hand as well and combed his right fingers through his locks. Soon, though, both brothers sat on the lounge chair to her right. She wiped away any tears that were left on her face as Woodlily left the room and closed the doors behind her. "To be clear, both of you have known about me since I was sixteen?" Both Diamond and Heart nodded and waited for her to continue. "Why didn't you tell me?" she inquired.

"My dear lady, do you honestly think that you would've taken the information well?"

"Yes, please imagine what you would do if you arrived in a strange world and suddenly two men, who you have never met before, came up to you and exclaimed that they have known about you since you were sixteen," Diamond added, resting his chin on his intertwined hands.

"I probably would've run off extremely creeped out. My main issue is that you two expect me to follow your demands, yet you keep vital information from me. Either of you could've explained the situation to me before I started playing any of your games. Besides even if I did run off, I doubt either of you would've let me escape. Frankly, I just want to understand my situation better. I've been finding out more about this world as I'm here longer, but I still know so little it seems."

"There really isn't much more to understand, Miss Nix. You've discovered the letters, which indicate that both of us know a lot about you. If you look at the last letter, you'll see that it merely told us where to find you on your day of arrival."

"Likewise if we didn't have that letter, my dear lady, I'm afraid that you would be dead right now. Despite you being our plaything, we have kept you alive as well. We've told you before that we won't let you die on us."

"Yes, I'm well aware of that contradictory argument. Let's imagine that I didn't meet you two where I was supposed to be, what would've become of me? Would I have been thrown into life threatening games? Would I have bandages covering my limbs?"

"If that had occurred, we would've searched for you, but you would probably have died as soon as you walked into any of those areas that you've been in."

"I almost got killed on several occasions. I ran into that thing in the woods, I dealt with spirits, a strange statue, etc. None of that would've happened if it weren't for you two."

"Miss Nix, you would have never encountered the Crier or the spirits if you had gone through one of our doors back then. You were the one who chose the hard path. Furthermore, you would be dead if it weren't for my brother rescuing you from the spirits in the underground. Likewise if you somehow made it past the village and reached the carnival, the manager would have killed you. Do remember that we saved you back then too. We have been guiding you through this world, making sure that you don't die in the process."

"Then, why play the games if you don't want me to die? Surely both of you could've just guided me through the dangerous areas to the safe ones without playing any of those games. And, don't give me the excuse that it's part of your nature. I merely want a more understandable explanation."

"My dear lady, we've been over this. It's in our nature. You just have to accept it. We've already asked you to look past our twisted nature and search for the good."

"Tch, you two are so vexing," she muttered, dropping the letter and placing her head in her hands. What was she supposed to do when she couldn't do anything? She had two maniac brothers, who supposedly didn't want her dead but couldn't explain their desire for games. "Fine, for right now, I guess that I want to know why you two had received these letters. Why are you two so obssessed with me being your entertainment?"

"Miss Nix, we chose you to be our plaything because of those letters. We had been receiving them for about two years, and, well, the two of us found ourselves intrigued by you. Through those letters, we got to know you beyond any level we achieved with our past playthings. Besides, it seemed like you would give us a chance, and we were eager for your arrival. As for why we received the letters in the first place, I don't know. We don't even know who sent them."

"I happen to know who sent you these letters." The two twins looked up at her utterly amazed by her statement. She was taken aback by their reaction since she had thought that they would've had some logical guesses at least. "It's simple; it's the sunhat girl, and I want to know why she sent the two of you these letters. It's for something more than her mere amusement; it has to be."

Each brother glanced at the other, worry evident in their eyes. "Are you sure that it's her, my dear lady?"

She nodded in response. "All the pieces point towards that. She attained all of this information on me because she was watching me through my music box. I had seen her appear there back when I was sixteen. I never questioned it since I didn't wish for my aunt and uncle to accuse me of stealing. So, I still talked to my music box like usual. It was my stress reliever from my aunt and uncle. I could vent all of my emotions and listen to its soothing music.

"Plus, she's the one who summoned me into the music box and brought me here. Not to mention the encounters that I've had with her here. Back at the carnival, she mentioned that she told you two about me because she figured that both of you needed entertainment. Then at the circus, she came in and stopped Em before he could do anything else. She told me that she didn't want me dead at the moment and that my circus performance was just for a bit of fun, but she would've stopped the performance before I was killed. She has some plan for me, and you two are involved in it."

"Diamond, that does make sense. Most people don't wish to associate with us, and, with the sunhat girl, she would never communicate with someone unless she had something to gain from it."

"Yes, this is a matter of great concern. Miss Nix as of now, one of us will be with you at all times until we can figure out what the sunhat girl has planned. If she wants something from you, she won't stop until she has it."

"What?! I'll be fine on my own in this castle. I don't need a guard; I need time away from you two. Besides if she's so dangerous and if you two saw her with me at the carnival, which I'm sure you did, why did you never warn me about her?"

"Listen to me, Miss Nix, space is the last thing that you need. We're not going to let the sunhat girl take you away from us. As for why we didn't warn you sooner, it's because we didn't think that she actually had something planned for you. We thought that she only wanted to amuse herself for a bit and send those kelpies on you. We thought that it was temporary interest. Sometimes when she shows herself, that's all she desires: temporary amusement. That's apparently not the case here, so please try to understand the danger that you're in."

"I've been in danger the whole time that I've been here!" she yelled out.

Diamond stood up from the lounge and swiftly walked up to her. Grabbing her chin, he forced her gaze to his. "Don't make us restrain you, Miss Nix."

"Fine, you win. Of course, you would resort to that tactic," she remarked, swatting his hand off of her. Withdrawing his hand from her, Diamond nodded at his brother before vanishing. "So, I guess that you're taking first watch," she grumbled out, looking over at Heart.

For once, Heart didn't smirk or grin at her. His expression was one of seriousness, and he looked deep in thought. Without any warning, he got up and took the letters from her. He proceeded to head over to the sofa before taking a seat and reading through them.

"I doubt that you'll find any informatin on the sunhat girl's plans in those letters," she commented, resting her chin in the palm of her right hand.

"You don't not know that, my dear lady."

Leaning back into the chair, she glanced at the bookshelves and looked for a spell book. She also desired to know what the sunhat girl was up to, but, at the moment, Nix thought that it would be helpful to learn what type of magic the sunhat girl had.

Standing up, she walked over to the book. Of course, the book was on one of the topmost shelves. Resting her hands on her hips, she bit her bottom lip in irritation. It ended when she saw an arm reach up to the book and grab it for her. Looking up at Heart, she watched as he set it in her hands. "My dear lady, you're ours, and I won't let that child lay a finger on you," Heart uttered as he lifted up her chin.

Backing away from him, she mumbled, "Whatever. Thanks for getting the book, though."

"You're welcome," came his reply.

She turned the other way, went back to the chair and began to read the book. Heart made his way back over to the sofa, scanning the letters again. While Nix immersed herself in the book, she recalled what Chroma's past actions were.

Chapter Twenty Five: Rain of Hours

As the hours passed, she continued to read the book while Heart read through the letters. At one point, she rested her head in the palm of her left hand, staring outside. The grey clouds rolled by slowly as rain started to hit the windows. It was a calm rain, creating the perfect mood for reading. Her eyes trailed over to Heart, and she noted how intently he was studying the letters. Did his twin and him really care for her that much even though they played those games with her? Her mind had trouble wrapping itself around such an idea.

Staring at the page she was on, she asked aloud, "So, Heart, from my understanding, the sunhat girl possesses the magic capabilties of teleportation."

Heart almost seemed startled by her question, like he wasn't expecting her to talk to him. He set down the letter that he was currently reading and turned around on the sofa to face her. "Yes, that is true. Why the sudden interest, my dear lady?"

"When I encounter her next, it would be helpful to know what she's capable of. Obviously, though, your brother and you know more about her, yet beforehand you told me that you only really knew of her and that she will essentially take what she wants."

"By knowing of her, we also know of her magic. You just didn't ask a more specific question. Still, she doesn't only possess teleportation. She's an air user as well and a sorceress, meaning that she has a mastery of spells. Granted, that doesn't mean that she knows all spells, but the ones that she does have knowledge of she can cast them at their full potential."

"That would make sense, given how those kelpies suddenly came alive back in the carnival and how she summoned me into the music box. Still, wouldn't she have needed portal creation to summon me to this world, but that wouldn't have worked either since the book states that they can only form a portal to another part of this world," she mused.

"Correct. The sunhat girl utilized an advanced spell to bring you here probably, and it most likely has something to do with her hobbies. I don't know what spell books she possesses, but they must involve some of the chained texts."

"Wait, what are her hobbies and chained texts?"

"That girl has been known to sacrifice people, and there are spells that require such things. She probably sacrificed a few individuals to get to your world and to bring you here. As for chained texts, they're spell books that were supposed to be locked away in hidden places throughout the world. They were placed there since some individuals in the past didn't desire that knowledge to be spread throughout the world. Sacrificial spells would be among those books most likely, and she must have gotten hold of some of them."

"Let me guess. You didn't tell me about this hobby of hers because I didn't ask a specific inquiry."

"That would be the case."

Rolling her eyes, she continued, "Despite your vague details on these texts, I'm surprised that you know these facts. You don't seem like the book type to me."

"I'm not, but I had a mentor who taught my brother and me these things. I didn't bother to remember all of the details. Still, don't forget that I've been around for more than three centuries. Even if I don't like studying, I still collect knowledge whether I want it or not."

"And, what about this mentor of yours?"

"She's not important. What is important is that we keep you away from that girl. You now know of her hobby, and her plan for you might involve something of that nature. It might not, but we cannot throw that option out."

"Things just keep getting better," she muttered, sarcastically. Hearing movement, however, she looked back to the blue-haired male and saw him coming towards her. She raised an eyebrow and asked, "What?"

Instead of a response, he grinned and ruffled her hair some. "Don't worry too much, my dear lady. My brother and I aren't going to let the sunhat girl win. I'm not going to permit some child to take you away from me."

"Yeah, whatever," she mumbled, fixing her hair. He grinned at her once more before returning to his seat. This left her to continue with her book. Technically, she now knew of the sunhat girl's powers, but she was still interested in the spells. Another hour passed, and she glanced at one of the picture frames on the desk. Once again, it bore no picture inside. "What happened to the pictures in the frames?" she questioned aloud, hoping that Heart would be able to answer her.

Still reading the letter, Heart remarked, "Diamond and I removed the images."

"Why?"

This time Heart set down the letter he was reading and peered back at her. "Simple, those used to be pictures of other people. We claimed this castle after the owners died. The pictures were the images of the previous owners. Diamond and I didn't see any reason in keeping them; however, we liked the picture frames, so we left them on the furniture."

Nodding, she went back to reading the book and was almost finished with it. She could hear Heart pick up another letter. The rain increased in intensity as both continued with their reading. Another hour finished, and she had completed the book. Closing it, she stood up from the desk and headed over to Heart. Nix took a seat next to him and picked up one of the letters. "Maybe, I can help you find something," she suggested as she glanced over to him.

"I appreciate the offer, but you look like you need a break from reading. How about I distract you with something. I could use a rest myself."

"That's okay. I'd rather read."

In response, he smirked and grabbed her right hand in his left. He stood up and pulled her off of the couch. The action sent pain through her shoulders, and she winced immediately. "Hey, be careful! And, what do you think you're doing?"

"My apologies, I had no intention of harming you, but I thought that I would repay the favor. You've interrupted me three times today. So, now, I'm going to divert your attention away from your work."

He guided her to the center of the main floor of the room before stopping and holding both of her hands in his. Facing him, she looked up to see what he was doing. He released her right hand and snapped his fingers. Instantly, she heard the piano start to play in the background. Little balls of light bounced on the keys. "They're music pixies. When presented an instrument, they'll play what music notes come to them," the male explained.

Taking her hand back in his, he placed her left hand on his shoulder while holding onto her right hand. Recognizing what he was doing, she tried to protest and started to become embarrassed by the second. With his own right hand on her lower back, he kept her in place. "You know that this isn't comfortable for my shoulders," she voiced, trying to get out of the situation.

Heart lowered his head to her right ear, whispering, "Sometimes, you need to experience a little bit of pain before pleasure."

Heat erupted in her cheeks, and she hurriedly looked away from him. She heard a chuckle escape his lips, and his breath tickled her neck some. Nix muttered for him to just start the dance already, and he gladly did so.

Rain pounded against the windows as the piano played on in the background. She didn't know how long the two of them danced, but, part way into the dance, she felt Heart press her closer to him. Her cheeks continued to burn, and she kept her gaze downwards, so he wouldn't see her embarrassment. The dance continued while the music continued to play in sync with her every move. Heart, to her surprise, was an excellent dancer, but she would never admit that to him. He didn't need a boost in his self-confidence.

When the piano music died down, Heart slowed the pace of the dance. He let go of her right hand so that he could move his own hand to her face. Using her hands, she pushed him away and took a couple of steps back. "You're always so stubborn, my dear lady."

She huffed and seated herself back on the sofa. The male sat down next to her and rested his right hand on her left cheek. Immediately, she went to push his hand away, but he stopped her with his left hand. Leaning closer to her, he was about to kiss her, but she wrenched her right wrist from his grip, grabbed a nearby pillow and put it between the two of them. "Two can play at that game, my dear lady."

He grabbed her right wrist again and glided his lips along her arm as he moved closer to her face. She was about to bring the pillow down on his head, but he seized it from her, with his right hand, and threw it across the room. Swiftly, he crashed his lips against hers, and she could feel the longing in the kiss. Heart bit her lower lip before pulling away, which sent a thin trickle of blood down her chin. Wiping it off with his right thumb, he grinned in satisfaction. Her cheeks burned as she wished to get away from the male.

"My dear lady, I believe that it's time we head down to dinner." With that, he picked her up and took her out of the study. "I'm glad that I could make you so bashful," he whispered as he opened a portal and walked through.

Chapter Twenty Six: Night's Feast and End

The two of them appeared in front of a stone arch, which led to the dining room. It was a grand room, like the other rooms she had seen in the castle. A well polished table with porcelain plates, crystal goblets, red roses, and blue candles on top sat in the middle of the room. Wooden chairs with blue floral patterned cushions outlined the table. A simple silver chandelier hung above the table, illuminating the crimson walls. Blue drapes hung over lace curtains. Two elaborate china cupboards held detailed painted plates, which appeared ancient and mystical.

Placing her on the chair at the head of the table, Heart pushed her chair in and went to take a seat on her left side. Diamond was already sitting to her right. Woodlily was flying over the table, placing dishes down for the three of them. The pixie finished by lighting two blue candles, which smelled of blueberries. Hovering in front of Diamond, she grinned ear to ear. "Your food will be out in a moment, Woodlily."

Beaming, she flew up to the chandelier, sat upon it and waited for her meal. As soon as she sat on the chandelier, a wooden door swung open. Aberrous walked out and had a bottle of what looked like some sparkling drink in his hands. He wore a chef's outfit, and Nix found the attire adorable on him. Passing the two brothers, the frog came up to her. "Your glass, Nix."

She grabbed her goblet and handed it to him. He filled it with sparkling apple cider and gave the glass back. Aberrous poured some for Heart as well. Once Heart's glass was filled with the drink, the frog disappeared back behind the door. Aberrous soon returned with a crystal teacup and saucer, and it was already filled with tea. Diamond took them from the amphibian while Aberrous annouced, "Salads will be out in just a few minutes."

"Thank you, Aberrous," Diamond remarked as the frog bowed and started to head back into the kitchen. Woodlily flew down from the chandelier and waved her arms in front of the amphibian. Motioning the pixie to follow him, Woodlily flew behind the frog back and into the kitchen.

"Does Aberrous cook most of the meals?" Nix questioned before taking a sip of her drink.

"Indeed, Miss Nix, but, sometimes, my brother does the cooking. He's a very talented cook after all."

"I see," was all she managed to say. It was just one surprise after another one with these two.

"Is it that shocking? My dear lady, I hope that you didn't think we only played games. We have other hobbies of our own."

Peering into the bubbling drink in her glass, she felt suddenly sheepish. Due to the brothers' nature, she never actually expected them to have much in the way of hobbies besides the games. Then again, Heart proved himself to be a good dancer, and they probably had to do something in their spare time when they weren't bothering her.

When the kitchen door opened once again, Aberrous came out with three salads. Woodlily was nowhere in sight, and she was most likely already eating. Besides the abundant amount of greens in the salad, she saw that the salads had chopped up carrots, radishes, crutons and apples while a light dressing sat on top. After setting the salads on the table, Aberrous once again vanished into the room filled with the smell of cooking food. Poking at her salad with the fork, she glanced over to Diamond, who was sipping his tea. "Do you not like apple cider?"

"I don't like any sweet drink."

"It's true, my dear lady. One time, I put just one cube of sugar in his coffee, and he nearly vommitted in disgust."

She really didn't need to know that last detail, so she just nodded her head. Stabbing an apple and carrot at the same time, she placed the food in her mouth. As she continued to eat, the two brothers ate as well, with no one talking. It felt somewhat awkward until Diamond started up conversation."Heart, did you find anything of use on the sunhat girl?"

"No, I didn't. I looked through all of the letters, but nothing pertaining to the child's plan revealed itself. Were you able to discover anything, brother?"

"No, that child has kept her plan quite secretive. I doubt that we'll ever be able to find anything on it. I'm afraid that she might make the next move before we get a chance to act."

"Isn't there some way to get information on her?" Nix questioned, looking between the two.

"Most likely, but where do we look is the current question at hand, Miss Nix."

She let out a sigh and nodded in understanding. Stabbing the fork into a piece of apple, she went to eat it, but before she could bite into the apple, Heart snatched the piece from her. He grinned and swallowed the stolen food. "I must say that your salad tastes better than mine, my dear lady."

Just as she was about to yell at him, she noted another fork stab the last carrot in her salad. Diamond bit into it before mentioning, "I must agree with you, Heart. It does taste better."

Pushing the almost finished salad away from her, she glared at the two brothers. Heart merely smirked while Diamond smiled. They were completely unbelievable. Taking another sip of her drink, they ate the rest of her salad on top of their own. Aberrous soon came back out and checked to see if the salads were finished.

Noting that they were, he picked up the dishes. Nix thanked him, and he nodded in response before he went to retrieve the main course. Her eyes shifted to glance at the salt and sugar shakers. An idea popped into her head as she saw Aberrous bring the next dish out. While both brothers were distracted by the amphibian, she hurriedly snatched up the two shakers. Not waiting a second, she tested which was which. Once she had this knowledge, she carried out her plan.

Heart and Diamond were still looking the other way. So, she tapped the salt into Heart's apple cider while putting the sugar into Diamond's tea. She tried to keep her face straight as she awaited for her plan to work. Aberrous set down the beef and vegetable stew. Bringing the spoon up to her lips, she watched as Heart took a sip of his apple cider while Diamond went to drink his tea. The results of her revenge were quite delightful.

Both brothers reacted in amusing ways. Diamond covered his mouth with his right hand, looking like he might puke. Heart, on the other hand, was coughing into a napkin, obviously disgusted by the new taste of his drink. When both had recovered, they stared at her with displeased countenances. She stared back at them innocently and continued to eat her food.

"Diamond, it would seem that my drink tastes dreadful."

"Indeed, my drink is quite intolerable."

With no warning, Diamond picked up his tea and dumped it into her half eaten stew with Heart following soon after. She gazed at her now ruined stew, annoyance taking over her facial features. "Miss Nix, you haven't eaten all of your dinner. You should finish it before it gets colds."

"I think that I'm full," she responded, shrugging her shoulders.

"That's a shame. It's a pity that we don't care," Heart chuckled out, and, in one swift movement, he took her spoon, filled it with stew and held her mouth open.

Before she could knock his hand away, he shoved the stew into her mouth. She had no choice but to chew since Heart proceeded to hold her mouth shut. The stew tasted disgusting, but she kept a straight face. Heart released his hand from her face and awaited her reaction. "It tastes delicous," she lied, swallowing the disgusting mixture of flavors.

"Then do continue eating it, Miss Nix."

"Fine, it tastes disgusting," she admitted.

"Then, don't put sugar in my drink again or salt in my brother's drink. I'm sure that we could think of a suitable punishment if you attempt to do such a thing again."

Crossing her arms over her chest, she frowned before she heard movement coming from the other end of the table. "You know, this food is quite good," came an all too famliar voice. All three of them turned their heads in that direction and found the sunhat girl sitting at the table. She had food in front of her while a wide and wicked grin stretched itself across her lips.

Chapter Twenty Seven: Plans do indeed Change

The sunhat girl stabbed a piece of beef in her stew, biting into the perfectly cooked meat. She swung back and forth in her chair, loving every moment of their surprised and angered expressions. Both brothers had rested their hands on the top of their sabers, ready to draw them at a moment's notice. "I heard that you two intend to stop your games for a week," the girl chirped out, still paying attention to her food.

"That doesn't concern you, child," Heart growled.

"Oh, it's so cute how you think that you're in control of the situation," she giggled, kicking her feet back and forth.

"What do you want? We know that you sent the letters to us," Heart stated, his eyes narrowing.

"Do you? Well, that makes things easier for me. Anyway, I merely came to tell you all that your plans will have to be modified," she mentioned innocently, but her eyes displayed only evil intent.

"Like that's going to happen. Now tell us why you sent us those letters and why we would have to change our plans," Diamond ordered, him being as tense as his brother.

"I merely sent those letters so that you two would become obsessed with Nix, which worked out quite well. As for why there will be a different plan, it's because Nix will be coming to my territory in the next few days. Don't argue about this either. You two don't control me; you're not my puppeteer, but you two can easily become my puppets. In fact, you two have been my puppets this entire time. Nix, on the other hand, is my favorite doll; she will aid me in my end goal."

"I'm not your doll. Don't give yourself such authority over me."

Bursting into laughter, the sunhat girl's eyes gleamed in delight. Heart and Diamond swiftly stood out of their chairs, sabers pointing at the golden-haired girl. She only laughed more as she clutched her sides due to her laughing fit. "Ah, Nix, you always are so stubborn yet so foolish. Of course, you're my doll, silly. Now, lower your swords and comply with my demand; bring her to my territory in a few days. I've grown tired of this entertainment, and I wish for it to be over so that I can have some new fun."

The brothers seemed to have not heard her as a strange look fell over both of their faces. Heart looked to be the definition of insanity while Diamond seemed to have a hazed look as though he only wished to kill. Their terrifying expressions had no effect on the sunhat girl. "You two wish to play? Well, I suppose that's what you two are best at."

In that instant, the two brothers ran at the child. She remained completely calm. As the two blades went to sever her head from her body, she vanished into thin air. Appearing on top of the chandelier, a childish grin graced her lips. Heart jumped up into the air with the saber extended out towards the sunhat girl. Once again, not a single sign of fear fell across her face. Instead, she disappeared and reappeared two inches to the side of the approaching blade, dodging its lethal intent. This left Heart exposed.

His face nearing the sunhat girl, she extended her right index finger and went to flick him on his forehead. Hurriedly, Heart vanished and appeared back on the ground. She landed on top of the table while both readied themselves for another attack. They charged at her, and she extended out both of her hands. Blasts of air burst forward towards the twins, and they evaporated into thin air. Diamond soon stood behind the girl and Heart in front of her.

They went to go for her head again, but it was her turn to fade away. This continued between the three of them for some time, and Nix could barely keep up with their movements. Objects on the table were long destroyed while she had to run for one of the corners in the room. She would cover her face from the blasts of air when they occurred, and the sound of metal cutting through the air filled her ears constantly.

It didn't end until she felt something sharp press against her right side. Staring down, she saw the sunhat girl right there. She had her typical smirk of malice on her lips while the twins came to a dead stop. "This changes the situation a little bit, doesn't it?" she chuckled out. "Now, you two will bring her to me, or I'll proceed to make these wounds on her look like child's play. After all, I just need her alive; I don't need her to be a pretty little package for me."

"And, what makes you think that we can't kill you before your attempt to injure her. You, like us, can't teleport her, but we can come over to you in less than a second," Heart threatened.

"It just depends on whether you wish to test that theory or not. Can you reach me before I severely wound her?" she asked, moving the knife up closer to Nix's face.

Noting this, Nix speedily grabbed the girl's right wrist and tightened her hold. She could tell that she caught the girl off guard, and she used that opportunity to steal the knife from the girl. Before she could attack, she was thrown against the corner. The knife dropped from Nix's hand as she coughed up some blood. Both of the twins reacted immediately and appeared in front of the girl.

By then, she had already grabbed the knife once more and had it mere centimeters from Nix's face. "She will lose something if either of you take another step," the girl warned while beads of sweat began to form on Nix's face. Neither of the twins moved. "Good. Now, for what she just pulled, I'm going to have to punish my little doll. Both of you will take your sabers and stab them through your twin's chest. I know that both of you will survive the action."

"You can't be serious. That's a ridiculous request to make. They'll die!" Nix shouted, but the knife was only moved closer.

"Do be quiet doll," the girl voiced, keeping her gaze focused on the twins. "Well, go on. You have ten seconds to act, or I'll take something from her."

Speechless, Nix watched the two twins plunge a saber into the other. Her mouth gaped open, and her mind couldn't comprehend what she just had witnessed. Maybe, she had screamed; maybe, she even had cried. She didn't know, but she did wish to move forward. The knife stayed close to her face, however. Both of them soon pulled the sabers out, but they collapsed to the floor in the process.

"Now, to avoid any other resistance," the sunhat girl mumbled before disappearing. She appeared next to the brothers and quickly knocked them out. "Much better," she chuckled out until she glanced over to Nix. "Since the twins continued to resist, I now ask you to proceed onward. Travel through the forest behind this castle, taking the train to the Land of Amusement. If you refuse this demand, I will take the two brothers and use them for my own personal entertainment. Their allowed freedom in this world will vanish, and they'll suffer. You will have doomed two people to a fate worse than death for your own selfish need."

"What makes you think that I care about the brothers' safety or freedom?" she barked out, not glancing at the twins.

"You may be unwilling to admit it, my dearest Nix, but I know that you care for them even if that feeling is buried deep within your heart, especially with your reaction to their previous action. Even if you say this isn't true, can you really send two people to an eternity of torture? Can you really commit such an act of evil?"

Glancing to the two bleeding males, she clenched her fists and glared to the small girl. "You win; I'll head to the Land of Amusement. Now, leave us alone!"

"I look forward to seeing you there, my favorite doll," she voiced as she disappeared from the room.

Upon her disappearance, Nix called out for Aberrous and Woodlily while she rushed over to the twins. The two soon exited the kitchen. Seeing the brothers, they rushed towards them. Woodlily's hands flew up to her mouth as tears already started to form at the corners' of her eyes. "Nix, remove their shirts while I go grab some ointment and bandages," Aberrous ordered as he dashed back into the kitchen.

She only nodded and hurried with it. After ripping the fabric on both of their shirts, she tilted each one upwards and pulled their shirts off. If they were awake, they would be teasing her about this. Such a thought sent a small smile to her lips, but she brushed it aside quickly. The amphibian dashed back into the dining room and put down the medical supplies. He went to work quickly. "Will they be okay, Aberrous?" Nix asked, sitting on her knees now.

"They'll be fine as long as we slow down the bleeding. Their bodies are already repairing the wounds due to their quickened healing ability. Once I'm done treating them, I'll help you take them to their rooms. Hopefully, they'll awake this evening or early in the morning. Then again, it would be better if they rested longer."

"I understand," she answered, sighing and picking up their sabers. She stood up and asked, "Where should I put these?"

"I'll take them, Nix," Woodlily responded, flying over and taking from her. She flew off to presumably the brothers' rooms. Staying with Aberrous, Nix waited for him to finish. When he did, he went to pick up Heart. He was having a hard time, but Woodlily flew in and sprinkled some pixie dust on both of the brothers. The brothers now floated some, making both Aberrous's and Nix's job easier.

With Diamond's left arm over her shoulders, Nix asked, "How do I get to his room?"

"I'll guide you, Nix," Woodlily offered, and Nix nodded in response. They proceeded to exit the dining room along with Aberrous. While Aberrous took a left, they took a right. Granted, Diamond's weight on her shoulders was uncomfortable, but his injury was more serious. So, she dealt with it.

The pixie opened a door and behind it were a set of stairs heading upwards. Red wall fixtures illuminated the stairwell as the two of them ascended the stairs. When they reached the top, she saw a hallway with two doors. One of the doors was right in front of her while the other was further down. Woodlily went past the first door and continued onto the second.

Only a worn maroon rug went across the stone hallway. A small rectangular window, at the end of the hall, let in the pale starlight. Woodlily soon opened the second door as Nix thanked her and walked in. Nix headed over to the king-sized bed, which had a gold and black canopy, pulled the sheets back and laid Diamond down. She draped the sheets over his form and took a step back. "He'll be okay," Woodlily called out from the doorway.

Nix nodded. "I'll stay in here and wait for him to wake up. Can you check on Heart for me and see how he's doing?"

"Of course," the pixie answered before flying off and closing the wooden door behind her.

Brushing back strands of her hair, she wondered why she was being so caring all of a sudden. She took a seat on the edge of the bed and glanced out over the room. The bed was close to the paned window, and red curtains hung over the glass. A checkered red and black rug went across the floor of the room while a black dresser with crystal red diamond knobs sat opposite the bed. Next to the dresser was a wooden door, which probably led to a bathroom. Towards the wall opposite of the main door was a black round table, with matching chairs that had red cushions. On top of the table rested a chess board. The pieces were in proper place, indicating its readied use for a new game if two people desired to play.

Her dark brown eyes glanced back to Diamond. "Why do I care?" she asked herself as she looked over his features. It didn't make sense to her. They put her through horrendous games, but they promised not to let her die. Back at the circus, they looked worried sick for her when they found her in that tent. Tonight, they had even stabbed the other so that the sunhat girl wouldn't harm her. Facts really did point to the truth that they cared for her deeply even though they were obsessed with twisted games. Perhaps, she cared because she finally recognized that they had a redeemable quality behind those jester masks of theirs.

Chapter Twenty Eight: Recovery

When she awoke, she found herself cuddled up to something warm. Something soft lay over her, and she felt something glide through strands of her dark brown hair. Pale morning light fell on her eyelids, and she snuggled more into whatever was next to her. A soft laugh hit her ears, and she jolted up. Heat rushed to her cheeks, like water breaking through a dam. She scooted away, heading towards the edge of the bed's right side.

"Good morning, Miss Nix," Diamond greeted with a small smile on his lips. "Woodlily wished for me to tell you that my brother is doing fine. You fell asleep at the foot of the bed before she could tell you herself. So, she stayed until I woke up. From there, I moved you up next to me since I figured that you would be more comfortable. It was kind of you to bring me to my room, so thank you."

"Yeah, well ... you're welcome. You're obviously doing better," she mumbled, getting out of the bed and heading over to one of the chairs in the room. She took a seat and kept her gaze off of him.

"Yes, though, Woodlily told me that we worried you. I'm sorry for that, and I'm sure that Heart feels the same."

"I wasn't concerned. Aberrous told me about your healing ability. Anyway, I'm heading to the Land of Amusement the day after tomorrow," she responded, playing with one of the queens on the board.

Fingers rested under her chin and turned her head. She was forced to look at Diamond. "No, you're not going there," he answered resolutely.

Whacking his hand away, she met his stare. Unwavering, she announced, "I'm heading there, Diamond. The sunhat girl needs to be dealt with. I'm tired of her appearing out of nowhere. This is only my fourth day here, and I'm already tired of her. She thinks that she's in control of my life, but she doesn't understand how wrong she is. I'll go to her and stop her."

Standing up straight, he frowned. "And, how do you intend to put an end to her plans? You saw her fight against my brother and me. You don't possess the capabilities to stop her. Be realistic, Miss Nix."

"I'm being realistic! She'll just attack us all again if I don't follow her demands. So, I'll do things the way she wishes and find a flaw in her plans. I'll stop her when she least expects it."

"So, you do care for my brother and me."

"I agreed because of the reasons I just gave you, and I do owe your brother and you for last night."

"Miss Nix, you don't owe us for anything," he replied, taking a seat in the other chair. "We acted the way we did last night because we didn't wish to see you harmed. We couldn't risk your safety and try to attack her. The idea of you falling into that girl's arms is nightmarish to us."

"Let's just go see how your brother is holding up. I don't think that I can convince you." She stood up from her chair and glanced over to him. He merely nodded and got up from his chair as well. Diamond opened a portal and signaled her to walk through. After she did, he headed in.

Both of them appeared in Heart's room. There were four paned rectangular windows in the room, each with their own set of blue and silver curtains. Three mirror dressers lined the wall opposite of the bed; each had a glass lamp sitting on top. The lamp shade itself was a pure white while blue feathers fell from the end of the shade. On the left side of the bed was a white writing desk and blue desk chair. Next to the bed rested two mirror nightstands. Lamps sat on top of the stands. The bed itself had vibrant blue and silver sheets while various blue pillows were stacked at the back of bed.

Neither of them saw Heart, but the door, next to the writing desk, opened. Heart walked out in some blue pajamas before he turned his attention to them. His dark blue eyes softened upon meeting Nix's gaze. "My dear lady, thank goodness that you're alright."

"You should be more concerned about yourself, Heart, but you look to be alright just like your brother."

He grinned some before looking to his brother. "Did you wake our dear lady up, then?"

"Actually, she woke up on her own. I just made sure that she was comfortable in her sleep while she was in my room."

Some heat danced across her cheeks as she huffed and looked out one of the windows. "Be quiet, you pervert."

Heart's eyes widened some. "Wait, you two slept together in my brother's room?!"

Cheeks burning, Nix abruptly turned back to the blue-haired male. "It wasn't like that! I merely fell asleep in his room after I brought him there last night. Your pervert of a brother pulled me under the covers when I was asleep, but nothing else happened!"

Diamond couldn't help but break out into laughter while Heart began to chuckle. "You're so cute, Miss Nix," the red-haired jester laughed out, covering his mouth with his right hand in amusement.

"That's it. I'm leaving," she huffed out, turning to exit the bedroom, but the door opened before she reached it. Aberrous walked into the room and carried a tray filled with tea sandwiches.

"I decided to bring you all some breakfast this morning, and Woodlily told me that you would all probably be in Master Heart's room," he spoke, looking between the three humans. He appeared confused, though, and asked, "Did I interrupt something?"

"No, you're alright, Aberrous. We're just having some fun teasing our dear lady," Heart managed to say between laughs.

Placing the tray on Heart's bed, the amphibian looked between them all and nodded. "I shall bring a pot of tea and some teacups. I'll be back in about ten minutes." He bowed and left the room, closing the door behind him.

Alone with the brothers again, she mumbled some curses under her breath. She walked over to the bed and took a seat on the foot of it before she snatched up one of the sandwiches. Biting into it, she watched the brothers take a seat on either side of her: Heart on her left and Diamond on her right. The blue-haired jester picked up the tray and set it on her lap before he grabbed a sandwich for himself.

"What am I? Your table?" she muttered, glancing over to the male.

"No, you're our lover," Heart answered, biting into his sandwich afterwards.

She nearly choked on her own spit. "Wh-what?! When did that ever happen? I never agreed to that."

"You don't need to agree to it, Miss Nix. You told us that you didn't want us to refer to you as our plaything, so this will be your new title. Don't you like it more?"

"Technically, it's better than being a plaything since I'm not being considered an object, but it's still terrible. I'm not your lover. I'm merely ... well, I don't know. I'm just a person who happened to get dragged into a ridiculous mess."

As if completely ignoring her response, Diamond mentioned to his brother, "We probably should summon a table here, especially if we're going to have tea."

"That is a good idea, brother," Heart answered, and he snapped his left index finger and thumb. A simple round wooden table appeared in front of them. The blue-haired male picked up the tray and placed it on the table's surface. "Is that better, my dear lady?"

"Yeah," she mumbled, picking up another sandwich. Before she could take a bite, however, both of the brothers leaned towards her and took a bite from either side of it. She blinked a couple of times before shouting, "Eat your own d*mn sandwiches!"

"Technically, Miss Nix, they're our sandwiches. After all, this is our home, and Aberrous made them using our ingredients. So, we're doing just what you want us to."

"You know what I mean," she retorted.

"Do I? Maybe, you should teach my brother and me a lesson," the red-haired male countered.

Giving up, she ate the rest of her sandwich and overlooked the fact that the brothers were staring at her oddly. She picked up another sandwich and finally noticed. Glancing between the two, she questioned, "What?"

"You ate the sandwich after we had already taken bites from it, my dear lady."

A light amount of heat touched her cheeks, and she grumbled, "Oh, grow up you two." She proceeded to take a bite out of her new sandwich and managed to avoid the brothers' attempts to eat from hers. Honestly, they could act like little kids at times. Maybe, it was a balance to their more sadistic sides. Whatever the case, it was better than playing another disturbing game of theirs.

Aberrous soon came in again and set down a silver tray on the table. Steam rose from the spout of the teapot while a bowl of sugar and a bowl of cream sat nearby. She thanked him before he bowed, left the room and closed the room door again. Wondering what kind of tea it was, she went to pour herself some, but Diamond beat her to the teapot.

He proceeded to pour everyone some tea, and the scent of earl grey met her nose. Diamond set down the teapot and took a sip of his tea plain. Heart began to add sugar cube after sugar cube while she merely poured some cream into hers. Nix kept a careful eye on both brothers, not wanting to experience something like she did on her first day of being in this world.

Thankfully, the twins didn't attempt anything like that, and she was able to enjoy her tea in peace. When she finished her first cup, she went to get another, but Diamond rested his right hand over her right. "Miss Nix, before you have another glass, why don't you try some of my tea or my brother's?"

There it was. She knew that they would try something like that. Her moment of peace faded, and she looked over to him. If she didn't take a sip, she feared what they would try to do. So, she forced back her pride and took his teacup from his hands.

Bringing it to her lips, she took a sip of the plain tea before she handed the cup back to him. It tasted rather delicious without anything added. She peered over at Heart and saw him holding his out to her. Nix could easily see that all of the sugar cubes hadn't dissolved in the liquid, and she really didn't want to try it; however, she took the glass and drank a little bit.

She nearly gagged on the amount of sugar as she gave it back to the male. Coughing some, she heard Diamond laugh a little. "It seems that she likes my tea better, Heart."

"Well when she tries my cooking, she'll like that better than your tea or cooking," the other brother countered.

The two males began to argue what she would like better, and, eventually, the two of them stood up and started to debate even more furiously on the topic. She took that as an escape signal. So, she quietly moved off of the bed and made it for the door. Reaching the door, she opened it steadily before sneaking out.

Chapter Twenty Nine: The Girl with the Vial

Once she was in the hallway, she went over to some nearby stairs and made her way down the steps. She never reached the bottom of the steps, though. To her right was a locked door. It was painted in a bright red hue and had a blue heart doorknob. Nix understood that she probably shouldn't try to open it since it was in the brothers' castle, and who knows what messed up games they could be hiding behind closed doors. Still if they were hiding something from her, it would be better if she learned about it.

Wondering how she could get it open, she wished that she could summon something to her hands like the brothers. A bobby pin would be useful. Hearing a door open and her name being called, she figured that she would have to keep moving and come back here somehow. Maybe, she should try to head to her room, and she might find a bobby pin in the bathroom.

Acting quickly, she hurried down the stairs and found herself in another hallway. She took a left and sped down it as fast she could. Her legs still weren't healed, so her running ability was compromised some. Nix continued to hear the brothers call her name, and they would probably catch up to her soon.

She would need to find a hiding place and have them pass her. Glancing around, she spotted an unlocked door and opened it. Cleaning supplies filled the area, and she got down onto her hands and knees. Nix crawled towards one of the corners and placed some buckets and supplies in front of her in order to hide better.

Footsteps raced by while another stopped. "I'll check for her in here, Heart. You head back and check her room," called out Diamond. She covered her mouth and nose with her hands and forced herself to calm down. Closing her eyes, she heard the door open while he walked in.

The noise of a light switch being turned on filled the space. Some objects were moved around, but she stayed as perfectly still as she could. When she heard the light switch being flipped again and the door being closed, she settled down some. Still, she didn't leave the closet immediately. Diamond could be trying to set a trap for her.

After allowing a few minutes to pass, she got out from her hiding spot and carefully opened the door. No one was in the hall, and she stepped out. She closed the door before she made her way quietly down the hall. Eventually, she reached the end of it and saw neither of the twins in sight.

Looking around, she noticed that she must be in the entrance hall of the castle, for large wooden doors lay opposite of her. Tapestries of rich dark and light colors displayed scenes of dreams and nightmares. One showed a castle surrounded by the colors of the sunset as another showed a corpse lying in treacherous woods. A long red carpet with silver embroidery graced the stone floor. Chandeliers of blue and gold hung above. To increase the amount of light in the room, three huge stained glass windows were on her end. A throne chair sat on a raised platform, but, for some reason, it was severed horizontally in two, giving the chair a haunting presence.

Pulling her gaze away, she wondered if she had come in the right direction. She knew that the hallway across from her led upwards to Diamond's room. Recalling what Diamond had said to his brother earlier, she realized that she had went in the opposite direction. Hurriedly, she spun on her heel and went back the way she came.

Since she heard no footsteps, she continued on her way and sped up the stairs. The problem would be if Heart was still in her room. Slowly, she made her way to the door and pressed her right ear against it. She didn't detect any movement on the other side. That was the case until she noted that the doorknob was turning.

Cursing mentally, she stood off to the right of the door. There wasn't anywhere that would allow her a decent hiding place. When the door opened, she was blocked from the person's view. She remained silent and still as they closed the door. Heart's back was turned to her, and she hoped that he wouldn't turn around.

To her luck, he sighed and raced off down the stairs. Not wasting another moment, she went into her room and closed the door behind her. She directed her feet to the bathroom and began to search the drawers and cupboard beneath the sink. Smiling, she found what she was looking for. After she took out a bobby pin from the container, she put it back and closed the right-hand drawer.

Before she left the room, she listened for any movement on the other side. There was none. So, she left her room, closed the door and went back to the stairs. Reaching the desired door, she crouched down and went to work. When the lock came undone, she unlatched it from the door and entered. The brothers would find her as soon as they passed the door again, but she didn't want to lock herself in some room. She merely set the lock on a nearby table while she placed the bobby pin in her right shorts' pocket.

Examining her surroundings, she seemed to be on the second floor of the room since a wooden railing lay ahead of her. Soft blue carpet covered the floor and her toes curled into some before she headed over to the railing and looked over. Below her was dark wood flooring, which had an intricate red carpet sitting on top of it as well as multiple pieces of furniture. There was a blue chair and red foot rest. Shelves of books were highlighted by a window, which had chocolate colored drapes. Opposite the wooden staircase lay a marble fireplace. Above the fireplace was a rather large mirror. The mirror reflected her presence in the room and gave her an uneasy feeling in the pit of her stomach.

Off to her right was a sitting room. She passed under the archway and opened up the red curtains in the area. With more light in the space, she smiled some before she took a seat in a brown leather armchair. This room was quite peaceful, and she wondered why it had been locked. Granted, she still felt uneasy about that mirror.

Tapping her fingers against the left armrest, she figured that she would go look at the books on the shelves. Personally, though, she was surprised that the brothers hadn't found her yet. Well, it worked in her benefit. She left the sitting area but stopped upon hearing footsteps or rather a clicking sound on the wooden staircase.

Immediately, she took a step back and tensed. If it was the brothers, they would've utilized the door or just appeared in the room. So, she backed up more and hid behind one of the walls supporting the archway. Peeking out from behind the wall, she froze with terror.

A cloaked figure crawled up onto the second story of the room. Long brown hair cascaded down its head as its tattered cloak hung to its every movement. Long pale arms extended out from under the cloak while long nails began to tear up the carpet. Seeing this, she tried to work out a plan.

She could try for the door, but that thing was practically now in front of it. A second idea would be to try and attack it with the side table that was next to the leather chair, but those nails looked like they could slice through any material. For a third plan, she could jump over the railing and try to land on the chair below. Of course, she would have time her jump correctly. It would be best to wait until the monster was closer to her so that it would take it longer to reach the first floor of the room. With is in mind, the third option seemed to be the best one. Hopefully, there was another door on the first floor.

Nix waited for the creature to near her as her hands trembled slightly. Its long arms carried the creature across the blue carpeted floor as its hair covered its face completely. Rip after rip, it came closer until it was close to the sitting area. At that moment, she climbed up onto the railing and jumped onto the chair below. Landing on the soft surface, she quickly looked and saw the monster staring at her.

Hair no longer covered its face entirely as midnight eyes stared back at her. A sickening toothy grin stretched across the creature's face while a crooked nose rested on its face. Horrified, she leapt out of the chair and searched for an exit. Right across from her was a simple wooden door. Propelling herself at the door, she tried to open it but discovered that it was locked. In a desperate attempt, she threw herself at the door. Instead, she was thrown backward. About to pick herself up, she found that terrifying face right above hers. Swiftly, she clenched her right fist and punched the thing in the face. With it momentarily distracted, she rolled away from the creature and got to her feet.

Recovering itself, it reached for her right wrist but missed as she dodged the attack. The monster grabbed the blue chair and threw it in her direction. Nix moved out of the way, and the chair collided with the mirror. Glass shattered and descended to the floor along with the chair. Something else fell to the floor, though. On top of the chair and glass lay a glass vial, which was filled with a strange purple liquid.

Catching sight of the vial, the creature's behavior suddenly changed. It no longer looked at her but seemed only fixed on the small item. The creature raced over to it and picked it up. Soon, the monster peered back at her while holding the vial between its teeth as its grin widened in delight.

All of a sudden, it charged at her and pinned her to the ground. She didn't dare move for fear of having the creature's nails cutting off her hands. Nix watched as the thing fiddled with the vial in its mouth, using its grey tongue to pull out the stopper in the vial. Once the stopper was off, it lowered its face to hers.

The door on the top level burst open, however. For once, the creature's grin slackened. It looked towards the upper level as it tightened its grip on her. From her perspective, she could see both brothers gazing over the railing. Spitting the bottle out of its mouth, it darted for the twins.

With sabers no longer in their scabbards, the brothers waited for the attack. When the monster swiped at them, they dodged and brought down their weapons on the creature. Picking herself up, Nix went over to the small vial. It was now empty as its contents were spread across the floor.

Hearing a feminine scream, she saw a long-nailed hand fly onto the floor next to her. The hand writhed on the floor until it stopped its movement completely. Looking back up at the brothers, she noticed that Heart had pinned the monster to the wall. With a saber plunged into its neck, the monster thrashed around furiously. Heart removed his saber, allowing his brother to cut off the creature's head. As the body fell to the floor, the two brothers hurried down the stairs towards her.

"Miss Nix, are you alright?"

"Yeah, but what was that thing, and what was the liquid in this vial? It tried to shove it into my mouth."

Heart went over to the foot rest and sat on top of it. "It was something we thought dead, but we weren't sure. That's why we locked it in here. As for the vial, let's just say it's a good thing that you didn't swallow any of its contents."

"I think that I deserve a better explanation than that."

Diamond let out a long sigh as though this was the last thing he wanted to explain. "Yes, you're right. Miss Nix, we had playthings before you: two to be exact. The creature that we just killed was the remnants of the second one."

"Wait if that's the case, why did she look like that? Was it the cause of the contents in the vial?"

"Indeed, it was, Miss Nix. We thought that it would change her but not in that way. At first, it worked out fine, but, after the fourth day, the transformation took place. We thought the pain of the transformation had killed her, but, just in case, we sealed her in this room since we have never really used it. Additionally, the door on the first level leads to a bathroom. Apparently, in her new form, she didn't need food, though."

"So, you just thought to starve her to death if she didn't die from the pain?"

"Please, understand Miss Nix. She tried to kill us time and time again. We gave her multiple chances, but, by that point, our sympathy for her had run thin."

Thinking this over, she proceeded to ask, "Why did you give her such a risky formula, then? Was it another game of yours? Or, was it because you could care less for her at that point?"

"It wasn't a game, my dear lady, and it was leaning more towards the second. We gave her that formula, so she would behave a little more to our liking. She had a habit of trying to kill us. Unlike you, she didn't try to escape by finding loopholes in our games. After a time, her behavior merely annoyed the two of us, so we tried to adjust it."

"So, you're saying that you would've used that on me if I started to annoy the two of you."

"No, we would never give you such a thing, Miss Nix. We know that you would never kill us; otherwise, you would've let the sunhat girl kill us. Or, you could've killed us after she knocked us out. You've had many opportunities to end our lives, yet you haven't."

"I suppose that's true. I have another question, though. Why hold onto the vial, then? Were you two expecting another disobedient individual before me?"

"We gave up after the second one. By that point, we had already a reputation of being cruel in general. Most stayed well away from us, and we figured that one wouldn't be able to look past our sadistic nature, my dear lady. Granted, we kept the vial in case we ever wanted to make modifications to it. At one point, my brother and I considered testing out some new spells on the ingredients in that bottle so that we could use it on ourselves. We thought that maybe we could change our nature into a less violent one, but we never went through with it."

"You two actually considered that?" she asked in disbelief.

"Yes, but we decided that this is who we are and that there's no need for us to change. We decided to not give up and to wait for someone like you to come along. You may not like us, Miss Nix, but you're conversing with us like we're not monsters. You're respecting us as people despite what we've done to you. The two before you only saw us as nightmares."

Thinking this over, she pushed back some strands of her dark brown hair and got up from her sitting position. "You two keep surprising me, but, on the note of your past relationships, do you need help with her?" she questioned, pointing up to the fallen body.

"We were probably just going to throw her into the fireplace and turn her to ash," Heart mentioned, standing up from his seat.

Crossing her arms over her chest, she shook her head. "Despite what she did to you two, she deserves at least a proper burial. I noticed that this castle is surrounded by a large grassland. There should be room for her there. I'll bury her myself if you two want."

"That's not necessary, Miss Nix, but if you want to bury her, we'll help you. Let's get this over, shall we?"

Nodding, she followed the two brothers up the stairs after she picked up the hand. Diamond grabbed her body while Heart took the head. They both summoned a large cloth bag and put her in there. Nix dropped the hand in, and they all made their way outside.

Chapter Thirty: Courtyard of Intrigue

The burial took several hours, but the deceased could now be laid to rest. They had buried her beyond the wall which surrounded the large grey stone castle. A few loose stones lay at the head of her grave, and Nix had asked the brothers to summon a few flowers. With the pink roses in hand, she placed the stems under the rocks so that they wouldn't blow away.

After the process was over, she wished to just take a long shower and wash the scent of death off of her. The brothers shared the same idea of taking a shower. So, they headed off to their rooms.

Once in the shower, she let the warm water flow down her body and enjoyed its comfort. She combed her fingers through her hair and thought back to what Diamond had told her. In truth, she was really talking with two sadistic jesters as though it was something natural in life. Despite her seeing them as that, she understood that they were still people and should be treated as such.

If they were true monsters, she wouldn't be able to reason with them in her opinion. They would easily put her in constant misery, but, instead, they did care for her on a level that she never experienced with her aunt and uncle. Despite their games, she couldn't picture them as something less than human. Even if she did try to escape from them in the future, it would be better to understand all of them. By cooperating to some degree, she could figure things out that she wouldn't have learned through completely resisting. Then again, did she desire to get away from them anymore?

Part of her screamed yes while the other yelled no. She bit her bottom lip in frustration and rested her head against the shower wall. Why did they have to be so confusing to her? Nix was about to slam her right fist into the shower wall, but she figured that wouldn't be too bright an idea. So, she forced herself to calm down. This shower was supposed to be relaxing after all, not cause an internal battle.

When she finished, she grabbed a towel and dried herself off. Afterwards, she tended to her usual bathroom routine and wrapped her wounds before she headed into the wardrobe. She put on some new undergarments, a grey, short-sleeved shirt and some light purple jeans. Nix braided her hair and tied the end off as she left her room and went towards the kitchen. Before her trip to the Land of Amusement, she would need a pack to bring with her, and the amphibian would most likely help her with that.

Sadly, both of the brothers met her in the entrance hall. They looked over to her as she entered. "My dear lady, we were waiting for you. We planned an early dinner for the three of us," Heart declared with a wide grin.

"I'm guessing that I don't have a choice in the matter," she sighed out as both of them nodded in response. They soon went over to her and took her hands in theirs. Diamond held her right and Heart her left. She would have to talk to Aberrous later, then.

They took her through the right passage and towards Diamond's room. Granted, they stopped at the first door in the hallway. Heart opened it and revealed a small stone room. The only things in the room were the vines covering the walls and ceilings. Up ahead, however, were three intricate pillars, which were in the middle of an archway. Light shone on the courtyard beyond, illuminating its beauty.

Flowers and bushes of various kinds were rooted into the earth while grass covered the remaining dirt. In the center of the courtyard was a strange tree. Its branches twisted and turned. Leaves weren't abundant on the plant, but glowing yellow apples were. As she observed the area, the brothers guided her closer to the awaiting courtyard.

A glass table, with three glass chairs, appeared out of thin air under the apple tree. When she was seated on one of the chairs, she glanced over to the late afternoon sky. They had quite the view of the grasslands and the sky. It was utterly breathtaking.

"My dear lady, what do you think of the dining arrangements?" Heart asked as he sat in his own chair.

"They're pretty nice," she answered, still gazing out at the view.

"We're glad that you like them, Miss Nix."

Within a few minutes, Aberrous walked out onto the stone courtyard with three glasses of iced peach tea. Setting them on the table along with a bowl of sugar and a teaspoon, he left the three of them alone once again. Heart put in several teaspoons, stirring the sugar around in his drink. Diamond, not placing any sugar in his tea, took a few sips of his own drink. Like the red-haired jester, she didn't add any sugar.

Leaning back in her chair, she glanced up at the glowing apples. Lifting her left arm up, carefully, she grabbed one and pulled it from the tree. The apple glowed in her hands, and she examined it some more.

"Miss Nix, we also brought you up here to discuss your plans about leaving the day after tomorrow."

"I'm going there, Diamond. I'm not changing my mind on that."

"I understand that. That's why before you set out, the two of us have agreed on giving you a weapon for protection. We trust that you won't kill us with it," Diamond responded simply.

"We would rather you not go to the Land of Amusement, but since we figured you wouldn't take no for an answer, we're arming you. This way if for some reason we can't protect you, you have a way to fight back, my dear lady."

She was shocked to learn that they would give her a weapon, but she could finally defend herself properly. Her eyes shone at the prospect as the apple illuminated her excited face.

"Your smile is a lovely sight to see, my dear lady."

"Indeed, Miss Nix, you should smile more often for us."

Hearing their words, a light amount of heat touched her cheeks, and she intensified her gaze on the apple. Thankfully, Aberrous came out with the dinner. He set each plate of lobster risotto in front of the three of them. When the amphibian left, she merely glanced between her plate and the two brothers. She waited to see if they would try to steal from her plate again. When neither made a move towards it, she hesitantly went to eat the food. After a few minutes of this process, she decided that they weren't going to try anything. Taking another bite of her food, a sudden curiosity popped into her head. "The two of you mentioned that there were two others before me. You already told me what happened to the second one, but what about the first one?"

"She lost her mind after awhile," Heart uttered, stabbing a piece of lobster.

"How so?"

"At first, she was fine. Only after the first game, however, she was on her knees begging us not to send her through another. My brother and I found it amusing and continued on with the games. I believe her mind couldn't handle it. In the first few games, she only cried," Diamond explained.

"We would have to come and retrieve her almost every time. It would then take several hours to calm her down. Eventually, she just tuned everything out until she broke down, my dear lady."

"Yes, for a few months, she was like a lifeless doll. Afterwards, she started to act quite strange. She would roam the halls of this castle, mumbling undecipherable things to herself. At other times, she would go outside and just start digging with her bare hands while laughing crazily," Diamond continued.

"Did you two kill her?" she questioned, taking another bite of her meal.

"No, we didn't, my dear lady. It would've probably been a better fate for her, though. One night, she managed to break out of the restraints we kept her in since she was unstable, and we had to keep her from trying something. Having broken out of her restraints, she left the castle and headed out into the grasslands."

"I take it that something else killed her, then."

"Quite right, Miss Nix. The next morning, we found her in multiple pieces. It took us the whole day to recover her entire body. The most disturbing part, though, was finding the insane smile on her face. She appeared to be laughing as she was being torn apart."

Nodding her head in response, she could imagine someone going crazy under the brothers' watch. The fact that she was laughing during her death, however, did indeed trouble her. What was also worrying was the creature that caused her death. What if she encountered something like on the way to the Land of Amusement? Knowing that she would have a weapon, though, reassured her a bit. "May I see the weapon?"

"Of course," Diamond answered, looking over to his brother, who nodded in return. Heart snapped his fingers as he set down his fork. In his hands appeared two daggers, one with a silver handle and the other with a golden one. Amethysts were throughout the handles while the stainless steel blades glinted in the afternoon light. Heart handed them over to her and watched as she examined them.

"We thought that daggers would suit you. Seeing your previous combat situations, we noticed that you attack directly, but you also use your surroundings to your advantage. A weapon that will allow maneuverability will do you well, Miss Nix."

The two daggers were crafted wonderfully, and she felt a sense of pride in holding them. These would definitely increase her chances of beating the sunhat girl. "Thank you both for these."

Heart smirked while Diamond smiled in reply. She set the weapons to the side as she finished her dinner and drink. About five minutes passed, and the three of them were now done with their meals. The glowing yellow apple still sat on the table but was soon removed. Heart held it in his hands before tossing it over to Diamond. Within seconds, Diamond had it cut into multiple pieces, having used his dinner knife. He handed three of the pieces to her.

Once in her hands, she noticed that the flesh of the apple was a light pink color. She stared at it questionably until she saw the brothers bite into their own slices. Seeing them eat it, she bit into one of the pieces and was surprised by the taste. It tasted just like apple crumb cake. Delighted, she finished the piece and ate the remaining two. When she looked back up, she noticed that the two brothers were gone. In their place was a simple piece of parchment. Picking it up in her hands, she read its message.

We hope that you enjoyed the dinner. We must retire for the day, though. We're quite tired, and we suggest that you get a goodnight's rest as well.

Setting the note back down on the table, she decided that the suggestion was a good one. So, she picked up her daggers and made her way back to her room. Upon entering, she placed her daggers on the left nightstand and headed into the bathroom and attended to her routine. Afterwards, she changed into a comfortable pair of purple and black checkered flannel pajamas. Exiting the wardrobe and bathroom, she went to get into her bed; however, there was already a figure in her bed. She stood frozen in place. "What the ..."

"Ah, my dear lady, I see that you're finally ready to go to bed," Heart yawned out as he sat up in the bed.

Her cheeks heated up, and she noticed that Heart no longer had a shirt on. She instantly turned away from him and went to head for one of the chairs in the room, but her movement was halted. Arms wrapped around her waist from behind her as long nails tickled her skin. Diamond's chin rested on her left shoulder as his calm breathing tickled her neck. "Surely, you're tired, Miss Nix."

"I am, but I'm not sleeping in the same bed as you two."

"My dear lady, think of it as repaying us for the daggers."

"You should've told me the cost before you gave them to me."

"We hadn't decided upon the cost yet, Miss Nix."

"Of course, you didn't," she grumbled before letting out a cry of surprise. Diamond lifted her off of the ground and carried her over to the bed. He pushed the covers aside and set her down. He got in after her and pulled the sheets over the three of them. Heart wrapped his arms around her waist and pulled her closer to him.

Diamond grabbed her left arm as he pressed himself closer to her. This left her head nuzzled into his chest. Both of their actions made her cheeks burn with bashfulness. Surprisingly, though, the two of them fell asleep quite fast, and, despite the awkwardness of the situation, she managed to slip into unconsciousness pretty fast. Their warm bodies pressed against hers, and the three rested peacefully.

Chapter Thirty One: Forest's Shroud

Waking up to pale morning light, she found herself on the edge of the bed. Her left arm and leg were hanging off of the side, and she was no longer in the brothers' hold. Realizing this, she quietly made her way out of the bed. When she got up, however, the sight she saw was rather amusing.

Since there was now no one between the two brothers, they ended up in each other's arms. Diamond had Heart in his hold, which left Heart cuddled up to his brother's bare chest. She didn't know how she managed to get out of their grasp last night. Maybe, she was somehow able to roll her way over to the edge of the bed. Whatever the reason, it worked to her benefit. So, she quickly and quietly made her way into the bathroom to start and finish her morning routine.

As she was doing this, she thought about her plan to leave for the Land of Amusement tomorrow. The brothers would be going with her, but would they really let her head there? If they so decided, they could prevent her from going quite easily. Right now, though, they were fast asleep, and she could sneak away.

There was the issue of how she would beat the sunhat girl without their help. They had magic, and she didn't. She now possessed daggers, but she doubted that the sunhat girl would take an attack without defending herself. Still if she waited, the twins might stop her, which would anger the girl. Nix didn't want that girl coming back into the castle like she owned the place.

Sighing, she came out of the bathroom and went into the wardrobe. When she left there, she had on a purple v-neck and a simple pair of black pants. Purple and black boots were on her feet while a simple purple jacket covered her arms.

She had put her dark brown hair into a clip, so in case she needed to run it wouldn't get caught on any branches in the forest. Her daggers were attached to her hips in their sheaths, and the amethysts glimmered slightly even without a light source shining on them. Luckily, she had also managed to find a small purple and black checkered backpack in the closet.

Before leaving, her gaze fell on the two sleeping brothers. She couldn't help but smile a little at their sleeping positions. In a way, they did look rather adorable, but that opinion would never leave her lips. Nix turned away and walked out of the room, having decided to leave early. Moving as fast as she could, she made her way to the kitchen to see if Aberrous was there. Thankfully, he was.

Hearing someone come into the area, the amphibian turned around and peered up at her curiously. "Nix, you're up early. May I ask why?"

"I'm headed out to the forest, Aberrous. When Diamond and Heart wake up, please tell them that I already left and headed there."

"The brothers informed me that you were going there with them. They wouldn't much appreciate you going on your own. That place is quite dangerous."

"I'm aware of that, but if I stay, the brothers might try to keep me here. So, I was wondering if you would help me pack my bag with some items."

"They would most likely try to stop you since they're quite protective of you. That would only bring that wretched child back here, and I don't wish for my masters to be harmed again. Very well, I'll give you one of the packs that I already prepared for the journey that was supposed to be tomorrow," he responded, opening one of the cupboards and pulling out a pack.

Appreciative of this, she took off the backpack and set it on the counter. She took the one he offered her and slipped it onto her back. "Thank you for this, Aberrous," she voiced, crouching down and hugging the frog to her.

"You're welcome, Nix, but you better be off before one of them wakes."

Still smiling, she pulled away and nodded. She waved at him and turned on her heel to make her way for the entrance hall. Soon, she reached there and left the castle. Nix looked out over the grasslands and relaxed under the gentle breeze that swept through it. Closing her eyes for a brief moment, she took a deep breath in before exhaling. When she opened her eyes, she made her way to the back of the castle. The sunhat girl needed to be dealt with, and she wished to get such an encounter over with.

As she walked around the castle, she noted the various stone statues in the courtyard. It seemed like they were watching her, and, at one point, she turned around to see if they had moved. Ever since the manager, she was quite wary of any statue in this world. When she looked back, she almost had a heart attack. The statues were indeed staring back at her.

All of them had their heads turned towards her. Her hands reached for her daggers, but she never drew the weapons. Instead of attacking, the statues merely waved at her as if to say goodbye. She gave a timid wave back before increasing her pace to the back of the castle. Reaching it, she saw a narrow dirt path, which led into the forest beyond.

Probably about five minutes passed before she came to the entrance of the forest. She stared upwards in bewilderment. The forest was raised above ground level and started on the edge of a cliff. Nix didn't understand how she was supposed to reach the entrance until her eyes fell on a rocky path that led upwards. Walking over to the beginning of the path, she observed the cliff's wall and the elaborate designs etched into it. The detail was so clean and precise that it made her think of a castle wall rather than a mere cliff.

Stepping onto the rocky path, she took careful steps so as not to trip and fall. This path wasn't traveler friendly, and one false move would mean death due to the sheer height of the cliff. With this in mind, she felt relieved when she finally made it to the top.

The entrance made it seem like she was entering a completely different world. Before her were two giant ancient trees designed into an elegant gateway. The two trees reached up into the sky, and their thick branches, which were filled with leaves, made a sturdy archway into the forest. Their trunks had details as intricate as the cliff walls. Beyond this otherworldly entrance lay tall trees devoid of leaves.

As she took her first step into the forest, she spotted a shrouded form in the distance. It stood still while Nix froze in place, waiting for it to make a move. Giving one last glance towards her, it turned away and disappeared on the path beyond. Her mind kept screaming at her to turn back, but she pushed forward, entering the mysterious forest. She made very little progress before she heard giggling behind her. Before she could look behind her, a form appeared in front of her.

"I'm glad to see that you're keeping your end of the bargain, Nix."

"What do you want?" Nix questioned in a harsh tone.

"I wanted to enjoy the show that's about to unfold before my very eyes. You didn't think that I was going to stay in my castle and miss all of the fun. You know how boring that would be, my doll. Oh, how are the brothers holding up?"

Biting back her urge to stab her, she replied, "They don't concern you."

"I see that my doll is developing feelings for them, how delightful."

Ignoring her comment, Nix walked around the sunhat girl and went further into the forest.

"Nix, you may never admit to such a thing, but I can see it in your eyes. Remember, I control the situation; you're only making it easier for me to break you, and you know how much I love to break people. Until later, doll."

Glancing over her right shoulder, she saw that she was gone, but the girl was viewing her progress from somewhere within the forest. Pressing forward, she heard many strange sounds coming from the trees, but she had encountered nothing yet, except for that shrouded figure. With the fog in the forest only increasing, she reached into her pack and grabbed the lantern. She wound it up, and her path became clearer. Nix noticed that the trees were becoming more compact as their abundant presence caused the path to be narrower. At one point, she had to crawl on the path due to the tree branches overhead. Thankfully, that didn't last long.

Water soon hit her face as thunder sounded in the distance. A storm was overhead, which only darkened the ominous forest. Pulling the hood on her jacket over her head, she stopped as something moved in the trees next to her. The movement halted as soon as it began. Right as she was about to proceed forward, something rolled out of the trees. To her terror, it was a rotting head. Its eyes rolled back and forth until they landed on her. It opened its mouth as if to scream, but no sound escaped its lips.

When at last it closed its horrid mouth, trees began to sway back and forth as branches in the distance snapped. Something was coming. She could run or fight, but which would prove the better option? Squinting, she tried to decipher the form. Instead of one form, there were many. As they neared, she noted that the creatures looked bug-like. With their number, she ran for it, charging down the path and refusing to look back.

Suddenly, she heard a loud buzzing behind her, and she guessed that the creatures were not far behind. Millions of tiny legs ran after her as knife-like teeth chattered with a hungry desire. In the distance, she could once again see the shrouded figure. They stared at her before outstretching a gloved hand of theirs. She could accept their hand or continue down the path and take her chances with the creatures behind her. Nix wouldn't be able to outrun the creatures for long, so she made her choice.

Now six paces from the figure, she jumped forward and grasped their hand. Upon contact, the figure drew her to them as the swarm of bug-like creatures charged past. She noticed their jewel-like bodies and beady red eyes. Horrendous hooked legs supported the creatures, with each creature having ten of their own. As they passed, she peered up at the figure. "Thank you for the help."

"I may have just saved you, but I may kill you yet."

Chapter Thirty Two: Bargain of Death

Vines wrapped around her wrists, binding them together. Her daggers flew out of their sheaths and into the hands of the hooded figure. She tried to struggle out of the restraints, but they only grew tighter and stronger. Looking back up at the hooded figure, she saw them disappearing into the trees. Nix didn't know whether to follow them or not, but she needed the binds off. They stated, however, that they might kill her. While she was debating the pros and cons of each choice, she didn't notice that her feet were already moving after the cloaked figure.

It wasn't until she almost ran into a tree that she noted her movement. Startled, she attempted to turn around, but she couldn't. It was as if some invisible force directed her forward. As the trees went by, she could spot something in the distance. Ahead lay a huge boulder, which had a small entrance to a cave inside. White and turquoise roses covered the rock and glowed in an eerie light.

The invisible force guided her through the entrance, making her duck in order to not hit her head. Upon entering, she saw a comfortable room. There was another cut out in the rock, which had a turquoise curtain covering it. It most likely led to a bathroom. As for the rest of the room, there was a simple wooden bed, which had white sheets spread across it. White and turquoise roses wrapped themselves around the bedposts. On the other side of the room were a small kitchen and a square wooden table with four matching chairs. White cushions lay on top of the chairs.

In one of the chairs sat the hooded figure. Nix noticed, however, that the cloak hung oddly at the chair as if the figure had shorter legs or no legs at all. "Sit," they ordered.

Not really seeing any other option, especially since that force was still behind her, she sat down in the chair. "Why do you want to kill me?" she asked simply.

"I don't want to kill you, and I haven't decided whether you should live or die yet. Your answers to my questions will determine your fate."

"Well, seeing as I'm restrained and have no weapons, ask away."

"First off, tell me how you know the sunhat girl?"

"She appeared in my music box when I was sixteen. One day, I wished to live in the world of the music box. That wish came true, and she trapped me here. She now wants me to go to the Land of Amusement," she replied, thinking that she might as well answer truthfully since her life was on the line.

"So you're the girl that she was talking about, the one to set her free. That's troublesome. Why did you agree to travel to her domain? What would cause you to make such a bargain?"

"Wait, you've talked to her, and what do you mean set her free?"

"You made the agreement without knowing its true meaning. That was a foolish mistake."

"You didn't answer my question. Why do you care so much about the sunhat girl and her agreement with me?"

"Because, I don't wish to see my sister ruin anymore lives."

Words escaped her as she stared in shock at the cloaked figure. The figure pulled their hood down, revealing a girl the same height as the sunhat girl. She had short hair, which was white on the left side while the right side was colored turquoise. Her eyes followed the same color pattern except the turquoise eye was on the left and vice versa. A simple black dress covered her figure as her bare feet swung back and forth.

"Before I answer your first question, please, tell me why you agreed to enter her domain in the first place."

"I agreed to go to the Land of Amusement because otherwise two people would've been captured by her. I owed those two my life. I had to make the choice then and there."

"You agreed in order to save another. I admire that, especially when you didn't know what you were agreeing to. As for your first question, my sister has grown tired of this world, and she intends to leave. Such a thing is near impossible, though, unless you're born with the proper magic. She isn't, however. My sister still managed to enter your world through the music box, but she could only stay in the music box. This didn't satisfy her.

"So, my sister hosted a tournament in her domain, claiming that the victor would be given power equal to her own. There was no victor, only sacrifices. These sacrifices were used to open the gateway to your world. However, she only ended up in a music box, forever observing your world. I'm assuming that she only sacrificed more in order to bring you into the music box."

"Wait, how did she end up in my music box, though?"

"I don't know. That's something you need to ask my sister directly. The important part is that in order for my sister to enter your world completely, she needs to make a sacrifice from that world. You happen to be that sacrifice. Tell me, what do you plan to do once you reach the Land of Amusement?"

Her statement rang in Nix's ears. A sacrifice, no, she wouldn't let that happen. "I intend to defeat her."

"I see, but how? Surely, you noticed how powerful my sister is. I need to know if you can defeat her. If you can't, I will kill you here. She can't be allowed to enter your world. If she does, more people will be turned into her puppets, her entertainment. There can't be a future where you become a sacrifice. The risk is too great."

"Why do you care so much about another world?"

"I witnessed the atrocities that she committed in this world. She messed with the minds of the original owners of the castle in the grasslands, making the household members kill each other in a manic frenzy. She murdered countless people in that tournament and even corrupted the mermaids near her territory. She is a child meant only for destruction, meant only to satisfy her selfish desires. I had wanted to stop her, but I suppose that I never had the courage to do so or the right opportunity to do so. She always seemed to be surrounded by people who would do her bidding, and I couldn't fight off that many. Presently, however, she has lowered guard since no one has made a major move against her. Now, is the time to strike, but tell me how you intend to defeat her?" Nix honestly couldn't think of way, and her silence gave the sunhat girl's sister the answer that she needed. "I thought so. I'm sorry, but you leave me with the task of killing you myself."

Seeing the girl getting out of her chair sent a wave of realization through Nix. She needed to get out of her bonds and defend herself. Swiftly standing, she grabbed the chair as best as she could and threw it at the girl. It seemed to be repelled by an invisible wall and was thrown back at Nix.

Throwing herself at the ground, she dodged the flying chair. The girl drew one of Nix's daggers and brought it down on her. Rolling out of the way just in time, Nix got back on her feet and headed for the kitchen area. Her fingers grabbed at the drawers, looking for something to cut her bonds and for a weapon. To her surprise, there were no knives in any of the drawers, but she found a pair of scissors.

When she attained the scissors, she felt a tug on her person. The unknown force pulled her back, and she noticed that the girl's cloak was no longer on her as her bare feet stood on the rocky floor. With no hesitation, Nix flipped the scissors around in her hands and cut at the vines, but they were too thick for the scissors.

Nix was now right next to the small child. A force sent the scissors flying out of her hands and across the room. In the girl's right hand glittered one of the daggers. The girl brought Nix down on her knees, ready to plunge the dagger into her neck. With nothing to lose, Nix reached for the hand with the dagger. Her contact with the dagger sent the girl's aim off its original course. Instead, it landed in Nix's upper arm. A surge of pain went through her body as she pushed the girl away from her.

The dagger remained in her arm as the girl came at her again with the other dagger. There was nothing Nix could do as she was held in place by the force. So, she held her arms in front of her face. Seconds felt like an eternity as blood dripped onto the rocky floor. The blade, however, never made contact. It was mere inches from her face, but it was stuck in the vines. This severed the restraints in half, freeing Nix from the bonds. Her hands flew at the girl's neck as she tightened her grip on the girl.

Eyes widening, the girl grasped at Nix's wrists as life escaped from her. The force faded away, and the girl would die soon. Something inside Nix, though, told her to stop. Maybe, it was the calm look in the girl's eyes, or, maybe, it was because Nix saw the good in her action. This girl wanted to save millions, who she didn't even know, and Nix wanted to preserve just her life, which might end soon anyway. She didn't want to give up on life, but she couldn't bring herself to kill the girl in front of her. As her hold relaxed, a smile found its way onto the girl's face.

"You have proven yourself, Nix."

"Wait, what? You mean that was a test. I thought that you wanted to kill me."

"I did, but you won over me even though you don't possess magic capabilities. Of course, I was going easy on you, but if my sister is weakened by me, you will have a good chance at beating her. Furthermore, you could've killed me just a few seconds ago, but you didn't. That mere action demonstrates that you have restraint over your emotions. You can keep your mind collected even in dire situations. That will help you survive against my sister. I don't know if you can win over her, yet something tells me to trust you. I will travel at your side to help you defeat her, and just in case you do lose the battle. This is one time where I can stop my sister, and I intend not to miss it. Along the journey, please, call me Fade."

"If you wished to kill me, though, why didn't you use your full power?"

"Yes, I desired to kill you, but I also wanted to test you. If I had used my full power, you would be dead. Like I mentioned, though, once my sister is weakened, you will step in and stop her. Since by that point, I will be exhausted by my fight with her. You'll deliver the final blow, which should be possible since she won't be at full strength, and you defeated me when I didn't use my full strength. Of course, there are differences between the two of us and our capabilities, but I believe that you can accomplish the task now."

Fade walked up to her, causing Nix to tense up. Instead of attacking her, Fade pulled the dagger out of Nix's arm, setting it on the ground next to her. As she went over to the kitchen, Nix's mind swirled in confusion. This child was just as frustrating as the sunhat girl; however, she knew that she had made the right decision in not killing her. Nix had gained an ally in her journey.

Besides, the girl could guide her through the forest. She would still remain cautious around Fade, yet she knew that the girl would no longer attempt to kill her. It was curious, though, that the sunhat girl hadn't interfered with the fight. Then again, Fade was her sister, and the sunhat girl might've believed that Fade wouldn't actually kill her. There was also the reason that the sunhat girl couldn't observe the fight without being in the house herself and that might've been too risky for her.

Coming back to her, Fade ripped off Nix's jacket and began to clean, stitch and bandage the wound. When the girl finished, she disappeared behind the turquoise cloth and left Nix alone before quickly returning. In her hands was a black cloak similar to her own. She draped it over Nix's shoulders and secured it around the injured girl's neck.

"We should head out. We need to make the next train," she said, holding her right hand out to Nix. Taking it, the girl helped Nix up before grabbing her own cloak. With it around her shoulders, Fade left the small home and waited for Nix to follow her.

Chapter Thirty Three: Meeting at the Station

Before she went outside, she reclaimed her daggers, putting them back in their sheaths. Once outside, Fade had once again returned to a height taller than her own. She soon realized, however, that the girl was still the same height. Fade was just hovering in the air with her cloak floating around her. Seeing Nix, she pulled the hood over her head and signaled her to follow. Nix clutched at her own cloak since her jacket was ruined, and it was quite cold outside. The rain had stopped, though, and some more light had returned to the forest.

As the two of them were traveling through the forest, Nix suddenly felt something grabbing at her pack. Looking behind her, she saw Fade reaching in before pulling out an orange. The girl zipped the pack up and returned to floating at Nix's side.

"Shouldn't we wait until we get out of the forest?"

"Why? If you're worried about the creatures of this forest hearing us, then you have nothing to fear. As long as you stay with me, none of them will harm you."

"Is that how you were able to save me before when all those bug-like creatures were chasing me?"

"Precisely, I happen to rule over this domain. The creatures here cannot harm me or anyone that I travel with. Do you want some orange?"

"I see, and, no, you enjoy the fruit. I have another in my pack."

"Alright, thanks. It has been awhile since I last tasted an orange," she remarked, peeling the fruit as she floated along through the forest.

With that, the two of them continued to press on through the forest. Pieces of orange peel trailed behind them. As some beams of light broke through the tops of trees, she could tell that it was late afternoon. Had she really been in the forest that long? Regardless, they could rely on natural light soon. For the moment, though, she reached into her pack and retrieved her flashlight. Just about to flick the device on, Fade's left hand stopped her. "That's not necessary."

Confused, Nix put the flashlight away and waited to see what she meant. Fade put the last piece of orange in her mouth before holding her hand out. Instantly, the forest floor began to vibrate lightly. When it stopped, tiny little mushrooms burst from the ground. Orange, yellow, pink, purple, and dark blue mushrooms glowed on the forest floor. Illuminating the surrounding area, Nix could see the figures of many creatures in the forest. It was amazing how she never had seen them before. This also reminded her of how lucky she was to be traveling with Fade.

Tiny little creatures with bright neon green eyes and thin haired bodies followed their every move as if waiting for her to step away from Fade. Their small clawed hands scraped across the floor in anticipation as their rotten tongues licked their yellow sharp teeth. She could see at least fifty of them around them. Turning her gaze away from them, she focused her attention on Fade's figure and tried to forget the terrifying creatures. Fade walked on as if not noticing them in the slightest. The tiny colorful mushrooms highlighted the girl's movement and caused her cloak to shimmer in the process. Fade truly did look like the ruler of the forest. During the long walk, Nix's feet were starting to grow tired, however, and she really wanted to float in the air like Fade. They walked further on, and the mushrooms disappeared back into the earth since more sunlight was breaking through.

"We're almost there. Do you see that large amount of light ahead, Nix?"

"Yeah," she answered as she noticed that it was probably almost dusk. "Let's hurry up."

"Eager to leave the forest?"

Nodding, they continued to head for the exit. Nearing the light, Nix saw that it was coming through a hole in a wall. When they stood in front of it, she noted that the wall went on for miles, stretching on into the unknown.

"That wall has stood for longer than when I became a resident of this forest. It helps prevent people from entering this place since there's only one entrance in the wall. Only those who must travel through the forest should enter its domain," Fade explained, seeming like she was recalling a memory or memories.

"I'm assuming that someone you knew died?"

"Some people that I have known have died but not because of this forest. Many have died in my domain, though, due to their foolishness. When there used to be more people around this area, people would dare others to enter. Those that entered rarely came back out. I aided some, but most who saw me claimed me to be a force of evil and ran away to meet death."

Thankfully, Nix had decided to not run away from the girl even though they had fought. Fade proceeded to go through the hole and onto the other side, with Nix following after her. Before them was a train station, but the train was absent from it. The sun would soon be below the horizon. Hopefully, the train would arrive soon.

While they waited, Nix walked over to one of the many bushes which grew throughout the station. She picked off one of the small pink flowers and twirled it between her fingers. As she glanced back towards the setting sun, she noticed two people suddenly appear in the station. Familiar heads of blue and red hair came walking down the stone pathway. Both brothers had back on their clothing from the first day that she met them. When they neared her, smiles didn't grace their faces. Instead, both looked less than pleased with her and seemed like they wished to murder Fade.

"So, these are the two that you saved from eternal torture. I was hoping that it wouldn't be them. I take it that you're their new plaything," Fade murmured to Nix.

"No, I've been upgraded to lover," she grumbled out. "Still, I take it that you know them."

Fade seemed a little shocked by that but didn't comment on the first statement. "Yes, they sent their last plaything into my forest. She nearly died. I had to tend to some of her wounds for Aberrous didn't know how to mend them. I'm surprised that you agreed to save them."

"Despite what they've done, they don't deserve a fate of eternal torment."

"That's a fair point."

Once the two brothers reached them, they turned their attention onto Fade. "What are you doing here, child?" Heart questioned in a rude tone.

"She's here to help me in the Land of Amusement," Nix responded, not giving Fade a chance to answer.

"Miss Nix, that's our job. Surely, you don't require her need."

"I intend to make sure that she doesn't fail in the task ahead of her. If she does, I will finish it for her," Fade added in, meeting both of their harsh gazes.

Heart scoffed before noting Nix's injured arm. She winced slightly as he held her arm up. Nix, however, pulled her arm away and took a step back from the two. "My dear lady, how did you receive such a wound?"

"I tried to kill her. I have decided, though, that she doesn't need to die," Fade remarked before the other female could reply.

In an instant, two sabers were at the girl's neck, but she showed no fear in her eyes. Before the brothers could attack, Nix stepped in front of Fade. "She's here to help, just accept it. Besides, she may have tried to kill me, but she also saved my life. If it weren't for her, I never would've made it out of the forest with as little injuries as I have."

At that moment, the train came into the station. Red and yellow paint on the train shone brightly as the headlights flickered on. The entrance doors opened, waiting for passengers to hop on. "Let's just get on the train," Nix suggested, glancing between the two brothers.

Lowering the sabers, the brothers put the weapons back in their sheaths. "Fine, we'll accept her aid. Granted, if you hadn't left us this morning, we could've transported you to this station without having to go through the forest."

"If I had stayed, you two would've tried to keep me from going."

"Diamond, it seems like she figured out our plan without our knowing."

"It would appear so, Heart. Let us board the train, then. Still, Miss Nix, we have some things to discuss once on. We won't forgive you leaving like that so easily." Nix nodded, and she didn't look forward to their discussion. As for the brothers, they glanced at each other; they didn't desire to have another protect their lover.

Chapter Thirty Four: Dining with Movement

Once inside of the train, Nix was surprised to see the engineer's car seat empty. She figured that it run on some sort of magic and turned to head further into the train. Entering the next car, the train began to move while she noted that the armchairs had a gold and silver checkered pattern. The feet of the chairs were covered in gems ranging from diamonds to emeralds. Elegant crystal chandeliers hung above in the car.

Fade continued to walk through to the next car but stopped when she didn't hear footsteps behind her. Looking back, she saw that the brothers had grabbed Nix and placed her in one of the chairs. The twins glanced to her, and she figured that they would come to the dining car later. If she tried to get in their way, she would only anger them more and would probably have to fight them. Besides, she knew that they wouldn't hurt Nix, especially since Nix had mentioned that they no longer considered her a plaything. So, she moved onto the next car and waited for the three of them there.

In her forced seat, Nix stared over at the two as they took their own chairs. She crossed her arms over her chest and glanced between the two of them. "So, let me guess. I'm going to have to play a game with you two for leaving this morning."

"No, we want something else," Diamond replied, resting his right cheek against his right knuckles.

Raising her left eyebrow, she gave them a puzzled look. "That's a first. What is it, then?"

"My dear lady, we wish for you to promise to never go off like that again. My brother and I were worried sick when we woke up to discover that you had gone off on your own."

"I left a message with Aberrous. Besides, I already told you that I suspected that you two wouldn't let me leave if I had left tomorrow."

"Miss Nix, we were thankful for the message, but beforehand, we had thought that you had run away on us. We had thought that we had lost the one person who would have given us a chance. Even after we had learned of it, we had been concerned that something in that forest had killed you already. We had entered in and searched for you. When we hadn't been able to find you, we had decided to head to the train station, and, luckily, we caught you in time."

"Well, it's a good thing that I met Fade, then. You two really should be easier on her."

"My dear lady, we have our reasons to be mad with her. Regardless, we didn't think to check with her since we didn't think that you would encounter her. She often keeps to herself, and, again, we don't like to associate with her. Now, will you promise us?"

"You were really that concerned that I had left you and were in possible danger?"

"Yes," they both answered with no hesitation.

Analyzing both of their eyes, she sighed in defeat. To her, it seemed like they were telling the truth. Then again, could she make such a promise? What if she wanted to escape from the two of them in the future? Still, there was the issue of her not having any magic to deal with the creatures that she would encounter. Besides, where would she go? Maybe, she could stay with Fade, but she was too close to the twins. Granted, they had mentioned, "like that," so she could technically try to escape, and she wouldn't be breaking the promise. She would just have to find another method to get away from them. With this in mind, she answered, "Fine, I promise to never go off like that again."

Hearing this, both of the twins smiled in their own way and stood up from their seats. "Thank you," they both uttered. "Let's go to dinner," they continued as she got up from her seat. Heart took her left hand and Diamond her right. Of course, they just took her hands without her permission, but she figured that arguing with them would get her nowhere.

Entering the dining car, she scanned over the design. Green carpet with a gold and silver diamond pattern lay out on the car's floor. There were rows of tables with freshly laid out dining ware. At each table were four wooden chairs with green cushions. Next to each table was a window with a set of greenish-gold drapes. Brass chandeliers illuminated the car.

Before the brothers could protest, she pulled her hands from them and sat down next to Fade, making them sit across from the two of them. Taking her pack off, Nix got comfortable in her chair. Remembering that she hadn't eaten in sometime, she reached into her backpack. Fade glanced over Nix's way to see if the dark brown-haired girl would eat one of the oranges. When Nix took out a bag of cookies, Heart snapped his fingers together. The cookies vanished as did the rest of the food in her pack. Nix became confused while Fade looked disappointed.

"What did you just do?" Nix questioned, looking to the blue-haired brother.

"My dear lady, we're in the dining car."

"We thought that you would like to enjoy a proper meal, Miss Nix."

"I guess that would be nice."

"Hmm, I wonder how long it has been since someone has cooked my meal for me," Fade muttered to herself.

"Tch, maybe, you won't receive any," Heart commented, rolling his eyes.

"You can always have some of my food, Fade," Nix offered.

"That won't be necessary. Everyone will receive food. The chefs on the train know how many of us there are," the small girl responded, making Nix wonder where the chefs were. They were probably at the back of the train somewhere. She kind of wished to see them though. Perhaps, she could look for them later on.

Still, Fade smiled in gratitude and began to play with her fork. Both brothers merely glared daggers at her while she seemed not to notice. Nix tapped her left fingers against the table's surface, the lack of conversation making her uncomfortable. The dark brown-haired girl's attention was soon caught, however, by the food that now appeared on her once empty plate. Food also became apparent on everyone else's plate. It consisted of a side of green beans with slivered almonds and roast beef with gravy on top. Iced tea was in everyone's glasses.

Heart took a sip of his drink only to gag and get up from his chair. "I'm going to go get some sugar for this," he grumbled, walking off.

Nix wished to go with him just to see the chefs, but she didn't want her food to become cold. She still had the rest of the evening to visit them. Fade noticed her looking at the male leaving and mentioned, "I can go with you later to see the cooks if you would like, Nix."

"Really? That would be great. Granted, I'm surprised that we don't have to pay for the food."

Cutting into the conversation, Diamond explained, "In exchange for not making their customers pay, they're allowed to purchase supplies without paying. They merely show their World Train employee card, and they're allowed to buy items of certain values."

"Are they the only workers on here?" Nix asked the two.

"Yes, this train is powered by a magic spell of continuity. In other words, this train will keep going, stopping only at the specific stations for its designated times," Fade narrated before taking a few bites of her food.

Diamond had an annoyed look on his face as though he wished to be the one to explain it, but he didn't say anything and quietly returned to his food. Heart soon returned and started to eat as well. Conversation went dead while the four of them ate. It was the first time the brothers had been so quiet around her, and they weren't messing with her either. Nix took this to her advantage. Having finished her own plate of food, she quickly snatched food from both of the brothers. Not surprisingly, her action seemed to bring them back to their senses.

"Miss Nix, it's rude to steal from another's plate."

"Consider it payback for the last time you two stole my food."

"My dear lady if you're going to eat our food, please do so properly. You have gravy on your face," Heart scolded as he reached across the table with a napkin in his hand. Bringing the napkin gently across the edge of her mouth, he wiped off the gravy. Heat swept across her face in embarrassment. "There, that's better."

"That reminds me, Miss Nix, do leave room for some dessert."

She merely nodded her head and pushed away her empty plate, taking a sip of her tea afterwards. Not a moment later, the plates vanished and were replaced by smaller plates. Double chocolate chip cookies lay under brownie batter ice cream, which was covered with whipped cream and a cherry on top. As Nix dug into the sweet treat, Diamond pushed his over to Heart while Fade ate hers slowly. When everyone finished, Fade asked, "Shall we go see the chefs, Nix?"

"Yes, let's go," she answered excitedly as they both stood from their seats.

Before they left, however, Heart questioned, "My dear lady, do you wish us to sleep in the same bed as you again?"

Just thinking about that made her face heat up, and she could only manage to shake her head until words found way to her mouth. "No, I'm quite fine on my own. Besides, you two looked comfy enough on your own."

"I don't quite understand you, Miss Nix."

"So, you two didn't find yourselves cuddled in the other's arms?"

What happened next shocked her. Both brothers' cheeks turned a light pink. Diamond glanced the other way, and Heart just took a sip of his tea, trying to forget her statement. Nix couldn't help but smirk slightly. "I'll take that as a yes, then. Well, Fade and I are going."

Beginning to float across the dining car, Fade left the car with Nix. The two twins followed their movement, not appreciating the fact that Fade was taking their lover's attention away from them. "Heart, let's play a game of matching cards to distract ourselves," Diamond suggested as he bent the fork in his hand into a ball.

"Good idea, brother," the blue-haired twin agreed, and the two of them began to play the simple card game.

Chapter Thirty Five: Not the Expected Evening

Exiting the dining car, Fade and Nix traveled down several cars. When they reached the door to the second to last car, the dark brown-haired girl could hear dishes being moved around and running water. Fade slid open the door and signaled for Nix to enter first. Walking in, the gazes of three people looked over to them. All of them wore green chef coats and matching green pants. There was one man with short, light red hair and green eyes while the other man had shoulder length light brown hair and blue eyes. As for the third chef, she had wavy, long black hair and dark brown eyes.

Nix stood there awkwardly and waved some as Fade came in behind her and closed the door. "She wished to see you three since she was interested in how you three operate," Fade explained, taking a seat on one of the few chairs in the car.

"We rarely meet people who wish to know more about us," the woman mentioned with a smile as she dried off a plate. "What would you like to know?"

"How can you tell how many people are in the dining car? I know magic is involved, but how does it work?" Nix asked, taking a seat as well.

"The dining car and this car are linked together by a communication spell. When one casts the spell, you state what you wish the spell to communicate to you. Its effect lasts for a year before it has to be renewed. Of course, another condition is that the spell is cast in two or more places so that the information flows and doesn't just circulate in that room. You also need to state which area is to be the sender and which the receiver," the woman explained, now working on drying another plate.

"Do all three of you take turns in casting it?"

"No, Will is the one who studies spells among the three of us," she answered, pointing with her right thumb over to the brown-haired male.

"Do you three have assigned roles here?"

"Besides Will being a spell caster, he's in charge of desserts and anything sweet. David and I work together on the other items. We all also have our own magic types. Will possesses earth magic, so he grows the herbs and such since they taste much better than those at the markets.

"David is an object manipulator; meaning that if we run out of a food item, he can turn certain items into the desired one. Of course, he can only do this to a degree. He can't turn a potato into a piece of meat. The items have to be in the same food group. As for me, I'm a fire user and teleporter. That's why you don't see any stoves or ovens in here and why the food appears in the dining car. Any other inquiries?"

"What's your name?"

"Jenna, and yours?"

"Nix. Well, thank you for answering my questions, Jenna. And, thank you all for the meal tonight. It was scrumptious."

Fade nodded in thanks as well while the two of them stood from their seats. They waved to the three, and they waved back. After the two left the kitchen car, they headed down a few more, and Fade stopped in front of a cabin. "I'll be going to bed since tomorrow we'll arrive."

"Alright, I'll see you in the morning, Fade," Nix answered before she turned and went to get a cabin herself. Still, she was worried about tomorrow. She didn't think that she would arrive at the Land of Amusement so soon. It was nerve wracking to think that she would face off against the sunhat girl already. Regardless, she would have to force the thoughts aside and get a good rest. Fighting half-asleep didn't sound like too good of an idea.

Sliding open a cabin door, she saw it empty and entered the room before closing the door behind her. The cabin was decent sized. It had a bedroom area with a wooden door leading to a small bathroom. Wooden walls surrounded the entirety of the bedroom space. Two windows, with wooden blinds, lay on the right hand side wall. A simple light fixture illuminated the room while there was a full-sized bed with dark green and gold sheets. In front of the bed was a green and gold chair.

Noticing a silver hook on the wall over the bed, she hung up her pack and headed into the bathroom for her night routine. Coming back out of the small bathroom in some purple flannel pajamas, she made for the bed. She collapsed upon it and hugged one of the green pillows to her form. Nix rolled onto her back and steadily reached up with her right hand to the blinds. After she opened one set some, she watched the world go by and enjoyed the peaceful atmosphere of the small room. Her alone time was soon interrupted, however, by someone coming into her cabin. "My dear lady, I came in just to check on you. You never returned to the dining car, so my brother and I figured that you would already be in one of the cabins."

"Well, I'm doing fine, so you can go back to your brother."

"You're so cruel," he practically whined out before he closed the door and took a seat on the bed. "No, I want to visit with you."

"Tch, well, I guess that you'll stay whether I want you to or not," she muttered, still staring out the window. "So, where is your brother?"

"Do you prefer him over me, my dear lady?"

"I don't prefer either of you. I was just curious."

"In that case, he's currently in the shower. I'm waiting for him to finish, so I can get mine. Would you like to join me?"

"No!" she yelled a little too loudly, with her cheeks heating up.

Heart chuckled at her reaction before lying down on the bed. She observed him closely, making sure that he wouldn't try anything. His dark blue eyes seemed to go out of focus as if he was in deep thought. "My dear lady, can you smile more for my brother and me?"

"Why should I?"

"Because, I just asked you to." Ignoring him, she continued to watch the world outside fly by; however, her view was soon blocked. Heart had pinned her to the bed, preventing her from struggling. "Now, smile."

"No. Now, get off. This isn't helping my wounds." Sighing, he released his grip on her before snapping his fingers. Her hands were soon tied together. In that moment, Heart grabbed her face with his hands. He placed his thumbs on the sides of her mouth, attempting to make her smile. "Stop it," she managed to growl out.

"You're no fun at times, my dear lady," he remarked with a pout. He did halt his attempt, though, and sat back on the edge of the bed, releasing the binds. "By the way, what did you think of me cuddling my brother?"

"What kind of question is that? I'm not answering that." Remembering the scene, though, caused a light smile to come to her lips. She was reminded of how adorable the brothers looked as well as the hilariousness of the scene.

"Finally, a smile graces your face. I take it, then, that you enjoyed the sight of us."

"I just thought it was funny; that's all there is to it."

Glancing at his hands, Heart snapped his fingers again. From her view, she could see that something blue appeared in his hands. When he turned around, she noted that the blue object was a blue teddy bear with a crown on its head. "Take it. I don't feel comfortable leaving you alone with that child on board. This way, I'm respecting your wish to sleep alone, and I'm still watching over you in a way."

"I'm fine really."

"My dear lady, I'm offering you a gift; accept it, or I will sleep in your cabin tonight."

Knowing he was serious, she took the blue teddy bear and examined it. It was pretty cute and extremely soft. "Thanks I guess," she stated. Heart nodded in reply before pulling her over to him. He gave her a quick kiss on the lips before he disappeared from her cabin. Heat danced on her cheeks, but her attention soon turned to another male entering her room.

When Diamond had come in, she had already set the teddy bear on the pillow next to her. His eyes glanced at it before he shook his head lightly in amusement. Diamond proceeded to head over to the chair and sit on it. She averted her gaze from him due to him just having a red bathrobe wrapped around him. "Did you come in here to visit with me as well?"

"Yes, I figured that it would be nice since tomorrow we have a battle ahead of us. Also, I have something to ask you. Why do you trust Fade?" he questioned, pushing his wet hair back some.

"I trust her because I know that she won't attempt to kill me anymore. Furthermore, her goal in stopping her sister is pure, and she intends to see it through. Unlike her sister, Fade doesn't wish to control others and make them her entertainment. You should treat her better. Besides, didn't she save your second plaything from dying after the two of you sent her into Fade's forest?"

"Yes, she did save our second plaything, but my brother and I aren't happy about that incident. We don't like relying on her."

"Why do I get the feeling that there is more to the story? Are you two jealous?"

"Is it wrong for my brother and me to be jealous?"

"No, I don't control your emotions. You can feel however you want to feel. Just don't expect me to stop talking to Fade. Still, there must be a reason why you two dislike her so much."

"There is, but I'd rather not discuss it. I'd rather you come over, sit on my lap and tell me exactly what Fade and you discussed while we were away."

"I won't do so unless you tell me why you two despise her."

"Oh, so you wouldn't mind sitting on my lap, then?" he asked with a smile.

Pouting, she rolled her eyes and glanced away from him. A soft laugh escaped his lips, and silence remained between the two of them. Oddly enough, she didn't mind his presence in the room too much, but, maybe, that's because he wasn't climbing onto the bed and invading her personal space. Regardless, she peered over to him after a time and discovered that he had fallen asleep. She didn't know if Heart would come back or not, but she didn't wish for the male to be in her cabin.

Getting up, she walked over to Diamond and attempted to wake him up by flicking him on the forehead. She tried shaking his shoulders. At one point, she even slapped him, but he remained fast asleep. Annoyed by this point, she turned around and left her room to find theirs. When she opened the cabin door on the right of hers, she shut it instantly. She could feel her face heating up; however, the door soon opened once again. "Did you change your mind on my previous offer, my dear lady?"

"No, I came to tell you that your brother fell asleep in my room," she responded, looking away from Heart, who only had a towel wrapped around him.

"Did he now? Maybe, I should have tried that tactic, but I'll go retrieve him for you."

"Thanks, but could you at least put some clothes on first."

Heart just smirked at her, but he still listened to her and went back into his cabin, closing the door behind him. He came back out in a blue bathrobe, following her into her room. Seeing his brother in the chair, he went over to him and lifted his brother's left arm over his shoulders. Dragging Diamond out of her room, Heart closed the door behind him. Now left alone, she finally climbed under the sheets and went to sleep. Tomorrow, the four of them would arrive at the Land of Amusement.

Chapter Thirty Six: A Little Secret

Feeling light shine on her face, Nix opened her eyes to see the blinds in her cabin wide open. Squinting, she looked for the person who had opened them. She saw a figure who was peering down at her. The familiar smirk upon their lips gave them away. "My dear lady, it would seem that you have grown quite fond of the gift which I gave you last night."

Looking down, she noticed that she was currently holding the teddy bear to her chest as though it was a life support. "Whatever," she mumbled, setting the object on the other side of the bed while a light dose of heat hit her cheeks.

"Ah, Miss Nix, I'm sorry for falling asleep in your room last night. I didn't realize how tired I was."

"It's fine. How long until we reach the Land of Amusement, though?"

"We'll reach the sunhat girl's domain around sunset, so we still have an eight hour wait."

She nodded in response, assuming that it must be around ten in the morning. Getting out of the bed, she walked past the two brothers, with her backpack in hand, and into the bathroom. Shutting the door behind her, she waited for the brothers to leave. Nix could hear her cabin door open and close as the sound of heeled shoes on the train floor faded. With the two brothers gone, she began her morning routine.

 Once finished, she walked out of the bathroom in a comfortable purple tank top and a pair of black pants. She put her daggers in their sheaths while she wrapped the cloak from Fade around her. Once she slipped on and tied up her boots, she left the cabin and headed for the dining car.

When she passed Fade's cabin, however, she opened the cabin door to see if the girl was still asleep. The girl's room was quite identical to her own. Regardless, she noted that Fade was still fast asleep. Tapping her lightly, she caused the girl to stir, and Fade remained unconscious. Sighing, Nix called out her name a few times, which seemed to do the trick. Stretching in her bed, Fade caught sight of her. Her short white and turquoise hair was all tangled. "Good morning, Nix."

"Good morning, Fade. I just came to get you for breakfast."

"That was unnecessary, but thank you. I was going to order food into my room. Would you care to join me?"

"Yeah, that sounds nice. Thanks."

Fade smiled and left the cabin for a bit. When she returned, she jumped onto the bed and motioned Nix to sit on the chair. Right as she sat down, one of the dining car tables appeared in front of them. A green and gold plaid tablecloth lay over the surface of the table. On top of the tablecloth were two cups of coffee. Cheese omelets with salsa over them and a bowl of cut fruit sat on two plates.

"There is another reason why the brothers aren't particularly fond of me. Would you care to hear it?" Slightly caught off guard by her question, Nix motioned for her to go on.

"Well, you see the encounter which I had with them in my woods wasn't the first time in which I had met them. I happened to meet them when they were children. At the time, they looked quite different. They were in possession of no elaborate clothes but were dressed in near rags, and they had no markings on their faces. When I had met them, I was wandering through the carnival.

"I was just about to ride on the Ferris wheel when the brothers ran into me. The three of us accidentally fell into one of baskets. This turned out well for the brothers since they were running away from the manager. Apparently, they had burned one of his favorite umbrellas. This action held the punishment of death."

"Isn't that a little harsh?"

"Indeed, it was a harsh punishment, but the manager despised children. He would make any excuse to kill one. Back then, though, the brothers still didn't have a good grasp over the magic that they possessed. Likewise, they didn't have any weapons on them. While I was stuck in the basket with them, they explained the situation to me, and I agreed to help them.

"After I had helped them in escaping from the carnival, I offered to aid them with their magic. They accepted the offer, and I became their teacher. Once the two of them reached adulthood, however, they became rather obsessed with sickening ways to amuse themselves. Beforehand, they liked their amusement, but it hadn't progressed to an extreme state yet. Their first victim was the manager, who had terrorized them as kids. I found out about this and tried to dissuade them from the path they were headed on, but they clearly didn't listen."

"So, you stopped aging when you were a child, then?"

"Correct. Regardless, they had attempted to kill me since they didn't want me to interfere with their games later on but failed. This obviously created the tension between us."

"Why did you save their second plaything then, or rather why didn't you stop them?"

"I saved their second plaything because I had no ill will against her, so I didn't see any reason not to save her. I didn't stop them, though, because I had been their teacher. Even today, I don't wish them dead; I just wished that I would never see them again.

"Moreover, their actions seemed miniscule to the ones my sister committed. The brothers, though, think that I'm going to take you away from them, but I don't intend to do this. As you know, that isn't my intent for traveling with you."

"I would imagine that they also know that they owe their lives to you."

"Yes, I suppose that's another reason why they hate me. As you know, both brothers like to be in control of the situation; they don't like owing anything to anyone."

Taking a bite out of her omelet, she tried to picture Heart and Diamond in tattered clothes and without markings on their faces. It was a strange image indeed, especially picturing them as kids or being students to Fade. "Fade, you must know some interesting stories then about their childhood."

"I do. Why are you interested?"

"Frankly, I'm kind of stuck with them, so knowing a little more about them might be useful."

"That's a fair point. I suppose that I could tell you that one story. I'm sure that you don't know what the brothers fear, Nix. Well, ever since they were little, they have had a great fear of owls. I believe the fear started after several of the owls in my forest attacked them. Of course, the animals had good reason. The two brothers were trying to steal the eggs from the nest. The owls kept up their attack for several days since the owls there are quite fond of holding grudges should they have one. So if you ever want to get back at the brothers ..."

"So, this is where you have been, Miss Nix. We were waiting for you in the dining car," Diamond voiced, coming into the room and noticing that she had already eaten since her plate was now empty.

"I forgot to mention that I decided to have breakfast with Fade. I must say that I never expected her to be your teacher."

The male sent a scowl in Fade's direction while she merely ignored his gaze, but Nix could see the traces of a smile on her face. "What else did you tell her, Fade?"

"I just told her how I met you two and became your teacher. That's all unless you want me to tell her more."

Nix could tell that Diamond was clearly angered. He walked over to her, picking her up in the process. "Hey, what do you think you're doing?!" the dark brown-haired girl cried.

"Miss Nix, you'll be spending the rest of the time on the train with us."

Sighing, she waved goodbye at Fade, who returned the wave. Diamond closed Fade's cabin door behind him and carried her until they reached the lounge car on the train. He set her down in one of the gold and silver checkered armchairs. As he did so, she saw Heart entering the room from the engineer's car. The blue-haired male seemed to notice the dark look on Diamond's face. "Is something the matter, Diamond?"

"The child told our lover of our previous dealings with her."

Heart approached her quickly. Gripping her shoulders, he scanned her eyes. "Did she tell you anything else besides the fact that she was our teacher?"

"No," she lied, taking his hands off of her.

"Miss Nix, could you please not lie to us?"

"I honestly don't understand why you two are so worked up over this. It's not like I'm going to judge you two for having a teacher who has the appearance of a child. Honestly, I don't think you should've tried to kill her, though, especially after she saved your lives."

"If you think that we owe her our lives, then you're wrong. We owe her nothing; don't think we're weak merely because a child decided to teach us a few things," Heart argued.

"So, that's the reason. You don't want me to think either of you weak. If that's what you're worried about then you're wasting your time. Like I said, I'm not judging either of you, nor do I think either of you weak. Frankly, the most shocking part was picturing you two as children with no markings on your faces."

"Well, I suppose that's good to hear. Should you ever relay that information to anyone else, though, we'll not hesitate to punish you severely," Diamond warned while a threatening look remained in his eyes.

Rolling her eyes, she turned away from them and glanced out the window. The rest of the time the two brothers merely talked among themselves, trying to engage her in the conversation. On some of the topics, she would join in.

As the time passed, the chefs transported food to them in the lounge car since Diamond had went back and requested it to be so. So, she had a late lunch with the brothers, who attempted to feed her the meal. This only resulted in them spilling the chicken soup all over themselves, which she found quite amusing. Her quiet laughing, though, only caused the two to smile. Both of the brothers left, though, to change their attire.

When they returned, Heart had on a simple blue coat, black dress shirt, blue pants and blue-heeled shoes. Diamond had on something similar but in red and black. She noted that Heart wore a smirk, and Diamond had a smile on his lips, which only meant something bad. They never had the opportunity to perform their plan, though, since the train had now reached their destination. The train stopped abruptly, sending her flying towards the two brothers. Both held her up, preventing her from hitting the floor.

Fade soon entered the lounge car, and she gave Nix a reassuring smile. Nix returned the smile before she glanced out the window, catching sight of the sunhat girl's domain in the distance. Hopefully, things would go positively for them.

Chapter Thirty Seven: Look beneath the Surface

Standing at the entrance to the train, Nix stared out at the scenery before her. In the distance, there stood what looked like a castle surrounded by amusement park rides. At the moment, she could only see the outlines of the structures, but how were they supposed to reach the Land of Amusement? Water encircled the entirety of the sunhat girl's domain. If the water wasn't deep, she could walk through it, but something about the water seemed ominous. The setting sun casting shades of purples, blues, oranges, pinks and yellows across the expanse of water and clouds still didn't hide this effect since the large body of water was too still.

"Well, Miss Nix, are you ready?" questioned Diamond, standing just behind her.

"We're already here, and it will only be worse the longer I wait. I just desire this mess to be over with. There's the issue of crossing the water, though."

"Just walk onto its surface," answered the red-haired male as he stepped onto the water.

She was expecting him to sink into the water, yet he stood on top of it. Fade went out of the train next, but like usual she just hovered. Nix continued to eye the water suspiciously, however. "Fade, do you know if there is anything in the water?"

"There is, but that is why we should hurry across it before the monsters sense our presence."

"I can carry you across if you would like, my dear lady."

"Thanks, but that would slow you down. I'll be fine on my own feet," she responded as she stepped onto the water below. Like Diamond, she didn't sink into the water but stood on top of it. "How is this even possible?"

"It's a hardening spell. It's cast upon the water's surface and causes it to be more in a solid state; however, anything underneath the water's surface can still pull us beneath if the being in question tugs hard enough. Also if something above impacts the water hard enough, it'll fall through," Fade explained while Heart stepped out of the train.

Nix nodded in reply, and once Heart left the train, the train
closed its entrance door and went off into the other direction. With
the four of them off of the train, they all proceeded towards the
Land of Amusement. Clouds rolled past them over the water's
surface, making them occasionally walk through them. She felt no
moisture in the clouds. They just felt soft against her skin as though
she was lying under a warm plush blanket during winter, and she
almost followed the clouds into the unknown before Fade grabbed
her right arm, pulling her back. Her action seemed to wake Nix up
from a trance-like state as Nix realized that she was about to walk
into the darkening water beyond.

"Don't follow the clouds. They only lead to death," the small
girl warned before she released her grip.

"Noted," Nix remarked as she cast one more glance at the
unclear waters. To her horror, she saw glowing eyes staring at her.
She tugged on Fade's cloak, getting the girl's attention. When she
looked down at Nix, the dark brown-haired girl pointed out into the
distance. The eyes were gone, however, and Fade examined her
closely.

"Did you see something, Nix?"

"Yeah, there were eyes out there."

The two brothers heard Nix as well, and she could see them
rest their hands over the weapons at their sides. Fade's expression
didn't change, but there was a sense of urgency in her eyes. "They
have spotted us; we should increase our pace this instance," the
small girl informed.

Seeing no reason to argue, the four of them walked faster as a
strange glittery mist began to creep over the water and neared them.
Thankfully, the setting sun's light seemed to keep the mist at bay for
the moment. Among the sparkling mist, though, she couldn't tell if
she spotted more eyes or if it was only the mist.

A splash soon sounded behind them as did another. After the
two splashes, they stopped altogether. This only made them quicken
their pace across the water, but Heart stopped Nix. Looking up at
him, he signaled her not to make another noise. Reluctantly, she did
as he ordered and glanced around her.

Nothing seemed to happen for the longest time until, in the distance, she noted a fish tail swaying back and forth in the water. Gold eyes stared up at her, and she rested her hands over her daggers, ready to attack. A second went by before the creature jumped out of the water. Revealing itself, she didn't know what the creature was. It looked like a mermaid, but its top half was skinned. The creature had no teeth, just a gaping hole for a mouth. Its golden fish tail glittered in the sunlight, but there was nothing beautiful about it.

Ripping out her daggers, they made contact with the creature's throat and sliced it open. Green blood poured out as the creature fell back into the water. The blood spread throughout the water while Fade looked around her anxiously, looking for more of the creatures.

"I think that it's time we proceed forward. The blood will attract more," Diamond advised. Everyone else agreed, and they all ran across the water.

"My dear lady, you did well on defeating that mermaid," Heart complimented, matching her pace and running alongside her.

"Thank you. So, that was a mermaid. Why did it look so ..."

"So deformed? My sister dumped the corpses of her victims into the waters. Some of her victims had been poisoned, and that poison leaked into the water. The mixture of poison, blood and human flesh is what ruined the mermaids," Fade mentioned while Heart seemed slightly peeved that she had joined in on their conversation, but at least he understood that now wasn't the time for arguing. So, he remained quiet and glanced forward again.

Disgusted by Fade's explanation, Nix shook her head. In the process, she looked down momentarily. Glowing eyes gazed up at her. Startled, she halted her movement before stepping back a little. Diamond, Fade and Heart stopped as well to see what was wrong. The mermaid took this opportunity to spring out of the water. Its skinless hands latched onto Diamond's right arm, pulling him down into the water. Diamond had no time to react as he was forced partially under.

Heart ran towards his brother and grabbed his other arm, pulling him back up or at least trying to. Nix ran over to them and helped Heart with the task. The mermaid lost her grip and retreated deep into the water below. Now standing, Diamond rubbed his right arm, but he remained uninjured. Hearing a loud splash behind her, Nix turned around and found herself face to face with one of the mermaids, and the creature was ready to latch onto her face. Its foul breath made her wish to vomit, but the creature went limp as a blade pierced through its heart.

"Are you okay, Miss Nix?"

"Yeah, thanks."

Picking herself up, the four of them continued to run towards the approaching structures. The water and clouds were cast in a full shroud of darkness as the mist now ran over the surface of the water. "Whatever you do, don't breathe in that mist. If you do, you'll stand still in a trance, permitting the mermaids easier access to you," Fade alerted.

Immediately, Nix covered her nose and mouth. She didn't need to be eaten alive by a monstrous mermaid and dragged to the depths of the unknown. Luckily, they were now near the entrance. It stretched high into the sky, and its grand gold doors, embedded with topazes and opals, slowly opened. Solid ground lay beyond as well did the amusement park. They all ran faster due to the prospect of finally getting off of the dangerous waters.

Her feet carried her into the park as Diamond and Heart followed in behind her. Just as Fade was about to enter through the doors, a mermaid leaped out of the waters and pulled the girl down. Cursing, Nix ran back and latched onto Fade. In her attempt to rescue the petite girl, she accidentally breathed in the mist. Nix's body refused her commands, and her mind became clouded; all she desired to do was remain perfectly still. Heart and Diamond swiftly ran back out.

When Nix's grip on Fade failed, Heart darted forward and snatched the girl's left wrist. Diamond picked up Nix and ran back towards the entrance of the park while his brother applied more of his strength and wrenched Fade from the mermaid's grasp. Before the mermaid could attack again, he bolted into the park right with his brother, and the doors closed after them.

With Nix still in a trance, Diamond seated himself on his knees and laid her across his lap. "How long until this wears off?" he asked Fade.

"I'm not sure of the exact duration, but it should wear off in a little while," she reassured, standing guard with Heart.

As the duration lessened, the far off look in Nix's eyes began to disappear. A pink figure, however, began to approach the four while humming filled the air. Heart took a defensive stance in front of his brother and Nix. Fade tensed but prepared herself for a fight as well.

Chapter Thirty Eight: Riding to Darkness

Pink fluffy ears flopped behind the pink figure while the humming increased. Nix steadily recovered to her senses while her gaze shifted to the oncoming figure. Her vision was a bit blurred, but she could tell that it was a rabbit skipping on two legs. The giant pink rabbit stopped in front of them, but couldn't move closer due Heart and Fade blocking its path. It rested its hands on the blade of Heart's saber and looked down at Nix.

"My mistress sends her regards to you, Nix. She hopes that you enjoy your stay here. Also, she wants me to let you know that you'll regret bringing the brothers and her sister here. Now, it's time for me to say goodbye."

The humming grew louder, and the three born residents of the world dashed away from it. In the rush, Nix had little choice but to clutch onto Diamond's coat in order to steady herself some. While they ran away, a loud explosion sounded behind them. When they stopped, she peeked around Diamond, and the sight made her insides twist and turn. The rabbit was strewn over the entranceway while flames danced on some of the pieces.

"The rabbit must have been a fire user, and, probably, the fire burst from their center. That's a perfect demonstration of my sister's cruelty, however. She plays with her followers' minds so that they willingly kill themselves for her."

"Let's just go towards the castle. This path should lead us to her," Nix voiced, motioning for Diamond to set her down. Reluctantly, he did so, but only after she reassured him a few times that she was alright.

"I'm afraid that it's not going to be that easy, my dear lady," Heart uttered, pointing at the path ahead.

Up ahead, the path was blocked by a blue stone wall filled with glowing gems. Irritated, Nix looked for another way. All around her were lampposts, shining brightly in whites and pinks. Blue stone towers and walls decorated the amusement park while a red and orange Ferris wheel turned slowly. In the distance, she noticed a well lit roller coaster that wrapped around a pointed mountain. "Where do we go now?" she muttered since she couldn't see any new route.

"Miss Nix, I believe that we must enter that domed building."

She glanced to where Diamond was pointing and saw an archway leading into a blue stone domed building. There really was no other way. So, the four passed through the archway. Large doors, which had been opened inward, slammed shut behind them. Nix peered back and thought that she saw someone standing there for a moment, so she continued to stare at the space until she was satisfied that no one would reappear. With entrance now sealed off, though, they could only go forward. White lights illuminated the path up ahead and displayed a right and left path.

"Fade, do you have any idea about which path we should take?" she asked since both looked to be identical in appearance.

"Sadly, I don't. Under no circumstances, however, should we split up."

Sighing, Nix nodded in agreement. Splitting up would just allow the sunhat girl to pick each of them off one by one. With the similar paths ahead, she closed her eyes and tried to listen for any sound that would distinguish them. Only the sound of her companions' breathing hit her ears. That was the case until she picked up a sound coming from above them. Footsteps neared them and continued before the sound faded away.

Concerned, Nix looked to see if anyone else had noticed the sound. Fade had worry written on her countenance while both brothers had moved closer to Nix. "I suggest that we move forward and quickly," Diamond voiced, his left hand gripping the handle of his saber.

"I agree with my brother. I suspect that both paths lead to something terrible," Heart stated, wrapping his hand around the handle of his blade.

"Fine, let's go right, then. I can't tell any difference, so it's as good as choosing the left. Any objections?" Nix questioned, and her companions shook their heads. With that in mind, she stepped forward and headed down the right path.

When the brothers and Fade tried to follow her, they ran into an invisible wall. Both brothers banged against the glass, but Nix couldn't hear any of their attempts to break down the wall. While they tried to break through, the footsteps above sounded again. They were directly over her. She couldn't wait around for the brothers or Fade. If she didn't move, the thing creating the footsteps might break through the ceiling and attack. At least, she wouldn't put that possibility past her. So, she mouthed that she would be fine to the three and progressed down the stone path.

~ ~ ~ ~ ~ ~ ~ ~ ~ ~

The brothers banged against the wall, cursing while doing so. Fade muttered curses under her breath at her sister. When the brothers saw their lover walk away from them, they attacked the wall more fiercely, but it didn't work. They knew that a glass gate spell had been used, and only the individual who cast it could disable it, yet they still desired to break through the unbreakable wall.

"It looks like my sister is forcibly separating us. We have no choice but to go down the left path."

"Unfortunately, I must agree with you. We must go down the other path. It's the only way to reach our lover now," Diamond grumbled out, beyond vexed that the situation had taken such a turn.

Heart wasn't fond of agreeing with the girl either and sighed in frustration as he went down the left path. Diamond followed after his brother as did Fade. The hovering girl swore that she could hear her sister giggling somewhere in the building, though. Already, her sister was controlling their movements. It would seem that her sister was going to hold none of her tricks back.

~ ~ ~ ~ ~ ~ ~ ~ ~ ~

Nix had her hands constantly over her daggers, prepared to attack whatever came at her. Footsteps now sounded on the same path as her, making her raise her guard even more. They were slow and moved in rhythm with hers while the ones from before were quicker. When she looked behind her, she spotted no one there. This frustrated and worried her. How long would she have to endure that thing following her before it showed itself?

Focusing on the path in front of her, she still saw nothing new. Only more blue stone walls and white lights decorated the path ahead. She wouldn't be surprised if the tunnel continued on for forever; it sure felt like it. The footsteps still stepped in sync with her, however. Not being able to take it anymore, she turned around once again. "Will you just show yourself? I'm tired of you tailing me!" she yelled at the empty path behind her.

"So, your patience has finally tired. I didn't expect it to last so long," echoed a voice down the tunnel. Surprised that the thing responded to her, she looked around her and tried to find the owner of the voice. She felt hands rest on her shoulders and warm breath on her left ear. "Do you wish to fight me?" Unsheathing her daggers, she spun around, and her daggers sliced through air. "So, you do want to fight me. Well, let's make things much more interesting. Come and catch me~"

A man appeared in front of her, but she couldn't get a good look at him since he took off running in the other direction. She had no choice but to follow since going back would lead to a dead end. With this in mind, she took off after him. He continued to run ahead at a faster pace, and light began to flood into the tunnel. The man didn't stop, however, but disappeared.

Coming to a halt, she glanced at the large roller coaster before her. The sound of the coaster charging towards her resonated throughout the air, and her gaze darted to it. Before she could react, a hand reached out towards her and pulled her on. She was set down in one of the middle cars while she saw a form vanish next to her. In a few seconds, she spotted someone sitting up ahead of her. They had a purple top hat on, which was adorned with black roses. A black suit graced their form while long bleached blonde hair rested on their head.

"Well, don't you think this fighting ground is much more interesting?" he asked, turning around in his seat. Yellow eyes stared back at her while a grin spread on the man's lips. Frankly, Nix was just wondering how she would fight on a moving roller coaster.

The ride was now approaching the upside down part. She quickly looked for a strap to tie herself in but saw none. Sheathing her daggers, she gripped the ride. The roller coaster zoomed down the tracks, going upside down. She held on for dear life as she felt her body being lifted into the air. Soon, though, that part of the ride came to a close. When she looked for the man once again, she noticed that he was gone.

"I'm right beside you," he murmured into her right ear. Taking out one of her daggers, she slashed it through the air next to her. "Too slow, darling," he chuckled out. "Do tell me, though; how do you plan to beat my mistress if you can't even land a blow on me?"

With the tracks twisting around the mountain, she felt herself slide around in the seat as she attempted to steady her balance. She ignored the man's comment and looked around for him. "You have one chance to kill me before I attack, darling. I would suggest checking behind you."

Only turning her body slightly, she kept a firm grip on her dagger and raised it upwards. She focused her attention back to the front of her and brought her blade down. Finally, the blade made contact with the man. It nestled itself into his right arm, and blood leaked out of his arm, but he only grinned insanely. "My turn," he breathed out.

His yellow eyes shined as his left arm wrapped around her waist, bringing her closer to him. Due to this, she couldn't reach her other dagger nor retrieve the one from his arm. He whispered undecipherable words to her, and she could feel her consciousness slipping. As the roller coaster raced down the mountain, the man jumped out of the ride and tossed her unconscious body over his right shoulder.

Chapter Thirty Nine: Childhood of Flowers

Fade and the brothers continued down the blue stone tunnel, further frustration kicking in with every second. So far, the tunnel remained the same until at last they reached a turn in the path. Making it, they came across a flight of stairs heading downwards. The white lights faded away down the stairwell as they were replaced by dull orange ones.

Heart was about to travel down the cement steps, but Fade stopped him. "Let's throw something down first. Knowing my sister, these stairs are holding a trap."

"And, what do you intend to throw down there? I'm sure you've noticed that there are two barriers in place, and they happen to block both our teleportation and portal creation abilities. Your sister must have cast a specific portal creation and teleportation barrier spells on us at some point when we entered this area. So, we shouldn't waste time in throwing something down there. I don't know about you, but I want to retrieve my lover before something happens to her," Heart snapped back.

"You'll do no good if you die, so I'm asking you to listen to me once more. I want to reach her just as bad as you, and we're only wasting more time arguing about this."

"Heart, I'm sorry to say, but I agree with her. If we want to reach our lover in time, we must trust her."

Cursing silently to himself, Heart turned away from Fade. She took that as an agreement. Reaching into her cloak, she pulled out a small peppermint candy. Throwing it down the stairs, she waited to see what would happen. Upon hitting one of the steps halfway down the stairwell, spikes shot out from the walls with one of them piercing the tiny candy. With it stabbed, the spikes retracted back into the walls.

"It appears that as long as we don't touch any of the steps, we'll make it past the stairs alive," the girl mentioned, glancing to the two brothers.

"How exactly are we supposed to do that? We can't hover like you," Heart remarked as he rolled his eyes.

"Actually, you can. You just have to grab onto me, and you'll hover. This requires more of my energy, however, which I was hoping to save for my sister. It seems like I don't have a choice in the matter, though. I should've expected something like this to happen."

"So, we could have went across that sea of water without ever touching its surface?" the blue-haired jester questioned.

"It wouldn't have made a difference. The mermaids would have still noticed us before we reached the gates. Now, should we proceed forward, or continue talking at the top of these stairs?"

Casting a rude glance at Fade, Heart reluctantly grabbed Fade's shoulder while Diamond grabbed the other one. Displeasure was written all over the brothers' faces as the three of them hovered down the stairs. No spikes came out of the walls, and they safely landed at the feet of the stairs. Beyond lay another tunnel, except this one was all cement while the orange lights emitted even less light. Going down the tunnel, the three of them reached a turn in it.

After making the turn, the floor, ceiling and walls were covered in white paint while huge pink polka dots decorated it. Crystal light fixtures lined the walls. Despite the brightness of the area, it was anything but pleasant. The silence in the tunnel ended as the sunhat girl appeared at the end of it. Both of the brothers were about to charge, but Fade managed to pull them back. "She wants you to run at her. So, calm yourselves, otherwise all of us will be killed before we reach Nix," Fade warned.

Much to her relief, the brothers settled down some while the sunhat girl giggled a little. "I'm so glad that the three of you could join me in my domain. It's a shame that your dear doll can't be with you at the moment, but she is currently preoccupied."

"Where is she, child?" Diamond demanded.

"Why, she is resting in the arms of one of my faithful servants."

Metal soon glinted in the light of the hallway. "I suggest that you to tell your servant to keep his hands off her, or we'll make sure he suffers," Heart threatened.

"You two are so fun to mess with. I'm afraid, however, that I cannot take your suggestion. So, how about we play a game? Reach the end of this hallway before the timer runs out, and you'll see your precious doll again. You two always enjoy games; I hope you like this one." She proceeded to giggle continuously until her voice could be heard no more.

Once her voice became scarce, a huge cuckoo clock appeared behind Fade and the brothers. The hands on the clock began to move backwards, and it seemed like it was set for fifteen minutes. Cautiously, the brothers and Fade set off down the pink polka dot hallway.

~ ~ ~ ~ ~ ~ ~ ~ ~ ~ ~

Darkness surrounded her, and she felt herself falling through an endless void. There was no distinction between warm and cold; she couldn't feel anything except her limbs floating like a feather. Her dark brown hair swayed side to side as an unknown force created a resistance to her descent. This strange state continued on for some time before a faint light hit her dark brown eyes.

Her eyes opened slowly as grey clouds surrounded her. The air's temperature was just perfect. Still, she knew that the ground was approaching, yet she wasn't afraid. Grass, blowing lightly in the wind, greeted her from below.

At last, she reached the ground, and she fell softly onto the awaiting grassy floor. Resting on the ground, however, she found that her body proportions were quite different. She had the body of a five-year-old while a simple grey dress graced her form. Her feet were bare, but dirt couldn't stick to them; they remained perfectly clean. None of this bothered her, though. Nix only wanted to lay on the grass undisturbed for centuries to come; nothing else mattered to her at the moment.

Soon, though, she heard the sound of wheels turning. Childlike curiosity caused her to get on her feet. Her grey dress swayed in the wind as she surveyed her surroundings. In the distance, she could see something small pushing a huge wheelbarrow. Its rusty wheels creaked as it moved across the floor of the plain. She noticed that something bright and colorful grew out of the wheelbarrow.

Nearing it, she saw flowers of various kinds in the wheeled device. She ran up to it, and the wheelbarrow stopped. Resting her hands on the edge of the wheelbarrow, she stepped on her tippy-toes. Her dark brown eyes widened in happiness since radiant flowers greeted her vision. A grin found its way to her face as her hand reached out to grab a purple rose that was nestled in the center of the wheelbarrow. Blue, red and yellow butterflies circled her hands. When she went to grab the rose, a thorn pricked her right index finger.

"You should be more careful young miss. Roses may be pretty, but they're dangerous too. Let's find a different flower for you," advised a voice from the other side of the wagon. A small brown bear made its self apparent. Various flowers covered one side of its face while a black bow tie was tied around its neck.

"Who are you?" she inquired, finding the bear quite adorable.

"I'm whoever you want me to be young miss."

"Okay, be my friend and play with me." The bear nodded while reaching into the wheelbarrow for a flower. He pulled out an orange akita daffodil. When he handed it to her, she accepted it gratefully. "Can I ever have the rose?"

"No, young miss, remember that its dangerous. Now shall we play?"

"Mhm, but do you know where we can play?"

"Yes, take my hand young miss. We shall go to a place where only happiness exists."

"That sounds nice," she voiced as her innocent dark brown eyes stared at the flower.

Something about the flower seemed wrong, but a land filled with the promise of eternal joy seemed too wonderful to pass up. A land where she could always play filled her with excitement. She took the bear's paw, and, with her hand in his, he dove into the flowers, taking her with him. Colorful petals flew around them as the light around them increased.

No longer was the area painted in hues of grey. Bright green grass grew on the ground while pink and yellow flowers covered the earth as well. Streams of crisp clean water ran through the fields of flowers and grass. Orange and yellow butterflies dominated the air right above the flowers. Her bare feet landed on the soft grass while her small hand held the bear's soft paw.

Scanning the area, her grin widened as delight filled her being. Her hand disconnected from the bear's paw, and she ran over to the stream. She jumped happily into the water, letting the cool liquid run over her feet. The bear stood on the edge of the stream, and she splashed him playfully. Butterflies flew around her head, taking in the droplets of water that flew out of the stream.

Eventually, she got out of the water and lay on the grass, playing with the flowers around her. The bear handed her flowers while she twisted them into a crown. Once finished with her headpiece, she smiled in utter delight at the final product. Grabbing it from her small hands, the bear placed the crown on her head. "It suits you, young miss."

"Thank you, but something is missing."

Her mind kept traveling back to the purple rose. It may have been dangerous, but maybe that's why it intrigued her. She wanted to take the risk of pulling it from the wheelbarrow. It called to her like it was hers and only hers: hers to claim. Curiosity tugged at her from every side and angle, but a voice pulled her back to the field of flowers and grass.

"What's missing young miss? Let me, your friend, assist you."

Staring at the bear, her thoughts of the purple rose evaporated from her mind. "Nothing, this crown works perfectly." The bear smiled at the statement as the two of them continued to play. A crown lay upon her head, but it didn't shine; it only tainted her.

Chapter Forty: Danger over Serenity

Their feet pounded against the pink polka dot floor as multiple traps attacked them. Bursts of fire would go off if they stepped on the white space of the ground in certain areas. Further down the hallway if they stepped on the dots then spikes would shoot up from ground and ceiling, stabbing whatever was on the dot. Fade and the brothers had no choice, but to progress down the hallway slowly. Time wasn't on their side, however, and the clock had gone from fifteen minutes to eight.

Upon reaching the eight minute mark, the pink dots on the ground started to move. Faceless creatures emerged from the ground, walls and ceiling. They had the appearance of a person covered in a pink body suit. They crawled on all fours, and their bodies contorted in ways not possible. An acidic substance leaked from their bodies. Seeing the creatures, the brothers unsheathed their sabers, ready for attack.

"This is ridiculous, they're blocking our path. Do you know some way to get around them?" Heart asked, looking to Fade.

"No, we just have to plow our way through them and run for the end of the hallway. Surely, you noticed that we don't have time to fight all of them."

"Of course, I noticed that."

"Then, let's move."

"Please, tell us that you have some way of fighting too," Diamond remarked, glancing to the small girl.

"I was your mentor. Of course, I have a way of fighting without using too much energy." Not a second later, she allowed vines to wrap around her right and left hands, allowing her hands to act like claws. With weapons ready, the three cut and sliced through the creatures. In doing so, blood painted the white walls while acid ate through parts of the hall. There was no end to the creatures, though. They kept coming out of the walls, but the end of the hallway was in sight.

They had almost reached it when one of the creatures jumped Heart. The two of them collided to the floor as other creatures slowly made their way up to them. Diamond halted his movement only to run over to his brother to aid him. Stabbing the creature in the heart, Diamond pulled the creature's body off his brother. Acid ate at Heart's jacket, making him quickly pull it off. Fade had run ahead in order to reach the end of the hallway in time.

She had managed to make it and was currently waiting anxiously for the brothers. There was one minute left on the clock. As the seconds ticked by, the brothers rushed towards the door. Before they could reach the door, one of the creatures had pinned Fade against the wall. Acid ate away at her dress sleeves and was about to reach her skin. With a blast of air, she shot the creature off of her. She proceeded to tear her sleeves off of her dress as the acid continued its work on the cloth.

Ten seconds were left on the clock, and the brothers had just made it to the door. The three of them hurriedly opened the door and shut it behind them. A huge explosion sounded in the hallway behind them. Up ahead, the three spotted a stairwell heading upwards and an orange door. Hesitantly, they neared the door. Fade rested her hand on the doorknob, turning it steadily. When the door opened, they gazed down upon the amusement park. A glass path stretched out before them. It led across the amusement park, heading directly for the sunhat girl's castle.

"There's no need to be afraid. I promised that I'd let you see your plaything, and you won my little game. Please, proceed ahead on the path which I have given you," called the sunhat girl from the other end of the walkway.

The sunhat girl smiled her wicked smile before turning on her heel and disappearing. Fade was the first one to step out onto the path, for if it was a trap, she could always hover in the air, preventing a fatal fall. When her feet hit the glass walkway, though, nothing happened; it remained quite solid. With the path safe, she once again returned to hovering. Both brothers walked onto the path after her, deciding that the path was indeed safe to walk upon. All of them made their way across the glass walkway as white and pink lights sparkled below them.

Heels clicked against the glass as the brothers followed Fade down the path. The air grew cold with the growing night, and more clouds rolled across the sky. Diamond tapped his long painted nails against the sheath of his saber as concern washed over him. Fade wrapped her cloak around her, and Heart placed his hands in his pants' pockets.

Soon a blue door came into view. Reaching the door, Heart turned the knob and revealed a well polished throne room. Gold-tiled floor sparkled under the bright light of an orange crystal chandelier. There were no windows in the room, yet orange velvet drapes hung all around the circular space. Gold stairs led up to an elaborate gold throne chair, which had orange velvet cushions on it. Upon the chair sat the sunhat girl. Her golden hair shined brightly under her sunhat. Brown eyes sparkled in delight as a wicked grin lay on her face. An orange dress graced her form. She giggled in joy when she saw the brothers angered expressions, for the brothers currently had their gaze on two other people in the room.

A man with long bleached blonde hair and yellow eyes held Nix's sleeping form in his arms. Her head rested against his shoulder as her chest fell and rose peacefully. The cloak that had been wrapped around her shoulders was used as a blanket. She slept serenely while the man stroked her dark brown hair. This sight sent the brothers into a rage of fury.

"Release her immediately, or do I have to cut off your arms?!" Heart commanded, drawing his saber.

"I suggest that you comply with my brother's demand. I show no mercy to those who touch what's ours," Diamond threatened as his gaze turned to one of bloodlust.

The man holding Nix merely disregarded the brothers and turned to his mistress. She smiled at him and nodded her head. A grin became painted on the man's face as he set her body against the sunhat girl's chair. He lifted her chin up with his left fingers, bringing his face closer to hers. Without a moment's hesitation, the brothers charged at him. Dodging their attack, the man jumped to the other side of the room and landed on his two feet perfectly; however, the brothers were now standing next to their lover's sleeping form. When Heart reached out to her, he instantly pulled back for a scythe landed between him and Nix. The weapon quickly vanished, and the twins glanced over to the male from before.

"Do you think that I would let you obtain your plaything so easily? She's mine now. Besides, you two shouldn't ignore my servant, Skull. You should worry about him at the moment."

Noting that the male had teleportation abilities, the brothers created some distance from them. They were weaker without their magic, but they still were superb fighters. Not only this but also one of them could cast a specific teleportation barrier on the male while the other fought him.

So when the man darted at them, Heart took him head on while Diamond moved back towards the door and started to work on casting the spell. Skull noticed and teleported over to the male. Heart cursed and cast a glass gate spell. The enemy's blade made contact with the small glass wall in front of Diamond. The bleached-blonde male teleported away from the area and behind Heart, and Heart managed to block the male's next attack. As the brothers fought with Skull, insanity shined in their eyes. They only wanted to get their lover back, and they wouldn't let the sunhat girl's servant stand in their way. He would die as his blood painted the walls of golden room.

While the brothers fought, Fade stared at her sister. Her cold eyes met her sister's insane ones. "I never thought that you would visit me, Fade. Have you finally decided to kill me?"

"I refuse to let you escape to Nix's world, where you can ruin the lives of more people. They're not yours to control Chroma! There will be no sacrifice today!"

The sunhat girl's eyes narrowed, and all humor left her face. She hadn't heard her real name said in ages, and it disturbed her greatly. A sickening grin plastered itself to her face as she got out of her chair. Fade prepared herself for battle while her sister descended the steps from her throne. When the second battle in the room took place, Nix still lay in slumber.

~ ~ ~ ~ ~ ~ ~ ~ ~ ~ ~

Nix watched the clouds roll by as a yellow butterfly flew around her face before landing on her nose. Her dark brown eyes examined it curiously while the bear laid out a picnic blanket for the two of them. When it was laid out, tea and cookies rested on top of it. Sitting up, she went over to the blanket and sat down next to the bear. Before she could put one of the jelly filled cookies in her mouth, though, she noticed two figures playing on the other side of the stream. Two kids her age were fighting with wooden swords. One had baby blue hair, and the other had blood red hair. Both wore no shoes and had simple clothes on. Tan peasant shirts rested on their shoulders while brown baggy shorts covered their legs.

"Who are they?" she asked the bear, who was sitting next to her.

"It doesn't matter. They don't concern you. Let's just enjoy this picnic."

"But, they seem so similar. I want to share some food with them," she uttered, standing up.

Her small hands reached for the plate of jelly filled cookies, but the bear stopped her. "They're dangerous, young miss. Please, stay here. Remember what I told you about the rose?"

"I don't care. I want to talk to them. Mr. Bear, don't stop me!"

Pulling away from the bear, she took up the plate of cookies, went towards the stream and intended to cross it. The bear, however, grabbed her and knocked the plate of cookies from her hands. "I can't let you go near them. You'll stay here, young miss," he ordered as the flowers on his face began to fall.

"Mr. Bear, I told you not to stop me, and, now, you ruined the cookies. You're being rather mean right now. You can always cross the stream with me and greet them as well."

"No, they're dangerous, and I won't let them win."

More flowers fell from his face; only a few remained.

"What do you mean by win? Are you in some contest with them? Tell me, Mr. Bear!"

"That doesn't matter to you, and I told that you that I won't let you escape."

The last flowers fell, revealing a face of rot. In parts of the bear's face, bone showed while rotten flesh clung to the bone. There was no eye in the socket, only the remnants of dead flesh. She backed away from the bear. Fear took over her small body, and she darted into the stream's water. The bear chased after her and latched onto her legs. This made her fall and land in the water.

Water soaked her as she fought against the bear. She somehow managed to throw the bear off of her. With the bear off, she bolted for the two boys playing. Taking a quick glance behind her, she saw that the bear had crumbled into a pile of bones and rot. While being disturbed by the image, she threw the crown from her head and left the corrupted object behind.

Chapter Forty One: Remember the Rose

Nix's small bare feet ran through the field of flowers as water dripped from her. The two boys playing were now very close. Not being able to remain quiet anymore, she called out to the two of them. For some reason, she had their names on the tip of her tongue, but she couldn't say them. Now standing only a few inches from them, they turned their attention over to her. Dark blue and fire-red eyes stared at her. Their eyes examined her before they glanced at each other.

"Who do you think she is brother?" asked the blue-haired boy.

"I don't know, but I think that we should keep her," the other answered.

"That sounds like fun; she is cute."

"Agreed, but what should we play first?"

At this point, she was getting frustrated with the two. They were acting like she wasn't there, and they made her sound like some possession. "You know that I can hear you!" she yelled at them with her fists clenched.

The blue-haired boy merely smirked while the red-haired boy smiled. They gave no reply to her, and they just continued to look amused by her outburst. "You know; I came over here to greet you two, yet you act like I'm not here. I was even going to bring you cookies, but they got ruined. I'm glad that they got ruined now!" she exclaimed, turning away from them.

"Don't go. We do want to play with you," the blue-haired boy called out.

"Yes, we haven't had someone to play with in awhile," the red-haired one added.

"Diamond, Heart, you're so frustrating," she muttered, surprised that she suddenly could say their names.

~~~~~~~~~~~

The scythe barely missed Diamond as Skull swung the weapon at the brothers. They had been at the fight for five minutes already after they had managed to put a specific teleportation barrier on Skull. It was a surprise for the male to be so powerful. Already, the blonde-haired man had several wounds, but he just kept coming. He kept shouting that he would please his mistress whatever the cost to him. This will to keep fighting made the battle more difficult for the brothers. Both of the twins had been expecting something that would end in a couple of minutes, but, clearly, they had underestimated him. If they had access to all of their magic, the male before them would've been dead already.

Still, Skull hadn't landed a single hit on them, and he would most likely not survive too many more wounds even if he was boiling with determination to win. Growing impatient, though, Heart grabbed a handful of the orange drapes and tore them off. He waited for Skull to approach him. Just before the scythe could fatally wound him, he dodged the attack and landed behind Skull. Taking the sheet, he wrapped it around Skull's head. With their opponent blinded, Diamond took the opportunity presented to him.

Skull swung the scythe's blade around furiously, trying to see once again, before he stopped and tried to listen for the brothers' movements. The male heard footsteps charging towards him and went to swing his scythe, but his weapon fell to the ground due to his loss of grip. His scream was muffled as he dealt with the pain of losing his hands. He turned back to the fast footsteps and knew that this would be the end of him. A couple of seconds passed before Diamond severed the man's head from his body. As the head rolled across the golden tile, the body fell to the ground, allowing a pool of blood to form around it.

During the brothers' fight, Fade was battling her sister. The odds weren't looking in favor of Fade. Only a few minutes had passed, which was enough to leave Fade battered and bruised. Her sister only had a few scrapes on her. Both of them possessed air magic, so neither could use air without the other deflecting it completely. Fade had earth magic, but her sister was a teleporter along with being a sorceress. If the brothers finished their fight before her, they could cast a barrier on her sister. Still, she needed to weaken her sister enough to where Nix could deliver the final blow if she needed to.

At the moment, Fade attacked her sister with vines which were both wrapped around her hands and sprung from the ground. Chroma would teleport from every attack and deliver a kick or punch to Fade before she could react in time. Only a few times had Fade reacted in time. After probably a little over five minutes of fighting, Fade's eyes glanced over to the brothers again. They had completed their battle, and their attention was back on Nix. She needed to get their attention over to her, but that wouldn't be easy since she couldn't make her objective known to Chroma.

She dodged a kick from her sister and grew some vines over by the brothers. Fade received a punch in the stomach from her sister next, but she continued to focus some on the vines. When she glanced to the twins again, she saw them glance over to her. They glanced to each other before nodding to her, and both of them focused on casting the spell, for Fade had written *barrier on my sister* in vines on the ground.

While the brothers worked on the spell, Fade could feel her energy deplete. Chroma had delivered a powerful kick to her right side, and she was picking herself up from the ground. When Chroma went to transport again, she found that she couldn't. The blonde-haired girl seemed surprised, and Fade smiled. Now, the fight would be easier. Fade glanced over to the twins and mouthed a thank you to them.

"Ah, depending on your past apprentices to help you in your fight. How pathetic," Chroma chuckled out as she began to close the distance between Fade and her. "I'll still win in this fight. You're too weak, and I can just cast a spells to stop you. Then, I'll kill the twins for killing my servant, or, maybe, I'll hold onto the younger and make him suffer an eternity without his older brother."

"That's not going to happen. I'll stop you before you can accomplish any of that," Fade countered, having the vines disappear from her hands. She placed her hands on the ground and had all the other vines disappear. In the next second, she caused them to all break through the ground and form a cage around her sister. Summoning the rest of her energy, Fade darted forward and leaped before a glass gate blocked her.

Jumping into the air, Fade looked down at her caged sister and shot vines from her hands towards her. Chroma's eyes grew wide, and she summoned a vast quantity of air to her hands, shooting it at the vine cage. The blonde-haired girl made it out of the cage just in time, but a few of the vines had cut her on the legs significantly. Before Chroma could recover, Fade bolted towards her sister. A vine went to aim for Chroma's heart, but she dodged and ended up being whacked in the left side. The girl slid across the tile and into her throne chair while Fade collapsed to the floor, exhausted. As the chair wobbled back and forth due to Chroma's impact, blood seeped down Chroma's head, and her eyes fell shut.

After the brothers had aided Fade, they became only concerned with Nix. They ran over to her and were relieved to find her still unharmed. Her body was unnaturally cold, though. Diamond and Heart called out her name, trying to wake her up. A light chuckle came from the throne chair. The two brothers instantly cast their gaze at the owner of the laugh. Chroma giggled, and a grin painted her face.

"She's trapped in a dream world. Even with my servant dead, the only way she can now escape is if she breaks out on her own. Skull could've let her out, but he's dead now, and he wouldn't have listened to any of your demands. So, she's as good as dead. And then, her sacrifice will activate the spell seal over our heads, and its activation will allow me to travel to her world to conquer it. Even if you two manage to kill me, she will still die!"

Fade looked beyond despair hearing this news. As for Heart, he stood up and walked over to the sunhat girl. He brought his saber down on her, but she summoned four glass walls around herself to allow her time for recovery. The sunhat girl continued to laugh while Heart tried to destroy the walls even if he knew his efforts were in vain. Diamond stayed by Nix's side and rested his head on her right shoulder, whispering in her ear for her to wake up. He pulled her body closer to him as if the action would wake her up somehow. Nothing seemed to work, though, as she continued to remain motionless.

~~~~~~~~~~~~

"She said our names brother," Heart mentioned.
"Yes, I guess that it's time she left then, Heart."

"What do you mean? I just got here. I don't even know how I know your names." The two twins shook their heads at her before standing at her sides: Diamond on her right and Heart on her left. They each gave her a quick kiss on her cheeks, and she felt her face heat up. "Hey, you can't just do that!"

They didn't answer her as they backed away from her. Suddenly, the field began to disappear around her. As the ground crumbled, the two brothers waved at her before they vanished as well. Scared at what was happening, she covered her eyes and waited for the earth to suck her in. Nothing of the sort happened, however. Instead, she still felt grass at her feet. Hesitantly, she uncovered her eyes and found herself back on the grey grassland.

With the clouds rolling by overhead, she heard the sound of wheels turning. In the distance, she saw the wheelbarrow of flowers once more. This time she would claim the purple rose. Running up to it, it stopped its movement. The same teddy bear came around the wheelbarrow to greet her. She wouldn't listen to it, though, and her hand reached for the purple rose.

"Young miss; you should get a different flower."

"No, I decide my own fate. You're not my friend, and you don't bring happiness. I will pick the flower that I want."

The bear looked angered by her comment and grabbed for her wrist. She had already reached the purple rose, though. Clasping it, she felt a thin trickle of blood run down her hand. It hurt, but she kept the rose firm in her grip. Pulling the rose from the wheelbarrow, she watched as the wheelbarrow and the teddy bear vanished from the grey world. She brought the rose to her lips, letting it glide over them. Its soft petals tickled them.

"Do you remember now?" asked Diamond.

"Yeah," she replied, now gazing at the two twins, who reappeared before her.

"Good, because your ours, my dear lady."

Nix rolled her eyes and watched as the world vanished once more. Darkness claimed her. A gush of wind rushed through her, and she opened her eyes. There was something warm next to her. Her dark brown eyes fell on a familiar man with blood red hair. Diamond hadn't yet realized that she was awake, and she could hear him muttering her name while his head rested on her shoulder.

"Soon, she will be dead. It' so much fun watching you all suffer. You know; I never would've thought that you two would become so attached with one of your playthings. Then again, I guess that I fueled your obsession with her. It's funny how I'm the one who brought her to you, yet I'll be the one to take her away."

"Be quiet child! Open your mouth for me, and I will slice off that tongue of yours," Heart exclaimed as he continued to slash at the wall.

She could hear Heart breathing heavily and could tell that he was exhausted. Diamond's grip on her loosened while he turned his gaze to the sunhat girl "You're one foolish child to think that you'll take her away from us," Diamond remarked while an ominous presence hung around him, and she could feel his grip on her tighten once again.

"No, you're the foolish one. Your calls for your plaything do you no good. She can't hear you. She's trapped in a dream world where you two don't exist."

"Actually, you're wrong on both those points. I can hear them quite fine and even in that dream world of yours I couldn't get rid of them," Nix countered, deciding it time to talk.

Everything in the room went silent as everyone's gaze turned towards her. She smiled inwardly at seeing the brothers' shocked faces. She smirked at the sunhat girl, however, as she saw anger flare up in the girl's brown eyes. The dream world couldn't make her forget the past and present, for she remembered every detail of it.

Chapter Forty Two: Sun or Light

"What ... how? What do you mean that the brothers were still in the dream world; that's impossible!" Chroma shouted, rising from her chair.

"Obviously, it wasn't. Apparently, you couldn't even understand the magic that was cast on me. Your servant was a dream sender, right? I read about that ability in one of the brothers' spell books. Surely, you know that the dream is formed from my memories, thoughts, dreams, etc.? Maybe, you should've treated Skull better, and he would've informed you of such a simple detail."

The sunhat girl fumed while droplets of blood fell from her head. Nix went to grab her daggers, but they were gone. Cursing, she saw the sunhat girl smirk slightly. "Can't find your weapons, my doll?"

As the sunhat girl walked towards her, with a knife in hand, she looked for something to defend herself with. In the process, she saw Fade breathing heavily on the tile a ways away from her. Seeing Fade's condition and the sunhat girl's injury, she put two and two together. Turning her attention back to the sunhat girl, she noticed that the girl was only a few inches from her. Before her attack could hit her, two sabers blocked it.

"So we were even in your dreams? I'm flattered, my dear lady."

"Indeed, I'm always pleased to be in your dreams, Miss Nix."

Nix rolled her eyes, knowing that they would torment her with this fact for quite some time. The sunhat girl, however, had backed away some and looked prepared for another strike. The brothers formed a protective shield around Nix and waited for the girl's next attack.

Chroma charged at them and leaped into the air. The brothers jumped up to attack, but she used a blast of air to push them away. Diamond flew to the right and Heart the left. She now descended upon Nix. Running forward in order to dodge her attack, Nix watched as the brothers recovered themselves to their feet. She turned on her heels and spotted whirls of blues, reds and oranges in front of her.

The brothers, however, made a miscalculation on Chroma's next spot of attack. She took this opportunity to blast air at both of them. In that instant, both brothers went flying in opposite directions again. They collided with the golden walls in such a way that knocked them unconscious. Turning her eyes onto Nix, Chroma approached Nix slowly as she threw the knife away. Nix was puzzled by her action until she saw the sunhat girl pull out two daggers from her dress pockets. Upon seeing them, Nix instantly recognized them as hers.

"I thought that it would be fitting to kill you with your own weapons, my little puppet. I really want to see your blood drip from your own blades. Now, stay still for you're only a doll."

At that moment, she ran for the brothers, the closest being Heart. The sunhat girl chased after her, laughing. Reaching Heart, she picked up the saber that lay by his side. Nix turned just in time to see the sunhat girl, bringing the daggers upon her. Blocking her attack with the saber, Nix kicked her in the gut and sent her sliding across the room. It was surprising that the sunhat girl wasn't blasting her with air, but, maybe, that last attack on the brothers had exhausted her. Peering closer at her opponent, Nix noted how tired she looked. Well, her opponent had a fight with both her sister and the brothers, so it made sense.

Turning to look at Nix, she glared intensely. "I may be weakened, but I'm still stronger than you, puppet! I will kill you and all your three companions as well. I hate all of you; I will make all of you suffer!"

An insane laughter left her lips, and the sunhat girl made her way over to Diamond. Immediately, Nix knew what she was about to do. Nix's feet pounded against the gold tiled floor as she ran towards the two of them. As she raised the dagger above Diamond's chest, she charged at the sunhat girl. She brought the saber down on the girl, but the girl blocked her attack. Nix had stopped her from killing Diamond, though.

Swiping one of the daggers, Chroma knocked the saber from Nix's hands before bringing the daggers upon her. Grabbing her wrists, Nix prevented the daggers from plunging into her, though; the blades were mere inches from her. Attempting to kick the sunhat girl in the gut again, Nix instead lost her balance and caused both of them to fall.

The daggers fell out of the child's hands. Seeing the opportunity presented to her, her hands seized up her daggers. Before she could stab the sunhat girl, Chroma darted for her discarded knife. Nix chased after her, but she picked up the knife before Nix could reach her. Chroma ran at her once more, but Nix dodged her next attack.

Tripping Nix in the process, Chroma brought a side kick to Nix's gut and kicked her into the throne chair. Upon impact, the chair crashed to the tile with Nix in it. While Nix coughed up blood, the sunhat girl came at her once more. Nix quickly utilized the chair as a shield and heard the knife tear at the fabric of the chair.

Running out from behind the chair, she saw the sunhat girl turning around to meet her. When Nix went to stab her, she missed and ended up knocking off her hat. Cursing, she threw herself to the ground when the sunhat girl made for another strike. With a lower attack position, Nix struck at the girl's ankles. Chroma didn't react fast enough, and one of the daggers made contact with Chroma's right ankle. She cried out, and Nix utilized that moment to strike at her other ankle. Hitting the sunhat girl again, the girl fell backwards.

Getting to her feet, Nix went to make a final blow, but her attack was deflected. Chroma brought her knife across her left arm and muttered something under her breath before the daggers reached her. A scythe appeared in her hands, and she smirked. "I didn't think that I would have to use my queen's weapon true form on you, but you will now stand no chance!"

Having no idea what she meant by queen's weapon, Nix backed up some and looked to the intimidating scythe. Nix reminded herself that it was just a larger blade than the last. It had its weaknesses, and she could still win. She had to win; otherwise everyone else's efforts would've been in vain. Holding the daggers up, she waited for the sunhat girl to come at her.

When the girl ran forward, Nix's eyes watched the blade and blocked with both of her daggers. Chroma proceeded to attack with the handle of the weapon, and Nix deflected it some, but she was pushed back some by the force. Nix managed to block the next attack as well, and she jumped back some.

Coming at Nix again, Nix blocked again and realized that she needed to make an offensive attack. She couldn't defend forever. Her stamina was fading, and she didn't know how long she would last against the girl. So, she put more strength behind her block and began to push back on the scythe. Before Chroma could create some distance between them, Nix lifted up her right knee and kneed the girl in the lower region. The sunhat girl cried out, and Nix noted that her grip on the scythe had loosened some.

Bringing her left leg up, Nix kicked downward and knocked the scythe from the girl's hands. She proceeded to kick it across the room. Nix knocked the sunhat girl to the ground and lowered herself to her. The dark brown-haired girl stabbed the daggers into the sunhat girl's wrists, holding her down. "Before I kill you, answer me this. Why did you come into my music box?"

She laughed insanely. "Isn't it obvious, doll? It's because I sensed a great amount of strength in you. I don't know what power is within you, but it's there, and I wanted it. Yes, I needed someone from your world to enter your world completely, but I also needed someone with great power in them. However, you're nothing special in my eyes. Only I hold power; only I control all. Only me, you're nothing; you're a doll, and you're my puppet!"

More laughter burst from her lips as Nix removed her daggers and brought them down on her heart. The girl soon faded into nonexistence. Upon her death, her daggers suddenly seemed to hold energy in them. Confused, she felt the need to put them together. Doing so, a bright light filled the area, and a purple sword appeared in her hands. A handle was in the middle while three glowing purple blades rested on the opposite ends of the handle.

Shocked, she didn't know what to make of this. What did the sunhat girl mean by her holding some power? Was this it? And, what was a queen's weapon? How was that different from a normal weapon? Her gaze turned to her three companions, and she saw the brothers beginning to wake up.

They got to their feet, and, soon, their heels clicked against the ground. A couple of moments went by before the brothers were kneeling in front of her. Heart had his left hand over his heart while Diamond had his right placed over his.

She looked at them shocked. Were they actually bowing in front of her? Disconnecting the blade and placing her daggers back in their sheaths, she glanced between the two brothers. Her cheeks became slightly warm as she suddenly felt awkward.

"To think that you would become a queen, my dear lady, it's truly remarkable."

"We're honored to have a queen as our lover, Miss Nix."

Words couldn't leave her lips as she was still in shock at their behavior. Both brothers stood up, each taking one of her hands in theirs. Each kissed the top of the hand that they held before releasing their grip on her. The brothers glanced at each other before turning their attention back on her.

"Nix, surely you understand that your still ours though right?" Heart asked. No answer left her lips while she stood frozen in place. He just called her by her first name. Just hearing her name leave his lips left her still. It sounded odd coming from him, yet at the same time she liked it.

"I think that you left our queen speechless, brother. Am I right, Nix?" Now even Diamond was calling her just by just her first name. There was no miss added to it, and it was nice to hear for once.

"I don't want to spoil you too much, my dear lady. I'll only call you by your first name when I think that you deserve it," he stated with a smirk on his face.

"I must agree with my brother, Miss Nix."

Before she could say anything or ask any questions, the ground beneath them started to shake as pieces of the ceiling began to fall onto the gold tiled floor. Her eyes landed on Fade, who was hunched over on the floor. She could tell that the girl couldn't move at the moment. Nix quickly darted over to her and called the brothers over. "Can one of you take Fade?"

Both brothers looked equally displeased by the request, but Diamond eventually tossed her over his right shoulder. Fade gave Nix a look of gratitude while glaring at Diamond for handling her so harshly.

"Fade, do you know what's happening here?" Nix asked, glancing at the shaking floor.

"With my sister gone, this place can longer hold itself up. She had built it using a series of spells. So, it's collapsing as we speak. We must hurry out of here."

As soon as the words left Fade's mouth, the four of them ran out of the throne room through the golden double doors that stood at the head of the room, with the brothers retrieving their weapons before they all left. Upon opening the doors, they ran across the glass path. The castle crumbled and fell apart behind them. Even the glass path was starting to break. Everyone's feet darted across it.

Once the path came to an end, Heart picked up Nix and tossed her over his left shoulder as both brothers hopped onto the roof of the building that the path led into. They began to hop across the rooftops until they reached the entrance to the Land of Amusement. By the time, they were at the entrance, though, the doors had already crumbled. This revealed the ocean of water beyond. No train laid in the distance, however, only water and the glittery mist. Luckily, the mist wasn't coming into the amusement park.

"How are we supposed to get out of here? When will the train arrive?" Nix questioned, trying to ignore the fact that she was on Heart's shoulder.

"We'll have to wait for the next train."

Looking back out at the water, she searched it for the mermaids that lived beneath its surface. She may now be considered a queen in this world, but she still hadn't gained any magic capabilities except for the queen's weapon. It still made little to no sense to her. Sighing in frustration, she looked at the brothers to see if they had any ideas. Sadly, they seemed as troubled as her.

Not knowing what else to do, Nix signaled for Heart to set her down since they were now on ground level. He reluctantly did so, and she unsheathed her daggers and formed the queen's weapon. She had no idea what she was doing, but she felt that the energy in the weapon could somehow help them. Plunging the blade into the pink stone walkway, a light surrounded the four of them. As the Land of Amusement fell apart, the ground underneath them stayed in one piece.

"Well, this seems to be working," she stated as water started to overtake the sinking rubble. When they returned to the castle, she would have to study this weapon's capabilities more, especially since it seemed that Chroma's queen's weapon appeared normal in comparison to hers.

"Miss Nix, it does look like it's working, but will you be alright holding it up for awhile?"

"We have no choice right? It's either this or be eaten by mermaids."

Diamond merely nodded his head in reply and set down Fade. As time ticked away, she could feel herself growing weaker. By the time the train reappeared, she was drained. After disconnecting the blade and sheathing her daggers, she saw only a glimpse of the train before she blacked out. She wanted nothing more than to sleep, however, and, so, she welcomed it.

Chapter Forty Three: Crowning Glory

Waking up, she found herself wrapped in soft purple sheets while pillows were under her head. Blinking a couple of times, she took in her surroundings and found herself back in her bedroom at the brothers' castle. She sat up and discovered that she was in checkered black and purple flannel pajamas. She was worried at first, but soon found Woodlily kicking her tiny legs back and forth on the fireplace mantel.

"I'm assuming that you changed me, Woodlily."

"Yep, I was also told to wait for you until you woke up. You've been sleeping in bed for a day and a half. I've been quite hungry, but Aberrous has given me some food while I've been waiting for you."

"Thank you for waiting. I'm going to go clean myself up, however."

She nodded and flew out of the room. Once Nix completed her morning routine, she got back into her pajamas since she was too lazy to wear anything else. Nix put her wet hair up in a clip before grabbing a bathrobe from her wardrobe. Wrapping it around her, she placed some slippers on her feet and went out of her room after grabbing her daggers from the top of the fireplace.

Now somewhat familiar with the castle, she walked onwards until she reached the entrance hall. Something caught her off guard, however, when she entered it. Instead of the severed throne, a new one sat in its place. The chair had a golden rim with intricate details on it while it was cushioned in purple velvet. Walking up to the chair, she ran her fingers over the right arm of the chair. The velvet felt smooth under her fingers.

"It's good to see you finally up, my dear lady." Hearing Heart's voice, she glanced over her shoulder to see his hair in a mess. He wore simple black pants and his blue peasant shirt. The male had probably just woken up as well. "You know; you can sit in the chair if you want. It's yours after all. My brother and I thought our queen needed a proper throne." Moving around the arm of the chair, she sat down and made herself comfortable. "How is it?" he asked, coming closer to her.

"It's quite comfortable. I really didn't need a throne chair, though. Anyway where is Fade? Is she back in the forest?"

"Sadly, she's still here and is recovering."

"She's in the guest room by the dining room if you wish to see her, Miss Nix," mentioned Diamond, who came into the room, looking like he just woke up as well.

"Thanks. So, what happened after I passed out?"

"Not much, we carried Fade and you over to the train when it arrived. After we boarded, we traveled back to the forest where the child guided us through. We soon ended up here at our castle, and you've been sleeping until now," the red-haired male explained.

Nix nodded and got out of the chair, wanting to see Fade. The brothers followed her, stating that they just wanted to be by her side. There really was no reason to argue with them since she figured that they wouldn't budge on the issue. When they reached Fade's room, Nix opened the door and was happy to see the girl awake.

Fade smiled at her as Nix pulled up a simple wooden chair. The room was quite simple with its stone grey walls and floors. Fade lay in cream colored sheets on a wooden bed. A single light fixture in the shape of a flower illuminated the room.

Both brothers stood at the doorway, keeping their eyes on their lover. Fade and she talked for quite some time. The two of them discussed the battle with the sunhat girl, how Fade was dealing with her sister's death and the responsibilities of a queen.

"There aren't any responsibilities for a queen in this world. It's more of a title and power symbol. It shows that you're a formidable foe since you wield a queen's weapon. Also, being a king or queen amplifies your magic capabilities. Granted, your weapon is a bit peculiar since you weren't from this world, yet there is all of that energy flowing through it. I'm not sure how that's possible, but, hopefully, you won't have to fight a battle any time soon. Regardless, the power of your title is yours, and you choose what to do with it."

"Your sister mentioned me having some sort of power that she sensed. Would that be connected to the energy flowing through my weapon?"

"Probably, but I haven't seen anything like it before. I can't say why your weapon is like that."

"That's fine. I'm sure that I'll figure it out eventually. I now have more time on my hands than ever, but I'm curious about something else. How many kings and queens are there in this world? And, does killing one mean that you become one?"

"There are four kings and four queens. You took over my sister's position of the Queen of Clubs. The titles are based off of a simple deck of cards. There is a king and queen for each suit. As for how you become one, you either kill the current holder of the title, or you become the holder's apprentice. Once the current holder grows tired of their title, they pass it onto their apprentice. Or if the holder dies, the title goes to their designated apprentice.

"The present holder has to announce formally to at least one other king or queen that the person in question is their apprentice. This makes it official, and a magic bond will form between the two, sealing the person in question as the successor to the title. If this is done, the successor can't change unless the successor is killed."

"Do you know any of the other kings or queens besides me?"

A light chuckle left her lips. "Well, I'm the Queen of Spades while the brothers are both kings. Heart being the King of Hearts, and Diamond is the King of Diamonds."

Glancing back to the twins, she raised an eyebrow. "Did Cirsis know that you two were kings? Or, did you take the positions from someone when you were older?"

"We were told that we received the titles before we were brought to the circus. Cirsis just thought that our names would be comical given our titles. Granted, we didn't find out that we were kings until after we left the circus. We don't know the names that were given to us by our parents," Diamond answered as he crossed his arms across his chest.

"Do you have any more questions, Nix?" Fade inquired, propping a pillow behind her back now.

"No, that answers my curiosities for now."

"In that case..." Fade glanced to the brothers before looking to her. Nix could tell that Fade wanted the brothers to leave, but they looked quite content with where they stood.

"Can you two leave for a moment?" Nix asked as she noted their hardened gaze on their past mentor.

"My dear lady, why would we do such a thing?"

"Miss Nix, we're not leaving you."

"Honestly, it's just for several minutes."

The two brothers looked at each other before leaving the room and closing the door behind them. Nix was glad that they were giving her some privacy, but she had the feeling that they would get back at her for asking them to leave. Regardless, she signaled Fade to continue with what she was going to say.

"Do you intend to stay with them? You can come live with me if you wish."

"I want to say that I'm going to run off and explore this world on my own, but, at the same time, I know that they would just bring me back. I have my queen's weapon now, but I don't think that I could kill either of them just so that I could escape. Besides, I don't know where I would go and if I could even defend myself against all of the dangerous things out there. And, thank you for the offer, but I know the brothers would become enraged if they found me living with you. I'm not putting you into that situation."

"You're too kind, Nix. First, you put your life on the line so that the brothers didn't suffer at my sister's hands. Now, you refuse my help so that I'm not harmed by them. It's refreshing to meet someone like you, and I'm happy that I didn't kill you back then."

"I'm glad about that too," she chuckled out, smiling to the girl.

"Nix, do you care for them, though? I know that's a personal question, but as their past teacher, I would still like for them to have someone to look after them."

Heat invaded Nix's cheeks, and she peered down to her feet. "I don't love them, but I have seen past their sadistic, violent sides. I understand that they can be caring individuals, and they've saved me on multiple accounts. Despite their games, I feel more at home here than I did at my home in my world. I don't even know if I could consider living with my aunt and uncle a home. In this castle, however, I feel safe even with the twins living in it. It's bizarre, but I'd be lying if I said otherwise."

"Then, will you look after them for me. I feel like I can trust you, and I consider you a dear friend now. I know that's a large request to make, but you seem like you can accomplish it."

"I suppose that I can promise you that, but I'm not giving them an easy time. They haven't earned that in the slightest."

Laughing some, Fade responded, "I wouldn't expect you to. Their egos don't need any more boosting. Still, thank you." Nix chuckled and nodded to her friend before the door to the room opened. The brothers walked in, coming towards Nix.

"I believe that several minutes have passed, so you'll be coming with us, Miss Nix."

"Yes, you've spent enough time with the child, my dear lady."

Fade waved goodbye to her as Nix was guided out of the room by the brothers. The rest of the day she spent with them. As for the next day, Fade had said her goodbyes and left for her forest. This left Nix alone with the brothers, who seemed all too happy at the prospect of having her to themselves once again.

~ ~ ~ ~ ~ ~ ~ ~ ~ ~

Two weeks had passed since Fade left. Some part of Nix thought that defeating the sunhat girl and being a queen would give her more liberty, but it seemed only the opposite. The brothers were constantly worried that someone would break into the castle and attack even though the sunhat girl was dead. They constantly seemed to be by her side. At times, they would even try to sneak into her room during the night, which they had succeeded in doing several times now. Whenever this happened, she would wake up only to find herself sandwiched between the two of them.

Along with keeping a constant eye on her, the brothers continued in playing games with her. Now, though, they only took place in the castle since they wouldn't let her leave the castle walls. Sometimes, they would be generous enough to let her into the courtyard, but that was as far as they would let her travel.

So, she sat in her purple throne chair, quite worried about the events that would unfold later on today. The brothers had previously forced her to play another game of theirs, which happened to be hide and seek tag. She had lost and was now anxiously waiting to see what they wanted in return for winning. After the game was finished, they merely looked at each other and grinned in delight before they had walked off simply telling her to meet them in the study at one in the afternoon that day.

Right now, it was eleven in the morning, and she had just finished breakfast. She kept tapping her fingers against the arms of the chair, trying to figure out what the brothers had planned. When nothing came to mind, she began to think of ways to stop whatever the brothers had in store for her. Nix could always summon her queen's weapon, but it's not like she desired to kill them or injure them. That's when an idea struck her.

Today was the day that Fade was going to visit her since the Queen of Spades had decided to visit her once a week. It was only for an hour, but that would be enough. The brothers made sure that it only stayed an hour because they didn't like her attention away from them.

A grin spread across her face as she waited for Fade to arrive. She only had to wait for ten minutes before she could pursue her plan. Time ticked away, and Fade arrived. The instant the castle doors opened for her, Nix charged out of her chair towards her friend. Luckily, the brothers would leave her alone when Fade visited. Nix didn't know how she managed to convince the brothers of giving her some space, but she was happy that she received it.

"Fade, I need to ask a favor of you. I lost at one of the brothers' games, and I need you to help me prevent what they have planned."

"Sure, I'll definitely help. What do you want me to do, Nix?"

"I want you to quickly go back to your forest and retrieve some owls for me. You said back on the train that the brothers feared them, so it's the only thing I can think of."

Fade smiled in delight before nodding in reply. She went back out of the castle and so Nix's plan had begun. Twenty minutes passed before Fade returned. When the castle doors opened once more, Fade walked in with four owls, two on each arm. The Queen of Spades let them fly onto the rafters before she walked over to Nix. For the remainder of the hour, they visited with each other until she left.

With Fade gone, Nix paced back and forth in the entrance room. When the clock struck one in the afternoon, she waited for the brothers to arrive. They would come soon, probably angry that she hadn't showed up in the study on the designated time. Just like she predicted, they appeared in the entrance hall, fuming. It was now a quarter past one.

"My dear lady, why didn't you meet us where we told you to?!"

"You made us worry! We looked all over the castle for you, Miss Nix!"

Ignoring them, she focused her attention on the rafters. The brothers soon noticed that she wasn't paying attention. Their own eyes traveled upwards. Their reaction was priceless. Both brothers went pale in the face as their eyes widened in fright.

"My dear lady, ho-howw ... di-did th-those ... creat- creatures... ge-get in here?" Heart stuttered as he stepped back a little.

"I'm not sure. They probably got cold and decided to come in. I don't see the problem. Maybe, I should call them down," she remarked, trying to keep a straight face.

Upon saying the last part of her statement, she saw the brothers look at her in horror. Before they could stop her, she called down the owls. She had learned how to do in the short time that she had visited with Fade. Their wings flapped as they swooped down. As soon as they neared the three of them, the brothers threw themselves at the floor, covering their heads in the process. At this point, she couldn't maintain a straight face anymore.

One of the owls perched itself on her right arm before she set it down on her chair. The other three owls chased after the brothers. Not being able to help herself, she began to laugh uncontrollably. The chase seemed to last at least for five minutes before the owls eventually perched themselves back on the rafters. Not a second later were the brothers standing in front of her, anger evident in their eyes.

"Miss Nix, please, tell me that you didn't let those owls in here."

"I didn't," she lied, attempting not to laugh anymore.

"My dear lady, lying to us is not a wise decision."

Nix stared at them innocently, backing away from them. Before she could get away, Diamond grabbed her and picked her up bridal style in his arms. "Let us not delay today's plans any longer. We'll think of a way to punish you later. If you ever think to bring owls into this castle again, however ... well let's just say that you'll regret it dearly."

Merely mumbling some insult under her breath, she turned away from his dark gaze and let him carry her to wherever they were going. The three of them soon stopped in front of a door she had never opened. Since they weren't saying anything, she inquired, "What exactly did the two of you have planned?"

"My dear lady, we have decided to move you to another room."

"Indeed, meaning that from now on you'll share a room with us. This is the prize we get for winning against you," Diamond commented like it was the simplest fact in the world.

Her mouth hung open as she peered between the two of them. "What! I'm not agreeing to that!"

"I'm afraid that you don't have a choice in the matter, Miss Nix."

Heart opened the door, revealing a luxurious room. The floor had black wooden floors and light purple walls. A red carpet with silver embroidery rested on the floor. Crystal light fixtures decorated the walls while a white marble fireplace laid on the wall across from the king sized bed, which was covered in blue and red sheets. A blue crystal chandelier hung on the ceiling, which was currently turned off due to the black drapes being opened. Three black and white checkered armchairs sat around a glass round table. To the right side of the fireplace was a black door, leading to a master bathroom, which also had wardrobe connected to it.

Carrying her into the room, Diamond set her down on the edge of the bed. "What do you think of the room?"

"I'd rather have my own room."

"That is no longer an option, Miss Nix. And, for your punishment, you'll remain in this room for the rest of the day. Before we leave to deal with the dreadful creatures you brought into this castle, though, we have something to give you."

Diamond's brother went into the bathroom and walked into the wardrobe. He soon came out with a box in his hand. Opening it, he revealed a gold and silver chocker. A red crystal diamond charm and a blue crystal heart charm dangled from it. Heart took it out of the box and approached her with the necklace.

"This is a symbol that you're our lover. You'll wear it for the entire day, my dear lady. If we find that it's not around your neck during the day, we'll think of a fitting punishment."

Staring at the necklace, she rolled her eyes. "I think that you two make our relationship clear enough without putting some collar around my neck."

"Oh, so you admit to being our lover?" they asked in unison as grins overtook their lips.

"What?! No, that's not what I meant! I meant that you two hang around me all the time. So, it's obvious that you consider me yours. That doesn't mean that I like you back," she tried to explain. "Look, I'm not putting that thing on unless we negotiate on the terms of that necklace."

"Miss Nix, you should know that we don't negotiate often."

"Just hear me out," she mentioned while there was a pleading look in her eyes. They sighed and motioned for her to go on. "Thank you. How about we drop the punishment of me not wearing it for one? Second, it's merely a gift from you two. I'll determine what that necklace means to me, not you two. Otherwise, I'll summon my queen's weapon and send that thing to oblivion. You should be able to tell that I'm serious on that threat."

"Well, we did have it custom made for you, and it would be a shame for it to go to waste. Will you still wear it every day, my dear lady? If you forget to wear it, we'll just put it around your neck with no questions asked. Will that work, or do we have to fight you?"

Thinking it over, she nodded. "That will be fine."

Both of the twins looked relieved by this, and Heart came over to her before he clasped the necklace behind her neck. His lips brushed against hers before he distanced himself from her and followed his brother out of the room. A light wave of heat touched her cheeks as she heard the lock in the door click. Just as she was about to grab her daggers and break herself out of the room, she heard the brothers stop walking.

"Ah, Miss Nix, don't try to break down the door or the windows; we placed glass walls in front of the windows and on the other side of doors now. Even your queen's weapon won't be able to break through."

Sighing, she set her blades down on the bed and heard the brothers walk away. She still smiled, however, since they had to deal with the owls. As for the rest of the day, she laid on the bed either sleeping or playing with her necklace before she decided it time to get a shower. After she was done, she changed into pajamas for the evening. Once she was changed, she went back to her boredom and lay upon the bed.

It was quite amusing, however, that it was evening, and the brothers still weren't back. Despite being locked in a room, she was glad at her decision to let the owls into the castle. She would never forget the brothers' facial expressions when they spotted the owls in the castle. Besides even though she was locked in a room, it was the most peace she had attained in quite some time. Soon, though, the doors to the room reopened and in walked the two brothers. Nix assumed that they had taken down the glass walls.

A light chuckle escaped her lips as she saw the condition of the brothers. Their hair was a mess, and their shirts were torn in several places while multiple feathers covered them. Heart went into the bathroom and closed the door behind him while Diamond sat on one of the armchairs.

"We're having Aberrous bring dinner up here in an hour. I hope that you don't mind, Miss Nix," Diamond uttered as he combed his fingers through his hair, pulling out a feather in the process.

"I don't mind," she replied, still chuckling.

Diamond narrowed his eyes at her before walking over to her. "Due to your stunt, Miss Nix, I now have a horrendous headache. Your laughing isn't helping."

She merely gave him an annoyed look and turned away from him. She felt, however, the weight of the bed shift and found herself being pulled at. Arms wrapped around her waist as Diamond brought her to his chest. "Let go," she muttered, trying to pry his arms off of her and pushing away the heat at her cheeks.

"Hmm, I'm tired, and, currently, I'm in need of a pillow."

"Then, grab one from behind you."

"You're softer."

By this point, she couldn't force the heat back from her cheeks and found herself unable to move. As Diamond rested his head on her right shoulder, she spotted a few owl feathers still in his hair. Laughing quietly, she managed to move her left hand and remove them from his hair. Diamond watched her, which only made more heat take over her skin. "I'm only doing this because I don't want them on me."

He smiled lightly at her comment before nuzzling into her neck more. The two of them stayed like this, though; she really didn't have a choice in the matter. When Heart walked out of the bathroom with just a towel wrapped around him like on the train, she shut her eyes and wished that Aberrous would hurry up with dinner. Diamond looked up at his brother and released his grip on her. Going into the bathroom, Diamond closed the door behind him. With his hold gone, she sat up, turned away from Heart and opened her eyes. She expected Heart to go into the wardrobe. Instead, he came over to her and picked her up.

Her face felt like it was going to explode, and Heart smirked at her as he carried her into the wardrobe. Setting her down on the purple carpet, she looked away from him. "So, tell me why you brought me in here?"

"I thought that you would like to help me pick out my evening attire. I want to look nice for you," he whispered into her right ear.

"Fine, let's just get this over with, but I'm not picking out your undergarments," she murmured, trying to hide the fact that she had practically jumped as a result of his action.

"I wouldn't expect you to," he answered as he guided her over to his section of the closet. Quickly, she grabbed the first articles of clothing that she saw, wanting to get out of the wardrobe. She didn't realize, however, that she had only grabbed a bathrobe. "You want me to just wear my robe, my dear lady? Well, I don't object, but I didn't think that you would pick out something like that."

Finding only a robe in her hand, she threw it back on the hanger before grabbing a pair of black pajama pants and a simple blue v-neck. Heart took them from her hands, smirking at the same time. "Can I go now?"

"Yes, but you're welcome to stay."

Scowling at him, she walked out of the wardrobe and back into the bedroom. She sat down on one of the armchairs, and Heart soon came back out, seating himself on her left. Heat was still present in her cheeks, but, eventually, the two of them agreed to play a game of cards. Before they could finish, though, Diamond walked into the bedroom. He wore a loose red cotton shirt and some black pajama pants as well. Sitting on her right, he rested his chin in the palm of his right hand.

Aberrous came in with dinner soon after, which consisted of baked potato soup and a small salad. Dinner went by quietly with the exception of Heart and Diamond trying to feed her. She had managed to grab her spoon and fork back after several attempts. When dinner finished, Aberrous came back into the room, retrieving the empty dinnerware. After he left, both brothers got out of their chairs and held their hands out to her.

"I'm sleeping on the chair," she resolutely stated.

Before she could protest further, both brothers grabbed her arms and pulled her out of the chair. She freed herself from their grip and walked over to the bed. Getting under the sheets, she created a fortress around her with the pillows on the bed. Heart chuckled slightly while Diamond smiled lightly. The pillows were removed from around her, but she tried to keep a firm grip on them. This still didn't work, however.

Heart's arms wrapped around her as did Diamond's. Diamond's fingers lightly grabbed her chin as he turned her head towards him. He closed the distance between the two of them, kissing her tenderly on the lips. On the other hand, Heart placed butterfly kisses along her left arm before reaching her neck. Soon, he found her soft spot and began to kiss the area roughly. The brothers switched places, and she could feel the bruises forming on her neck as her cheeks burned. When they stopped, they both pulled themselves closer to her.

"We hoped that you enjoyed that, my dear lady. You have such soft and delicate skin," Heart whispered into her left ear.

"Goodnight, Miss Nix. You have delicious lips," Diamond murmured into her right ear.

As she turned around in their arms, she hid her face in the pillows, hearing both brothers laugh at her attempt to hide her heated face. Eventually and thankfully, she managed to fall asleep between the two brothers. The kings had found their queen, and they intended to never let her go; she belonged to them, and no one else would have her.

Magic List for the Brothers' World

Note: One can have multiple magic types. Abilities are unique for each person in the world and are not passed down through birth. Thus, a child can have abilities completely unlike their parent. There have been exceptions to this rule, however.

Elemental:

*   Fire: Those with the ability of fire magic can cause already present flames to increase or decrease, can cause flames to be present at will, can warm their bodies at will and/or radiate heat from their forms and transfer it to other people/objects/etc. through touch.

*   Water: Those with the ability of water magic can utilize water in the area and bend it to their will, can suck water from the air and do the same, can use water from their own bodies and do the same, can turn water from its liquid form to its solid form and vice versa and/or can cool themselves down by cooling the water in their body.

*   Earth: Those with the ability of earth magic can cause plants to grow from the ground, can summon vines from their body and/or can manipulate any plant growth in the area.

*   Air: Those with the ability of air magic can manipulate the air in the area around them and use it to their will, such as sending a burst of air at someone. If they choose to do so, air manipulation can quicken their speed and can cause them to fly as well.

*   Light: Those with the ability of light magic can bend the light in the area to their will. This extends from forming the light into various shapes/colors/etc. to blinding their opponents temporarily to burning their opponents from the heat of the light.

*   Shadows: Those with the ability of shadow magic can utilize shadows in the area to help in areas of stealth and to become invisible at night. The shadows can also be made to attack one's opponent.

Non-Elemental:

* Portal Creation: These individuals can manipulate the space of the area itself and summon a portal to another part of the world. For example, one can open a door, which originally led to a hallway and find themselves looking at a forest. The skill of a portal creator determines how many places they can create portals to. Skilled portal creators can form a portal so quick that the action isn't caught by the human eye. Their power is ineffective if a specific or broad magic barrier is in place (see spells section).

* Object Manipulation: These individuals can essentially turn any item into something else of their choosing. For instance, a pen can become a sword. Ability to perform these transformations depends on the skill of the user.

* Teleportation: These individuals can teleport themselves anywhere in the world and summon any object they want to them. They can also teleport almost any person and/or object to another area. For instance, they cannot teleport another teleporter. Their power is ineffective if a specific or broad magic barrier is in place (see spells section).

* Dream Sending: These individuals can send someone into a dream state until they wish to release the person, or the person in question breaks free. The magic, from the user, utilizes the thoughts/memories/desires/etc. of the victim to form a dream world where the victim won't want to leave. This can only be done if the magic user has some form of physical contact with the person in question. Furthermore, the dream steals life energy from the

victim as it continues. If the victim is in the dream for too long, they'll die.

   * Illusion Creation: These individuals, depending on level of skill, can create illusions of nearly anything to fool their opponents.

   * Floatation: These individuals can cause an object to float in midair. What objects they can cause to float in air depend on their skill. Air users can perform this ability as well, but floatation users only have access to this specific ability. All other forms of air magic aren't possible for them.

   * Duplication: These individuals can duplicate not only themselves but other persons/objects/etc.

   * Prophecy: These individuals can watch scenes of things to come, but these mind films show only one possible future path. The seer cannot determine whether this will actually come true or not.

   * Quickened Healing: These individuals can heal faster than most. A wound that would otherwise be fatal heals within a matter of minutes. The longest healing time is thirty minutes. Of course, should the individual receive a wound in the heart or head, this ability won't save them. If a limb or organ is lost, it cannot be regenerated with this magic ability.

Spells:

   * Anyone in the world can utilize spells. The selection of spells is vast, and some require more practice than others. The ranks of spell users start at beginner before advancing onto the rank of caster. The third rank is mage, and the final is sorcerer/sorceress.

   * The following are some of the spells:
      1. Broad Portal Creation and Teleportation Barriers = nullifies these abilities of all users of this magic in the area that the barrier is over

2.   Specific Portal Creation and Teleportation Barriers = prevents a specific user of these magic capabilities. This spell can only last for a max duration of two hours.

3.   Glass Gate= allows the spell user to form an unbreakable glass wall anywhere that they please. Only the one who cast it can remove it. Granted, the user can't form a glass wall horizontally.

4.   Durability = strengthens the item in question and decreases the chance of it being ruined. It cannot be cast on a person's whole body.

5.   Continuity = causes the object that the spell is cast on to keep going unless stop times are added into the spell

6.   Communication = the spell user states what they wish the spell to communicate to them. Its effect lasts for a year before it has to be renewed, and the spell must be cast in two or more places so that the information doesn't remain in one room. Lastly, the sender and the receiver rooms need to be decided during the casting of spell.

7.   Hardening = causes a liquid to be more solid. The liquid can still be broken through either from the top or bottom if hit with enough force.

Made in the USA
Las Vegas, NV
02 November 2020